PEARL MOON

A RUN AND HIDE THRILLER

JJ MARSH

PREWETT
BIELMANN

Pearl Moon
Copyright © 2022 by Prewett Bielmann Ltd.

Cover design: JD Smith

Published by Prewett Bielmann Ltd.
All enquiries to admin@jjmarshauthor.com

First printing, 2022
eBook Edition:
ISBN 978-3-906256-19-1

Paperback:
ISBN 978-3-906256-20-7

To Neil and Elsa, for inspiration

1

———

Sitting in the departure lounge in Johannesburg, waiting for her flight to Pemba, Iris asked herself what the hell she was doing. Her optimism and excitement as she had prepared for her trip had shrivelled into remorse the minute she queued to check in at Lisbon airport. The people, the noise, the inability to flee for cover smothered her to the point she considered bolting through the automatic doors and hailing a taxi to the train station. Two things stopped her: the look on Lana's face when she arrived home and the bloody awful weather. Why was it always raining when she had to travel?

Lisbon was a shock but Frankfurt was utter hell. Her inbound flight was delayed by forty-five minutes due to storms and Iris had less than half an hour to race through crowds of tourists if she had any hope of reaching the transfer gate. It was almost enough to make her give up or turn into a complete misanthrope. She screeched to a halt at the passport control, one of the last to board the Lufthansa flight to Johannesburg. Even after she had settled into a luxurious First Class seat, her nervous system continued screaming alarm bells for another ten minutes.

"Good afternoon, madam. Orange juice or champagne?"

"Neither. I need a gin and tonic. Emergency measures, if you know what I mean."

"I'll see to that right away."

With two shots of Bombay Sapphire soothing her stress, Iris began to relax. The flight left on time, her neighbour wore headphones and never took his eyes from his laptop and the meal was a luxurious treat of salmon terrine, mushroom soufflé and cherry sorbet. Iris scoffed the lot, including the bread roll. This kind of cuisine had not featured in her recent past and was unlikely to make an appearance in her immediate future. Dinner over, she refused a coffee, accepted another glass of champagne and pulled up the privacy screen. She asked herself once again: *Iris Simons, what the hell do you think you are you doing?* Instead of an answer, she simply closed her eyes and retraced the steps that had brought her this far.

Dear Ms Simons

Thank you for your application. I am sorry to say it was unsuccessful on this occasion. The board acknowledges your enthusiasm for helping the disadvantaged girls and women of Angola. However, we seek individuals with immediately useful skills to offer. Self-defence training, fluency in Portuguese and being a native English speaker is not sufficient to become an instructor and/or teacher at our facility. Your combat experience appears little more than anecdotal, since you provide no official training records or references. Neither do you mention TEFL certificates or similar proof of your ability to teach languages. We strongly discourage charity tourism or 'voluntourism' as the long-term effects prove harmful to the work we are trying to do.

If you wish to support us in a practical sense, please find attached a blank invoice where you can donate to our charitable fund.

We thank you for your interest in our project.

The fourth rejection in as many weeks. For the first time in her life, Iris wasn't good enough. She threw the letter into the bin with a curse. It took a few minutes of wrestling with her ego before she retrieved it, smoothed it out and placed it on top of the others lying on her bedroom desk. She had to learn from these refusals and make her next application better.

She knew what an asset she could be to these NGOs, but to be fair, they didn't. Why should her truncated CV portray her as anything other than a hobbyist do-gooder, ticking items off a bucket list? Her difficulty was providing any kind of certificates for Iris Simons, an alias who had only come into existence at the end of last year. If only she were able to demonstrate the background, experience and qualifications of Olivia Jones, every one of these organisations would be competing to employ her. She frowned at her tediously repetitive thought patterns. *You are Iris Simons. Olivia Jones no longer exists.*

The heat of the afternoon subsided and within the hour, the three farmhands would return from their lunchbreak and come buzzing down the lane on their mopeds. Nestor had already fired up the tractor and Lana was probably already in the orchard, getting on with the fruit picking. The agricultural calendar could not be postponed, not for anything or anyone. Irritable and disappointed, Iris planted her straw hat on her head and stomped across the farmyard with her baskets. Against her will, her dejection lifted. This was her favourite time of day. The heady mixture of fragrance from the farmhouse roses mingled with honeysuckle, lemon verbena and bright pots of sweet peas. Lilac and buddleia bushes lured a buzzing crowd of various bees and silent balletic butterflies. Iris inhaled the warm afternoon air and gazed down to the river. The sweeping meadow was shorn of its swaying grasses, now cropped, baled and ready to be stored in the barn as winter fodder. Trees along the riverbank were beginning to change colour, hinting that last year's autumnal display might well be outdone by this year's fireworks. Squeals and shrieks from upstream made Iris smile. Teenagers at 'The Beach', or in other words, one of the widest and most accessible sections of the River Dão, were making the most of the long, lazy days of late summer.

In the orchard, the stepladder she had used that morning was still resting against a plum tree and Lana was yet to arrive. She layered a cushion of grasses in the base of her basket, climbed the ladder and continued plucking plums, humming a half-remembered tune.

"Someone's in a good mood." Lana, sturdy and calm, swayed through the knee-length grasses, wearing an apron and her hair tied up in a scarf. She reminded Iris of wartime photographs of land girls.

"Hard not to be when you're outside on a day like this. I've almost done this tree."

"A fine crop of plums we picked this year. Last year was even better but we had to let them fall and rot. Nestor and I couldn't manage the harvest alone. Since you took over the farm, everything's coming up roses." She smiled, shielding her eyes to look up at Iris.

"I hardly 'took over' the farm. You still have to tell me what to do and how to do it. Right, that's a basketful. Shall I give you a hand with the pears?"

"No, I can manage the pears and quince myself. I think we've got enough plums and our hedge fruits will last another week. Why don't you start on the peaches? You have a delicate touch so I trust you not to bruise them."

The two women worked in silence other than the odd altercation with a wasp. On the slopes above, Nestor and the farmhands moved up and down the vines, cropping enough A

Quinta Douro grapes to fill the community containers. Tomorrow, a truck would come around to collect their harvest, check its weight and give them a receipt which could be exchanged for money or the equivalent in local wine.

The sun sank and the air cooled. Thin clouds on the horizon took on hues of nectarine, apricot, fig and blueberry, or perhaps Iris had been in the orchard too long. She and Lana lugged their baskets back to the house amongst the sounds of cicadas and into the chill of the pantry.

"Tonight, we eat fresh fruit," said Lana, her skin glowing from the sun. "Tomorrow, we make cakes, jam, *marmelada*, pickles and jars for the winter."

Iris collected a bowl of plums and peaches for breakfast, marvelling that she was not yet sick of the things.

"That's assuming you will be here tomorrow?" Lana asked with a casual air. "I saw the postman came this morning."

The cloud of disappointment settled over Iris's horizon. "Not only tomorrow, I'll still be here this time next year. The letter was bad news. Yet another NGO refused me because my skills are insufficient." The bitterness in her tone was audible.

Lana finished wrapping apples, quince and pears in brown paper then stretched with a sigh and a creak from her shoulders. "Do you have something to eat for this evening? I can whip up an omelette with ham and tomatoes before I leave."

"I'm not completely helpless, Lana. You're very kind, but I can feed myself." They emerged into the dusky light of the kitchen. "Go home, look after your husband. I'll see you in the morning."

Lana cleaned the sink and work surfaces, then switched on the kitchen lamp. "Iris, you have so much talent and intelligence. You are a hard worker and quick learner. These charity companies must be desperate for someone like you. If they are turning you down, you've approached them in the wrong way."

Iris was affronted. "What do you mean by that?"

"Let me ask you a question. When applying for a job, are you selling yourself or meeting the employer's needs?"

"I'm not selling anything. It's a volunteer position! They should ..." Iris bit her tongue.

"They should be grateful? Perhaps. You want to work in a Portuguese-speaking country in Africa, yes? How much do you know about Angola, Mozambique or Cabo Verde? How can you be sure you have what they need?" Lana's voice remained steady and she seemed to be waiting for an answer.

"My problem is ..."

"Your problems do not concern them. They have plenty of their own. You must understand how these non-governmental agencies operate, who they want and why. You cannot send off your résumé and hope they will beg you to come and save them. That's not how it works. Take out your little computer, dig into the company ethics, find out which skills they seek and tailor your letter exactly like a job application. You need someone to pick fruit? I am an expert. You want someone to raise chickens? Not a problem. Dig wells, patrol fences, drive to market, plant crops, I am your all-round handywoman. Look at it from their side, Iris, not yours." She pulled her shawl over her broad shoulders and went to the door. "Don't eat much more fruit tonight or you'll spend half the night on the toilet. *Até amanhã.*"

"*Até amanhã.*" Iris sat on her own in the kitchen for another hour, until the sky turned inky blue, considering Lana's words. Then she made herself an omelette, took a notepad from the office and started again.

Her motivation came from the right place, of that Iris was sure. A slideshow of young female faces flickered across her eyelids at unexpected moments, but the result was always the same. A sense of injustice and impotent anger resulted in a vow to do something. The 'something' was never quite defined. But their names were never forgotten.

Paula was the most recent example. The farm's most energetic worker with a sunny disposition had a potential career in agriculture. Unfortunately, her father had strict old-fashioned views. After Paula got pregnant by her long-term boyfriend, she was sent away in disgrace to distant relatives, breaking more than one heart. Some months earlier, back in Brazil, beautiful teenagers Juliana and Alexandra should have been spending their youth on the beach, surfing, flirting and having fun. Not working as prostitutes servicing remote logging camps in the Amazon. Further back in time, grey-eyed young women like Krystina, Merle and Laine, lured from Eastern Europe by the promise of respectable jobs found themselves trafficked into Britain, forced into drug addiction and sex slavery. The defeat in their eyes still haunted Iris.

Now she was no longer in her role as an undercover cop, she could actually do something to help instead of turning a blind eye. She could never atone for her silence and tacit approval of what those women had suffered, but volunteering at a female refuge in Africa might equip other girls with the skills to avoid such a fate. As long as she kept herself off the radar, neither the London Metropolitan Police nor the Osman-Vargas organization was likely to track her down. That was exactly why she applied for the most remote locations she could find.

It was the perfect solution. Except no one wanted her.

Night sounds penetrated the open window; cicadas chirruped, moths batted against the mosquito screen, frogs burped down by the river and the rushing of the Dão soothed her mind. Every time she thought of the river, she glanced at the third finger of her left hand. The ring groove and paler skin where her wedding ring used to sit was still visible. In a month, maybe two, it would vanish completely. The band of gold which once occupied that space was lying somewhere on the river bed, buried by mud or carried downstream and washed out to sea. In a moment of wild paranoia, she had convinced herself the ring was a tracking device, torn it from her finger and hurled it into the waters.

Not a day had passed since without her regretting such a stupid, ill-considered gesture. Yet she imagined herself telling the story to Sal: 'I was delirious and dehydrated and very possibly having a breakdown'. He would have laughed, of course he would. Sal had always been about the present, enjoying life in all its reality and symbols were for the birds. Rings, he would have said, can be replaced. Husbands cannot.

Rings can be replaced. But for some reason, her finger was still bare.

Perhaps Lana was right. She was looking at the volunteer situation from the angle of how it benefitted her, not them. *If you wish to support us in a practical sense, please find attached a blank invoice where you can donate to our charitable fund.* She made four payments, one to each of the projects, and printed out three more job descriptions. This time, she read the detail of the roles in the mindset of the person who wrote them.

... mainstreaming of gender issues, collaboration with stakeholders, education for underprivileged girls, dissemination of information at governmental level, prioritising and realising female potential, securing funding, breaking the socio-economic vicious circle, promoting sustainable incomes, advocating for equality in local communities ...

The position, Iris realised, was less about teaching pubescent teenagers how to kick box or single mothers how to haggle over the price of a tie-dyed sundress, but had a far wider remit. The aim of this non-governmental organisation was to effect long-term change. That meant challenging deeply rooted attitudes, persuading local and national councils to become allies, and cooperating with journalists, lawmakers, politicians and influencers to support all their citizens. Not easy. Because those with the power to change the balance might well be invested in the status quo. Her fantasy of teaching combat moves in a circle of eager students faded in the flare of embarrassment.

She read the job advertisements once again, with clear eyes. Single mothers, orphaned girls, rape victims, teenagers with two living parents and an excess of siblings, disabled women with intelligence and ability did not require a well-meaning blow-in to sing them songs and take selfies. What they required was someone with the will to take on the establishment and set in motion a fundamental and permanent improvement in their own circumstances. Not just for themselves, but for future descendants. Iris quailed. Battling with the establishment was a hiding to nothing, in her experience.

Finally she made up her mind and pinpointed a job opening in Mozambique. Pemba was a port town on the northeast coast, around 250 kilometres from the border to Tanzania. The skills required were a mixture of pastoral and administrative, the kind of stuff Iris was easily capable of fulfilling. But she quashed any suggestion of overconfidence and spent two evenings researching the project, its history, aims and successes. There wasn't much. She delved into the country's political and cultural situation, informing herself as best she could on this former Portuguese colony. Then with great care, she set out how she would meet the challenges of the role. She'd never worked so hard on an application in her life. Only once she'd finished, sealed and posted the envelope did she allow herself to look at online pictures of the town and surroundings. So much water! On one side, the Indian Ocean in shades of navy blue to turquoise with coral reefs and long stretches of white sand. On the other, the natural harbour of Pemba Bay sprinkled with fishing boats. Water exerted an extraordinary pull on Iris. Much as she loved her farm with its walls on three sides and the river as its fourth perimeter, she yearned for the ocean.

All through the rest of the harvest season, she dared to

hope. This time she'd be lucky and repay her debts by being an asset to society. September was warm, and soft sunlight threw a glowing filter over turning leaves and terracotta roofs. In early October, the weather changed and two days of sudden storms made farm work sporadic. On the third day, Iris was repairing the gate to the kitchen garden under a sulky charcoal sky when Lana cycled down the drive, somehow balancing a trug of vegetables, an umbrella and a pile of post in the basket in front of her handlebars.

"Nice top," she said, as she cruised to a halt.

Iris looked down at the holey, frayed T-shirt she had flung on that morning. It had once been bright pink with the logo from A Pantera Rosa emblazoned across the chest. But it had faded to a weak hyacinth colour and the logo was gone. There used to be a time when she cared about clothes.

"Slugs ate half the lettuces," said Lana. A movement behind her turned out to be a little cat trotting behind the bicycle. "So I picked the rest for our lunch. It's not exactly salad weather, but I won't let them go to waste. The replacement bulbs for the barn have arrived and there's a letter for you from Africa. I'll go in and start cooking." She handed over a flimsy envelope with a postmark saying Correios de Moçambique.

Iris took it, staring at the handwritten address as the cat wove figures of eight around her ankles. She stroked the animal absently, already processing her disappointment. An acceptance would have been a fuller envelope with a contract, detailed information on travel, accommodation and dates. This was a standard rejection, she knew it. With wonderful timing, the first few raindrops darkened the thin paper. The cat raced into the barn and Iris followed. A port wine barrel cut in two provided a stool for goat-milking and other chores. Iris sat on it and ripped open the letter. A relentless drumming began on the roof.

Dear Iris

The position you wanted is filled, sorry. Your application was great — you know a lot about us, what we do and why we do it. We got no paid jobs right now, but why not join us as a volunteer? If you don't mind getting your hands dirty, you can start anytime you like. We don't pay much, just subsistence money and you'll have to fund your own travel. All we can offer is a room, food and basic training. Sorry I took so long to reply — it's crisis after crisis these days.

Kind regards
Mafalda Moutinho

2

———————

Six hours after leaving Frankfurt, she woke up in South Africa.

The change of continent had the same effect as a change of gear. She had come this far and would see it through. There was no contract or commitment, meaning any time it all got too much she could leave and run home to the farm. She shook her head – that was cowardly thinking.

Now for the last leg of the journey to Mozambique and her final destination – Pemba. The two aircraft could not have made a greater contrast. Her air-conditioned First Class reclining berth was now a knee-cramping economy seat beside two garrulous men in short-sleeved shirts, who found each other's stories thigh-slappingly hilarious. Her cotton shirt soon became damp and clammy in the draining heat. In her head, she balanced the trade-off: drink more water to rehy-drate and risk the demands of her bladder, or sweat and suffer. She compromised, drinking the occasional sip of tonic water.

One of her fellow travellers observed her swigging from the bottle and with a cheesy grin, offered to buy her a gin to go with it. She refused, patting her stomach. "Thank you, but no alcohol in my condition."

His smile snapped off like an elastic band. "Ah. Congratulations." He returned to his conversation, turning his back.

Two hours later, Iris regretted her brush-off. On arrival in Pemba, night had fallen and the airport was closing down. After passport control, the building was only half lit and in the moist evening air, not a single taxi waited at the rank. The two men who had been seated next to her collected their bags and stepped into a waiting vehicle, ignoring her plight. Fifteen minutes later, the place was practically deserted. She tried going inside to ask for advice but the doors were locked and the lights out. Voices at the end of the building caught her attention, one American accent louder than the rest.

"Will you give me a break, Josie? The shuttle bus should be here any minute. I get the fact you're tired, but all I can do is call the hotel one more time."

"Maybe we're in the wrong place, Carl?"

"Stop B, it says on my confirmation email. Where are we, people?"

"I dunno, Carl, I can't see jack shit."

The sound of an engine made the party shush one another. A minibus lumbered along the road, stopped at the airport entrance and flashed its lights.

"Finally!"

"Let's go!"

"He oughta come to us. This is Stop B."

"There's a bus at Stop A and seeing as it's got the name of the hotel taped on the front, I'll take my chances, OK, Carl?"

Iris scanned the party of around a dozen people and assessed them as a ragbag of divers or surfers who might not spot an interloper. As they passed, she attached herself to the rear. One blond with dreadlocks did a double take.

Iris rolled her eyes and shuddered. "Airport toilets are

gross. Take my advice, wait for," she clocked the taped printout above the driver's head, "Hotel Baia. Fewer cockroaches."

He gave a weary smile and waved a hand, inviting her to board first. The minibus was crammed with sweaty bodies, backpacks and suitcases. The driver stood outside smoking while Carl and Josie, bickering constantly, strapped their surfboards to the roof.

The journey took no longer than thirty minutes, amid an overcrowded group of tired, hot and fractious tourists. Iris could remember pleasanter journeys. Finally, they came to a halt on a well-lit street, right in front of Hotel Baia. Music pounded from a bar opposite and the travellers dragged themselves inside. Carl and Josie had still not resolved their dispute and judging by the faces throwing sour looks over their shoulders as they entered the lobby, everyone else had heard enough.

Iris hesitated, debating the wisdom of staying in a Pemba hotel for one night or trying to locate the refuge in the dark. Her courageous side told her to be resourceful, find a taxi and put her plan into action. Then again, Hotel Baia had a terrace overlooking the beach, with palm tree umbrellas, a barbecue wafting scents of grilled fish and waiters distributing cocktails. She heaved her backpack over her shoulder and made up her mind to enquire about a room.

Just as she did so, a taxi honked its horn and a young man poked his head out of the window.

"Where you wanna go, lady?" he called, in English.

She was about to name the refuge when an instinct stopped her. She answered him in Portuguese. "My friends have a place in Luguni, near the lighthouse. Can you take me there?"

He sucked his teeth. "Luguni, at this time of night? It's going to cost you."

"OK, forget it. I'll stay here tonight and take the bus tomorrow. Bye."

"Wait a minute! We can come to an arrangement, if we're both flexible." His voice segued from urgent to suggestive in a matter of syllables.

"What's your name and how old are you?"

"Tendai. I'm twenty-three and I've been driving taxis for years."

Iris got into the back seat, her backpack upright by her side, like another passenger. "Pleased to meet you, Tendai. My name is Iris and I've been teaching self-defence for years. The arrangement we will come to is this. You take me where I want to go and make sure I'm safe. I will pay you double the usual fare because it's late at night. That's it. Any suggestion of inappropriate behaviour and both our evenings will be ruined."

His eyes met hers in the mirror. "You want to go direct or along the beach route? Avenida da Marginal is a little bit longer, but a better road and sea air."

"Yeah, sea air sounds good."

The journey lasted around twenty minutes and Tendai kept up a cheerful monologue throughout. A bright guy, he soon learnt personal questions to a jet-lagged foreigner were unwelcome and likely to get no more than a monosyllabic response. He switched into tour guide mode, extolling the virtues of the peninsula and recommending the Quirimbas National Park.

Iris checked the map she'd printed in Portugal and made a rough guess as to the location of the refuge. Her stomach growled. Perhaps there would be a pot of beans or a plate of sardines with bread and a cold beer to welcome her. The journey had wrung her out. All she wanted was to eat and sleep. She was using the torch on her phone to illuminate the map when a sudden swerve caught her completely by surprise. One minute, Tendai was wittering on about endangered dugongs and the next, horns blasted, lights blinded them and she was thrown against her backpack.

The taxi stalled. "You OK?" Tendai asked, his own breathing shallow.

"What the hell was that?" Iris asked, twisting around to see the tail-lights of two vehicles disappearing into the night.

"Troublemakers, I guess. Some young guys like to harass the people at A Casa da Prata." He started the engine. "It's a kind of health centre where women can escape ..."

"I know what it is. That's where I'm going."

He hung his arm over the back of his seat and turned to stare at her. "You don't look like a lady in trouble."

"You don't look like a guy who judges on appearances. How far is it from here?"

"Just around this corner. No more than a minute. I'll drive you. Single females don't want to be walking the streets in the dark, believe me."

"Thank you."

He started the vehicle and after a moment's tyre-spinning, got them back onto tarmac. He pulled up at the end of an unremarkable driveway with lights in the distance.

"I'd better stop here. They don't like strangers."

"Yeah, that's best. I'll walk up the drive. Here's your fare and I appreciate your professionalism. I wish you a good evening."

He held a hand out of his window, offering a business card. "Iris! If you need a driver, or just a guy you can trust, call me, yeah?"

Iris tucked it into her back pocket. "Yeah, Tendai, I will. *Boa noite.*"

The long day's travelling settled on her like a dead weight as she watched the taxi do a three-point turn and take its lights with it. Moonlight provided the only illumination on the sandy road, although the night was alive with insects, frogs and the constant swishing of the sea. No traffic came from either direction, and the silence wavered between reassuring and sinister.

The track leading to A Casa da Prata was not marked and sported no gates or security system, but it was the only compound of buildings just after the lighthouse. Iris was initially disappointed the place did not overlook the ocean, and then rebuked herself. She was not a tourist but a volunteer, here to work and use whatever abilities she had to help.

Voices drifted down the track and in their tone something made Iris speed up. This was not a languorous conversation between folk on the veranda, but a frantic yelling, interspersed with tears. As she drew closer, she saw half a dozen women clearing up debris and fixing some kind of enclosure.

"*Olà!*" she called, as she drew closer to the kerosene lamps spilling a ragged circle of light across the yard. The women froze and one started crying.

"My name is Iris Simons and I am here to offer my services."

Someone stepped out of the shadows, wearing gloves and holding a bucket. "Right, yeah, the volunteer. I forgot all about you. My name is Mafalda. I won't shake hands because I'm covered in chicken shit. We just got raided by some boys from the village. They stole most of our chickens and trashed the coop. Unless we secure the place tonight, we'll have nothing left by morning."

"I saw their trucks! They nearly ran my taxi off the road."

Mafalda tilted her head. "A taxi? Most of them won't come out this far and definitely not to A Casa da Prata. You got lucky."

"Shouldn't we call the police? This is criminal damage."

"The police? Oh dear God, no." Mafalda sighed. "Jennifer, stop crying and find this woman a bed. I've got work to do. Sleep well, Iris, and we'll see you in the morning."

A young girl, wiping her eyes and nose, waved a hand for Iris to follow. She walked past the main building and to a low concrete structure which had once been a cowshed. Inside, the temperature was cooler and a baby was grizzling. Jennifer led her past half a dozen stalls and opened a stable door. Inside was a single bed on a cement floor. There was a mosquito net, a pillow and rumpled blanket as if the previous occupant had left in a hurry.

"*Bemvindo,*" Jennifer sniffed. "The t-t-oilet is at the end. *Até amanhã.*" She closed the stable door behind her.

Iris dumped her rucksack on the floor and sat on the bed. Hot, hungry, in need of a shower and underwhelmed by her reception committee, she rested her head in her hands and asked herself the same question she had formulated in Lisbon airport. What the hell was she doing?

3

———————

Flat-out exhaustion enabled her to sleep for a few hours until she woke with a dry mouth and tremendous thirst. After using a public fountain at Johannesburg airport and consuming mostly gin-less tonic on the plane, she still had a half-full drinking bottle. Iris swigged the lukewarm water as if she was a camel. The compound was silent and in total darkness, with no other sounds than far-off waves and a breeze whispering through palm leaves. For a moment, she could imagine herself on Praia do Pesqueiro, with Branca snoring at her feet and the call of a white heron as an ersatz alarm call.

The snoring was not a figment of her imagination. Someone nearby was breathing heavily, occasionally releasing a murmur. Flimsy wooden walls separated women and children with no more privacy or security than a cowshed. Iris curled up under the net, which at first had offered a sense of protection. Now realism intruded and prevented further sleep. She and all the women around her were sitting ducks. Or chickens. That was going to change. Seeing as any more sleep was unlikely, she might as well make plans.

A child's wail woke her with a start. The cowshed, bathed in morning sunshine, was a different prospect to the previous night. Women conversed in cheerful voices and the sound of a belly laugh made Iris smile. Her thirst propelled her out of bed, along with her hunger. Secondly, she was curious to see her new home in daylight. The crying child was soon comforted by a soothing voice singing some kind of lullaby. Iris made use of the basic bathroom to wash her face and clean her teeth. There was no mirror, a fact which pleased her. When she emerged, the scent of cooking food called her like a dog whistle. She dumped her dirty clothes on the bed and rummaged in her rucksack for clean underwear, shorts and a T-shirt.

Outside the main building stood a palm tree shelter, rustling in the morning breeze. Beneath it, a group of people sat around a makeshift table, two women tended a grill made out of half an oil drum and a trio of children ran in barefoot circles, giggling and chasing one another. Iris sensed she would not be afforded an official welcome and simply wished the party good morning as she sat at the end of the table. A few looked up and returned her greeting; others continued their conversations or ate their breakfast. Iris sat for a moment, assessing the situation, until she realised no one was going to serve her and she would need to fetch her food herself.

At the oil-drum grill stood Mafalda, slight, sooty and wearing a pair of dungarees. She saw Iris and seemed momentarily puzzled until her brow cleared and she offered a wry smile.

"Iris, right? Hi. Sorry we didn't roll out the red carpet last night. Your timing could not have been worse. But they didn't take all the chickens, so we have scrambled eggs, *xima* and some tomato salsa. You must be hungry."

Iris took in the blackened pan, the whitish mulch and bowl of salsa. At home on the farm, that would not have fed her six farm workers. But it was all they had.

"Not really, I ate on the plane. But I am thirsty. Where can I get some water?"

"Depends how brave you are. There's a pump against the wall or you can do like Demi and drink the boiled stuff. Foreigners are better off with bottled water otherwise you get the shits and use twice as much water cleaning it up."

It seemed the wrong time to mention her purifier bottle, so Iris merely noted the water pump and listened to Mafalda's instructions.

"Take some *xima* and eggs because we have a busy morning. Chicken coops, vegetable plots, fences and gates all need repairing before sundown. We work in the mornings and study in the afternoons. Demi, will you show Iris the ropes? I don't have time today." With that, she sliced off a chunk of *xima* the size of her hand, added a dollop of salsa and handed it to Iris.

The tallest woman Iris had ever seen emerged from the farmhouse, giving Mafalda the thumbs up. Her hair was white blonde and her skin red and peeling. She wore khaki culottes and a linen poncho over a pale grey vest. Her feet were protected by a pair of battered walking boots. She raised a hand in welcome and crammed a baseball cap over her head.

"Hello, Iris! Another lamb to the slaughter. I'm Demi from Rotterdam and counting down the days till I get out of here." She laughed without conviction. "Are you American?"

"American? No. I come from a small village in Portugal nobody knows. In winter it's quiet, so I wanted to volunteer, make myself useful. When do you leave?"

Demi beckoned her over and cast a glance at her food. "Hey, welcome to Pemba. That's not much of a breakfast. Eat as much as you can, you're going to need all your strength. My stint is over in January, unless I ask for an extension. How long did you sign up for? Sit over there and I'll bring us some coffee."

Iris found a place away from the heat of the grill, under

palm-leaf shade with an ocean breeze. She filled her bottle from the pump and pressed the filter. The advertisement promised 99% purification, eliminating viruses and bacteria. She hoped it lived up to the hype. Hunger overcame politeness and while waiting for Demi, Iris ate took a mouthful of moist tomato porridge. She chewed slowly, ignoring the savage signals sent by her stomach. Around her sat two dozen women of varying ages. Most were black and only Mafalda appeared Latina. Demi was demonstrably Northern European and the only other white face was her own. Three toddlers and two babies suckling at the breast brought the camp total to approximately thirty females.

Sandy ground swept down to the beach, where waves crashed onto the shore with all the arrogance of a breaker, only to fizzle into spindrift. Everything was different. The heat, the sand, the sky, the birds circling overhead, even the colour of the ocean seemed familiar yet not.

"I didn't ask if you want cream or sugar because we have neither." Demi placed two tin mugs and a bottle of water on the wooden surface with a smile more weary than friendly. "You're not the typical volunteer. Gauche, well-meaning liberals in their twenties, plenty of those. Hippie grandmas dispersing their children's inheritance are also pretty common. You fall somewhere in between. What cross are you bearing?"

Iris took a sip of the coffee and almost moaned with delight. Hot, strong and restorative, it was exactly what her body craved. "Thank you. I cannot tell you how much I needed this." She finished her eggs and drank her coffee, marshalling her response. "I'm trying to do something good. For other people, I mean."

"No such thing as altruism. You're trying to make yourself feel better. Don't get offended, we're all doing the same thing. Let me tell you something for nothing, it's harder than it looks.

OK, that's your newbie's briefing, now let's get to work. Help Jennifer clean the kitchen and join me down at the gate. Somehow we've got to patch up that shit again. Hey, nice bottle! You're smarter than you look."

'Kitchen' was a misleading term. The grill, some shelves covered with fabric and the water pump served as the facilities. Iris watched Jennifer and copied her efficient system of washing plates and mugs, using the minimum of water. All the utensils lay on the table to be dried by the sun while she scrubbed at the mesh from the grill with a handful of sand. Iris picked up an apple core and some watermelon rind, but there was no other litter. The women respected their environment, that much was clear. The weepy Jennifer of last night was no longer crying but gave off a morose air as she pointed out the compost area.

"Thank you for helping me," offered Iris. "You're very kind."

"'S-s OK. You done now?'"

"Think so. Demi wants me to help with the gate."

Jennifer stacked the plates and mugs on the shelves and drew the curtains. "Gate never s-s-stops them. Not before, not last night. They come and t-t-ake what they want, even when they don't want it. I gotta go fish if we want lunch. *Até logo.*"

"*Até logo.*" The question burned on her tongue but Jennifer had shuffled away into the barn before Iris could pronounce the words: *who are 'they'?*

The heat rose with intent and by the time she'd walked to the compound entrance, Iris was sweating and regretting the lack of a water bottle. Demi was hammering nails into two slats of pathetically thin wood. One well-placed boot would crack them in two. There had to be a better solution. Iris was bursting with ideas, but reminded herself to listen first and ask questions second.

"How can I help?"

Demi straightened, running the back of her hand over her brow. "Not sure anyone can help with this mess. Have a look at the hinges, will you? If they're bent out of shape, we'll need to wire the gates to the posts."

On the left, both hinges were torn from the concrete posts, one dangling like a Christmas decoration, the other completely missing. On the right, they had remained in place, wrenched and twisted into uselessness.

"No functional hinges, I'm afraid."

"I guessed as much. Go up to the house and ask Mafalda for some wire. It's going to be a make-do and mend job. Goddamn it all, this won't keep a goat out!"

Iris paced in the direction she had come, relieved to head into the shade. The sun was cruel, even at this hour. She searched for Mafalda, for Jennifer, for anyone, but only encountered the two women nursing babies who spoke no English or Portuguese. The only response she got to repeating Mafalda's name was a shrug and vague wave of the hand from the older of the two. Iris interpreted that as 'around here somewhere'.

Amid the clutter of broken wood, wrecked bedsteads, holey buckets and chicken wire stacked against the rear of the 'kitchen', Iris found nothing strong enough to support the weight of a gate. She filled her bottle from the pump, pushed the heel of her hand on the filter and strode down the drive.

"Demi, I can't find Mafalda or any wire to speak of. But maybe we can look at this from a different angle. The thing is, I don't want to waltz in here and start telling people what to do. I'd rather get the context from you before proposing solutions. Could we get out of the sun and talk practicalities?"

It took all of ten seconds for Demi to gather her tools and lead the way to the farmhouse. It was a low, one-storey building made of the same kind of concrete as the cowshed. Inside was far cooler than the grounds and even the kitchen. Pale green walls enclosed a row of benches, like a makeshift church. But the whiteboard at the end announced its function loud and clear in three languages and a diagram. Iris read the Portuguese and translated in her head.

School hours 15.00-17.00. No school, no food.

The other end of the house was divided into three rooms by means of tall woven screens. A storeroom containing catering drums of oil, sacks of flour, rice or beans and vacuum-packed bags of coffee stacked on rough pallets took up the furthest section. In the middle was a small room, half hidden by a curtain. A large metal desk overflowed with piles of paper and even had an old-style telephone. In the corner was a neat little camp bed, much like her own. Mafalda's office and sleeping quarters, Iris assumed. The front section was a kitchen housing a table, mismatched chairs, a gas ring for boiling water and a portable generator powering a fridge.

"Sit. This is what we call the boardroom. We can drink cool water and boil more to replace it. School doesn't start till three." Demi grasped a metal handle and yanked a jerry can from the fridge door. She poured its contents into two enamel mugs.

Iris raised her bottle. "I'm fine with this, thank you."

"Please yourself. More for me. Is this some sort of dodge to get out of working?" Demi asked, sitting on a wooden stool and stretching her long legs in front of her. "Because I fall for it only once."

The water, cold and clean, slaked Iris's throat and she had to force herself not to empty the whole bottle. "When I applied for this job, I asked myself what you need. Not what I can offer, because that might not match your requirements. What do you need? Let's start with the gate. Why do we need a gate and what for?"

"Are you some kind of idiot? Why do we need a gate? You saw what happened last night."

"For the purposes of this conversation, let's say I am an idiot. No, I didn't see what happened last night because I just walked into the aftermath. Explain it to me in simple terms."

Demi sipped at her water, the hint of a frown on her face. "Mafalda said you seem to understand what we're trying to do here. She said you gave the impression of being pretty smart. Not at all like an idiot."

Iris swallowed another gulp of cool water. "I do understand the theory." She parroted a few phrases memorised while completing her application. "A Casa da Prata is committed to the mainstreaming of gender issues, collaboration with stake-holders, breaking the socio-economic vicious circle, promoting sustainable incomes, advocating for equality in local communities ..."

"And there's our problem. Some, not all, of the local communities, or stakeholders in quango-speak, actively benefit from the way things are around here. Using women as unpaid labour is an established practice so ingrained it's like trampling over their culture to suggest there's another way of operating. The socio-economic circle is working fine, in their eyes. Our efforts to give their wives and daughters an education, an income and therefore some agency over their own lives is, as they see it, an insult."

"I take the refuge is not popular around here. My taxi driver said as much."

"Let's take an example. There's a man, we'll call him Pedro. He has a small farm with three cows for producing milk and working the fields. Some outsiders turn up, claiming one of his cows is maltreated and they take it away to their own farm. Pedro is bitter and angry. He goes to the local *barraca*, drinks a few beers with his neighbours and pours out his troubles. The same thing happened to Matteo, Luís and Chico. They rage at the injustice and convince themselves they are the maltreated ones, drink a few more beers and someone brings out a bottle of rum. Powered by alcohol, anger and the safety of numbers, they get into Pedro's pickup, drive out to the cow sanctuary and take something of theirs. It makes them feel better, at least until the next morning. But there are no repercussions. The refuge repairs the damage and we carry on. So it happens again, and again. We have no defences, not in real terms, and they feel their aggression is justified. What we are trying to do will take a generation to change, maybe two." The kettle came to the boil and Demi took it from the gas ring and set it on the floor. "Teenage boys often take a trip out here to cause trouble or sometimes out of curiosity. A group of women living together? It has to be a whorehouse, right?"

Iris shook her head as if she had something in her ear. "Cows?"

"That's how some of these guys view their women. Bought, paid for and meant to work."

"I get it. You have a very good way of illustrating the problem. Do you see a solution, other than time?"

"I'll be honest with you, Iris, I don't see any solution. Maybe Mafalda is playing the long game with A Casa da Prata, but I doubt it. She's just trying to survive and keep this place going. She and Faith are practical women, tough and determined, but strategic? Who has time for strategy when you're putting out fires? Jennifer is willing but hopelessly emotional. Look at the state of her last night. They stole some of our chickens while we were celebrating and she behaves as if she's lost her sisters. Anyway, today is your first day. Fill your flashy water bottle and let's go. We need to finish that gate."

Iris did as she was told, helping Demi tie the hinges into place and propping the gate up on a couple of stones. It was as resilient as tissue paper and they both knew it. But the stones gave Iris an idea.

"Demi? Do you know where we can get some white paint?"

Everyone slept after the midday meal of fried fish and rice. The hours from twelve till two were impossibly hot. The only option was to lie on one's bunk and try to doze. Iris had no problem whatsoever falling into a profound sleep, tuning out the languid conversations and sounds of fretful children. Her body needed rest.

When the women and girls of the camp shuffled into the schoolroom at three in the afternoon, Iris assumed she would be expected to teach or at least assist. Instead, Mafalda waved her away from the house and told her to begin preparations for dinner: slow-cooked beans and pounded cassava leaves stewed with onions, cashews and prawns, served with mango salsa. On a menu, it would sound fascinating. Unless you had to rinse, boil, stew, pound and peel the ingredients yourself.

Iris sweated over the hot stove for two hours, wholly focussed on the task in hand. It was her job and hers alone, since Demi had vanished. She boiled three pans of water while the stove was on, pouring the cooling water into two jerry cans. One she planned to keep for washing fruit and vegetables while the other was for Demi. Her purifying bottle was exactly what she'd hoped. Room temperature or chilled, Iris didn't care, so long as she could drink litres of clean water and keep hydrated. She stared out at the ocean, marvelling at how generous and yet hostile an environment could be. Fish and seafood from the country's long coastline, a rich natural abundance of mineral and vegetable in its interior, a diversity of fauna to excite naturalists and a multicultural populace living in one of the most beautiful places on Earth.

Another track of her brain was problem-solving. A Casa da

Prata had to function, feed, protect and defend itself. At the same time, its ambassadors had to open a dialogue with those who resented its very existence. That meant using every single tactic at their disposal. Tactics, she reminded herself, are nothing more than elements of a strategy. She needed to talk to Mafalda.

Before school finished, Demi came up the road on a push-bike, her pannier filled to overflowing with vegetables. She parked the bike in the shade and wiped her forearm across her brow. "Market day. If you get there when they're closing, you can score a bagful for under a hundred mets. I got sweet potatoes, string beans, two cabbages, green peppers, bananas and hallelujah, a pineapple. Guess what else I found?"

Iris eyed the limp-looking vegetables with little enthusiasm. "I don't know. Road kill?"

"White paint! Cost me twice what I paid for the vegetables, but I got two cans of bright white exterior paint. How about that!" She emptied her water bottle in two gulps.

"You're pretty resourceful, I have to say. How much do I owe you?"

The doors of the school opened and women poured out, some heading for the cowshed, others already parking themselves at the tables, ready for dinner.

Demi waved at the eager guests. "Can't blame them, whatever you're making smells pretty good. You owe me three Euros. I'm going to put the veg in the house and have a swim. Back in time to help you serve."

"Wait, three Euros? That's ridiculous. You said the veg cost a hundred!"

"Yeah, a hundred meticais. That equates to one Euro fifty. Pay me later or you can even buy me a beer at the bar one of these nights. I'll put the paint in the store, OK? Maybe after dinner you can tell me what it's for."

Iris was looking forward to that.

. . .

The meal was a success, more for quantity than quality, and the compliments boosted her confidence. Iris filled her own belly while her clientele ate every last scrap. Jennifer came to help with the clean-up operation and one of the other girls joined them, shyly informing Iris that Mafalda wanted a chat. This was Iris's opportunity. She hurried across to the house, aware she smelt of sweat and smoke, but determined to grab her chance.

The house appeared to be empty, so Iris waited in the doorway, snatching a moment of coolness from the concrete floor. Sounds came from the storeroom; rustling bags and deep sighs. Eventually, Mafalda came out and saw Iris standing in the doorway.

"Thank you for dinner. You worked hard, I see that. You also used half the food store for one meal. It's not your fault, it's mine. I should have told you to limit proportions. Now we have a problem to feed everyone for the rest of the week."

Shame crept over Iris like a heat rash, undoing any cooling effect from the building. "I'm sorry. I cooked for thirty people and Demi got some vegetables from the market today."

"She did. We could use them to flavour the sand we have to eat until I can buy more dry goods. Iris, we survive on government grants and charity. There is no money. Our vegetable patch and tiny farm grows just enough to support the children, unless it is stolen. More often than not, it's stolen. In future, you work with Jennifer on cooking detail. You have to go now. I need to prepare more funding applications."

"Mafalda, I'm sorry. I can buy some food to supplement what we have. I would consider it a contribution for letting me stay. Could we have a word about security?"

Mafalda rubbed her hand around her neck. "Tonight, no. I have to make some phone calls. This is the only opportunity I have to do all the things I cannot do during the day. Thanks for dinner. When Demi leaves, security will be Faith's responsibility. Go talk to the two of them. Listen, Iris, one piece of advice. Spend your first week learning, not trying to change the world. You'll fail and leave us worse off than before. Goodnight."

4

———————

Her words cut deep. Iris could not spend her money on food or security because she would not be there forever. What she could do was share her experience. She sought out Demi and they found Faith reading a book on her bunk. Their doubtful faces as she explained her concept made her worry the execution would be half-hearted. But Faith spoke for them both when she said with a shrug, "It's better than doing nothing".

They worked all night. Demi took the wheelbarrow down to the shore, Iris dug holes and Faith painted rocks. Bit by bit, they booby-trapped the driveway. First, they dug a gully half a metre deep just inside the gate. Secondly, Iris marked spots to excavate holes deep enough to embed a rock. Faith placed each rock so the white side faced the house and packed earth, stones and sea water around it to create a solid-ish base. When the women wanted to drive their battered Land Cruiser out of the compound at night, the driveway from Casa da Prata would be illuminated by its headlights as a snaking loop taking in three curves before approaching the gully. Not so from the main road. The drive from that angle was now a vehicular disaster.

Trucks and jeeps battering down the gate would fall into the gully and even if that did not wreck the axles and prevent them coming further, the rocks would cause maximum tyre damage.

Lastly, Demi and Iris layered a bed frame with broken pallets and hid it in the scrub beside the gate. It was easily dragged from its hiding place, strong enough to support a light vehicle and would act as an improvised drawbridge. They toasted their efforts with some warm water and as the sun came up, fell into their own beds.

Iris lay awake, energised with anticipation; half hoping a Jeep full of drunken locals would try making a dawn ambush.

They didn't.

The next thing she knew, her net opened and Jennifer shook her arm.

"Wake up, Iris, we're going to the city! We can try out your new security rocks."

Iris blinked her gritty eyes, stiff and aching. The scent of coffee wafted across the camp, indicating rest was over and work was about to begin. In the open-air bathroom, she washed off the dirt and dust of the night's activities, yawning like a donkey but careful not to swallow a drop of water. She wriggled into some combat shorts and a clean T-shirt, then hurried across to the kitchen before the coffee ran out. Mafalda offered her a steaming cup with a quizzical smile.

"You used your time wisely last night."

Iris drank, her need for caffeine greater than her yearning for Mafalda's approval. "Yeah. We worked till sunrise. Faith and Demi were both troupers."

Mafalda said nothing, squinting at the apparently random pattern of painted stones. She was wearing a denim shirt and black jeans, her abundant curls crammed under her baseball cap. The combination seemed suffocating to Iris.

"You offered to buy some dry goods for the compound, if remember correctly? Faith and Jennifer will take you into Pemba to do the shopping. Haggle, demand the best price and do not overspend. You Europeans think everything can be solved with a credit card. It can't. You splash the cash and set up an expectation we cannot meet. What you did to the drive is a smart idea, I agree, but we don't know how that will play out. If they wreck their trucks trying to scare us, how will they retaliate? No one knows, least of all you. Here, I saved our hunter-gatherers three pancakes. Take them to eat on the road."

"Thank you." Iris took the cloth-wrapped package and poured herself another bitter black coffee. "I'm trying to do the right thing, Mafalda."

"Until you know what 'the right thing' is, that means *nada*. Go now before the market gets too busy. And, Iris? Whatever you do, don't let Jennifer buy any more chickens."

The yellow Land Cruiser belonging to Casa da Prata was the definition of ancient and clapped-out. It took Jennifer four tries to start it and even then, it sounded raspy and weak, as if it might expire in a ditch at any moment. The girl seemed almost too slight to reach the pedals, but before Iris could offer to drive, they jerked away down the drive. Faith perched in the middle, directing Jennifer through the maze of stones. By some kind of miracle, they reached the main road and Jennifer swung the wheel hard right and onto the left-hand side. Only then did Iris realise she had been holding her breath.

She clutched the door handle as they bumped along the track, her focus on the road ahead. Occasionally, she sneaked a glance at her companions, astounded by their innocence and vulnerability.

Jennifer, hunched over the steering wheel, eyes wide and fists clenched, appeared no more than fourteen years old. Her hair was cropped close to her head, giving her a soft, youthful look. Her skin glowed like flames reflecting on a cooking pot.

Ahead, a Toyota Canter idled by the roadside as three men tried to cram twice its capacity inside. Jennifer made a faint humming noise through her nose and slowed.

"No, speed up," Faith hissed. "Iris, lean out of your window and wish them a good day. We will not be stopped. Foot down, Jennifer, foot down and do not stop."

The Land Cruiser came upon the men too fast for them to decide on a collective reaction. Iris called '*Bom dia!*' from the window as they overtook, one man raised a hand, another scowled and the teenager heaving tyres onto the roof gave them a dazzling smile. Jennifer was still making a keening sound through her nostrils.

"Jenni, it's fine. They didn't even see you because Iris distracted them. I looked all three in the face and I can tell you not one of them was him. You're OK. Concentrate on the road." Faith rested a hand on Jennifer's shoulder. "You're doing fine, *filha*, you're safe."

The intensity of Faith's voice made Iris turn away. Her staring could only add to Jennifer's distress. Instead, she gazed out of the window, observing both their reflections. Body language revealed so many secrets.

Faith could only have been a few years older than Jennifer, but her demeanour came from another generation. Her posture was proud, her jaw strong and her hair woven into tight plaits, the ends curled into a snail-shape at the nape of her neck. She'd stayed up all night to help prepare the driveway defences but still kept a steady hand on her friend, colleague or junior. Iris wondered why capable, calm Faith wasn't doing the driving but surmised everyone had to learn the hard way.

No one followed them and Jennifer seemed to relax, at least to one level lower than broken-molar tension. They parked in the shade of a fish market, locked the vehicle – a token gesture – and ventured into town. Faith led the way, with her list in her hand and an air of determination. She argued and spat and dismissed stallholder after vendor until she found a deal she could accept. Her courage in the face of downright disrespect and frequent insults struck Iris dumb. She would have confronted all these merchants, one by one, until they sold her the goods like any other buyer.

But she obediently followed Faith's lead, infuriated by inflated prices, yet playing the grateful consumer. Once everything on the list had been purchased and stashed in the vehicle, Faith bought a cold Sprite for Jennifer, an iced coffee for Iris and asked them to stay by the car until she finished today's business for A Casa da Prata. The two women leaned against the car, sucking at their beverages, pretending they were at ease.

Pasted along the walls of the fish market was a random assortment of election posters, all highly coloured and featuring the stiff grins of potential politicians. Each promoted a man in a suit with one exception: Amina Mecuande. A luminous beaming smile drew the eye to the focus point of a busy image. She looked like the centre of a clock, surrounded by green, yellow black and red ribbons, corn cobs, sunbursts, stars, and detailed elements of the national flag, such as a hoe, a rifle and an open book. Her slogan was 'Everyone Can Prosper!' and above her head banknotes fluttered like cherry blossom. Her body was swathed in a *capulana* with a headdress of similar material, and her skin reflected flecks of gold. The message was clear: 'I Am Every Woman' (Or The Woman You Want To Be).

"That's a good sign, no?" Iris asked Jennifer. "A woman running for office?"

Jennifer gave Iris a blank look and continued scanning the street for Faith. "They're all the s-s-same. No point."

"No point in voting?"

"No point. Not for us. There's Faith! Oh dear. She doesn't look happy."

That was an understatement. Jennifer scurried to get inside the vehicle, already welling up with tears, but Faith called out, her expression thunderous.

"Don't bother. We have to wait here until six. Let's go find a shady spot which doesn't stink. Get out, Jenni, and please don't cry."

Head down, Jennifer followed in Faith's long strides. The heat of the midday sun was like an iron, flattening them into obedience. But Iris never took anything at face value. Plus, she reasoned with herself, she needed to know the way things worked around here.

"Why six o'clock?" she asked, taking longer strides to catch Faith. "The shops open again at three, no?"

"Yeah, but that bastard at the pharmacy works the afternoon shift. He won't serve me so we have to wait till his wife takes over. She only does evenings. I hope to God she's working tonight or we're in trouble. No baby formula, no sanitary products, no medication for another week."

"Hang on." Iris came to a halt. "Why won't he serve you?"

Faith halted and gave her a sideways glance, but said nothing.

"I see." Iris exhaled. "He knows you're from A Casa da Prata. But he doesn't know me. In his eyes, I'm just another tourist. Why don't you let me buy what we need? I'd like to make amends for overcooking yesterday."

As if recalling the meal, Jennifer's stomach released a cat-like growl. She wrapped her arms around her middle and muttered, "S-s-sorry."

"Tell me what we need and take Jennifer back to the compound. I'll buy our supplies and take a taxi when I'm finished."

Faith's face was scornful. "A taxi? This isn't London, you know. I can't leave you wandering the streets of Pemba on your own. You're being naïve." From the town, male voices reached them singing a vaguely familiar dance hit from the '80s. Faith stiffened. With a glance at Jennifer, she thrust a piece of paper at Iris. "Why not? The prices are listed so just refuse to pay more. We'll see you at A Casa da Prata. Don't ... watch out for ... oh, hell, just be careful, yeah? Come, Jenni, we'll go back through the market." She tugged at Jennifer's hand because the girl seemed frozen in place. The movement triggered an urgency and the two women rushed away from the singing and into the gaping maw of the fish market. Iris watched as a group of boisterous youths emerged from a side street, performing some kind of swaying, hand-clapping dance while chanting women's names. These boys were looking for trouble. She recognised the look in their eyes at the same time she recalled the title of the song: 'Mambo Number 5'.

A cyclist rode past, laden with palm leaves. The rider slowed to wave at the singers and to make some whooping noises. Iris moved fast, lining herself on the other side of the branches and in the cyclist's blind spot. She broke into a jog as he sped up, pacing silently at his heels, her backpack thumping as loudly as her breathing. After he'd turned two corners and left the threat behind, she fell back, sweating from heat, humidity and adrenalin.

Faith's list was in her hand, moist and crumpled. The writing was still legible, but Iris had no idea where to find the pharmacy. She crossed the street to gain some shade and saw a hotel terrace with tables shaded by umbrellas. The urge to sit, rest and slug a Cuba Libre was hard to resist. She dawdled for a second, indecisive and slugging from her water bottle, until she heard two women berating a porter for scuffing their luggage. Their accents grated on her ear although they spoke good Portuguese and wore local dress. For a moment, Iris imagined one might be the politician whose poster she had seen, yet neither appeared the right age.

The long-suffering hotel employee placed their suitcases in the boot of a taxi, helped the still-bitching ladies into the back seat and slipped the driver a tip as he gave him their destination. Iris caught him before he returned to the terrace. She spoke in Portuguese.

"Excuse me. I'm looking for the local pharmacy. Can you point me in the right direction?"

He screwed up his face in concentration. "Pharmacy is by the hospital. Take a right there, and the second right. You'll see it on your left. Five-minute walk but it closes at one, so you better hurry, madam."

She held out her hand and palmed him a dollar note. An excessive tip for simple directions, but she felt an obligation to compensate for the horrible guests he'd just seen off. "Thank you. Have a good day." It was too hot to jog with her backpack and she wanted to arrive with her dignity intact so she strolled in the shade, practising her superior tone. Those snotty females departing the hotel had given her a touch of inspiration.

The pharmacy was a narrow building with the typical green cross on its illuminated sign. The interior looked clean and shiny, with an L-shaped counter, behind which stood shelves bearing boxes of brightly lit medicinal products. A teenage girl was serving a mother and daughter at the end, while the boss continued his telephone conversation. She hoped he would ignore her so she could be served by the young woman, but he gave her a curious once-over and ended the call.

"Yes?"

"Good afternoon. I'm from the UN office. We're in urgent need of certain supplies. Can you help or should I try somewhere else? I'm in rather a hurry, you see."

"UN? Really? Let's see some ID."

Iris didn't blink. "Do all your customers require ID?"

"If I ask for it, yes."

She held his gaze. The conversation at the other end of the room came to a halt.

"I'm on secondment from the Metropolitan Police in London. Here's my police badge, stating my full name, rank and security clearance. I hope that is satisfactory."

His eyes flicked from hers to the document she displayed. The photo was four years old and time had not been kind to her skin. But it was clearly the same woman.

He flared his nostrils and looked at his watch. "We close at one."

"So if we're quick, we can both get what we want – me, my medications; and you, your lunch. Can we start with feminine hygiene products? I'd like three boxes of sanitary pads and another three of tampons."

That did the trick. He scowled and addressed his assistant who was silently watching their exchange. "Aziah, stop your chatter and come serve this lady. I'm going for lunch. Lock up after these customers and open again at two." He switched the sign on the door to Closed and left the shop, without another glance in Iris's direction.

The other customer paid for her order, took her daughter's hand and with a knowing smile, wished Iris a nice day. The little girl stared as she passed by, her eyes huge.

The shop assistant stood in front of her, all smiles.

"Hello, how can I help you, madam?"

"Hello. Aziah, isn't it? I have a list, but I don't want to take up your lunch break."

"It's OK." Aziah gurgled a laugh. "I always take an hour from when I finish. He'll never know the difference because he sleeps until three. Give me your list."

Iris bought twice the amounts Faith had specified, paying with her own money and offering Aziah a little bonus if she provided a decent-sized carrier bag. Her next stop was a super-market where she used a phone booth in the entrance to call Tendai. He remembered her and offered to collect her when he'd finished his day's fares.

"Maybe four o'clock? Not too late?"

"Not too late," she assured him.

In Shoprite, she filled her trolley with rice, coffee, noodles, flour, various pulses and canned meat. Secondary items included a torch, a bike lock and a bottle of vodka. Cheaper than sleeping tablets, she told herself. She paid the bill with cash, Mafalda's words in her ear: '*You Europeans think everything can be solved with a credit card. It can't. You splash the cash and set up an expectation we cannot meet.*' Iris handed over the dollar bills with a shrug. She'd deal with that problem when it arose.

Her bags bulging, she stuffed everything in a trolley and wheeled it outside. An old guy was begging by the doorway, one leg entirely missing.

"Please help, madam, I am the victim of a landmine. Please help me, kind lady."

"I have no Mozambique money left," she said. "Can I buy you something to eat? Is there somewhere I can pay with a card?"

"Thank you, kind lady! I am very hungry." He pointed at a kiosk. "*Galinha asada e uma cerveja Dois-Em, por favor.*"

Iris returned his wide smile. "You know what, I think I'll join you. One roast chicken and two beers coming right up."

They ate together, her leaning against her trolley, him resting on his crutch. He managed to tell her his life story between glugs of beer and mouthfuls of chicken. She sipped water and gnawed on a drumstick, concentrating hard on understanding his accent. Berto was quite a raconteur. He'd lost his foot and thus his job as a bus driver over a year after the country was declared mine-free. Every time she opened her mouth to ask a question, his explanation had already begun.

"On the border with Tanzania. Forget about the official line, that's a fairy tale. I'm talking about 2016, after the land-mine charities declared us safe, took their charity dollars and left. The government were busy rebuilding our infrastructure, sure they were, but only for people near the cities. The rest of us had no chance. With one foot blasted off, how could I get to a hospital? On a goat?"

Iris glanced at his empty trouser leg, trying to find the right words.

He cut her off. "It was only your foot, she's thinking. Why the leg? I'll tell you, kind lady, if you have a strong stomach. And if you don't, feel free to give me the rest of the *galinha*. Yes, it was only a foot at first, but the shrapnel, you see, then the infections. Pain like you wouldn't believe. I swear it was the worst agony. The worst and I don't care if you've given birth to six children." Berto tore off a chunk of bread and dipped it in chicken fat. "The healer in my village did her best. Until she died of AIDS. That poor sainted woman treated us all and we ended up killing her." His emotion made him pause. "We killed her."

At a loss for what to say, Iris reached out to squeeze his shoulder.

He snatched his food away in a reflexive move and continued his story. "My brother-in-law strapped me onto his motorcycle sidecar and brought me to Pemba. A journey into hell, kind lady, and I am not ashamed to tell you I asked the Lord to take my soul. I could take no more. I passed out. He had to leave me outside the hospital as he could never afford my treatment." He laughed, a dry ironic sound. "I screamed for two full days and nights, calling on every cursed demon and monstrous deity and I know a few because we had a strange book in our village. It scared us senseless."

"Demons and deities?" Iris tilted her head, trying to ascertain how much of the old man's performance was a well-worn act or delusion.

"They cut it off eventually."

"Sorry?"

"My leg. No money. No treatment. This is why I trespass on the kindness of strangers. You know, Iris was my grand-mother's name. On my father's side. Wonderful woman, dearly loved. A storyteller, a singer, an angel!"

Iris wasn't sure how to phrase her next question. "Do you have some shelter, Berto? I mean, where do you sleep?"

"I'm not homeless, kind lady! No street sleeper, not me, not anymore. I had the very good fortune to meet a gentleman, a businessman with a heart of pure gold. I say a prayer for him every night before I close my eyes. Why, she's thinking? I'll tell you. That man gave me the gift of a home. Nothing luxurious, kind lady, don't get the wrong idea. It's a mobile home on some waste land but to me, it's a palace. Inside it's clean as a hospital and outside I built a shrine to the Virgin Mary so God will bless Senhor Samuel Albino for the rest of his sainted life."

"A mobile home? So you can change location if you feel like it?"

"Such is the irony of the name." He shook his head with infinite sadness. "A mobile home needs wheels and I have none. No wheels and only one leg, but I am content with my lot. Who could feel otherwise in this Garden of Eden?"

Iris was almost disappointed when a horn alerted her to the arrival of Tendai and his taxi. She gave Berto the rest of the roasted bird and thanked him for his life story. He had already lost interest in her and was hitting on the next shopper. She helped Tendai wedge her purchases into the back seat and climbed in beside the bags. With a wave and a blast of Tendai's horn, they were on their way.

"Was that man bothering you?"

"Not at all. He's a real character. I bought him lunch."

Tendai said nothing, his concentration on the traffic.

Iris looked at a couple taking a selfie outside a jewellery shop. Their joy was infectious and her cynicism gave way to a smile. She noticed Tendai's chatty tour guide banter was absent and wondered if buying a beggar some food was somehow frowned upon here, like feeding seagulls in Brighton. *You'll only encourage them!*

"You're not really a tourist, are you?" asked Tendai, watching her in the rear-view mirror.

She wasn't sure how to reply. Was being a tourist a good or bad thing?

"I mean, you speak Portuguese, you went shopping for those women and you bought Berto chicken and beer."

"You know that guy?"

"Everyone knows him. What are you, a charity worker? Where are you from?"

She kept it simple. "Portugal, in the north. My story is nowhere near as dramatic as Berto's. I work on my parents' farm. It's quiet in the winter and I wanted to do something useful with my time. That's why I came here to work at A Casa da Prata. To answer your enquiry, no, I guess I'm not a typical tourist."

Tendai said nothing, slowing to overtake a cyclist carrying a sack of something heavy. Iris looked out at the ocean, half wishing she was a tourist with nothing else to do but swim and sunbathe and read a book.

His voice interrupted her fantasy. "Can I ask you a question?"

"You already asked me three. Why the sudden formality?"

"It's a different question. You said you came here to work at A Casa da Prata. What kind of work? What do they do there? I've heard a whole lot of rumours. I mean, I'm not the type to listen to gossip but some people think it's strange, a bunch of women living together."

"*Some* people think it's strange?" She kept her tone even and calm, aware of the conversation as an opportunity. "What sort of people?"

He waggled his head. "Just people. I never get involved. Minding my own business is my superpower. That's why I'm such a great taxi driver." He laughed and Iris joined in. "I can't lie, though, I am curious. I mean, what's it all about?" He turned inland, leaving the expanse of the sea for dry and dusty earth.

"It's a farm, just like any other, but also a safe place. Not all women can or even want to live at home. You're a modern guy, Tendai, you understand. There's nothing strange about women helping other women in need."

He glanced into the mirror. "No, I guess women in need is OK."

"But?"

"I didn't say but."

"I heard it anyway, loud and clear. Tendai, we're being honest with each other, right? So finish your question. But what?"

He sucked his teeth and dodged a pothole. "Some of the girls, I don't know, their families say they get funny ideas, want to leave home, go to the big city, forget where they come from."

Up ahead was the farmstead she'd passed that morning, where Jennifer began hyperventilating. No one stood outside.

"When you were a boy, what did you want to be?"

Tendai laughed, his mouth wide. "I wanted to be a taxi driver! Meeting people, earning a wage for my skills and tips for my charm. I speak French and English, not only Portuguese. I'm reliable, friendly and know all the best places. Tendai's Top Tips! You were lucky to find me."

Up the road stood A Casa da Prata, apparently peaceful and undisturbed. Iris released a sigh. The place was still standing. "Stop at the end of the drive, please, and keep the meter running. Do you have sisters, Tendai?"

"Three, all younger than me. You have a lot of bags, Iris, I can drive you into the compound if you like?"

"No. Stop here, thank you. I can manage. Your sisters? Do they also want to be taxi drivers?"

He stopped the car and looked over his shoulder. "Taxi drivers? Ha! My sisters can't even drive the tractor. No, not a great job for a girl. They work the farm with my mother until they get married. Soon, I hope. You wanna pay in dollars again?"

Iris got out of the car and called to Demi, who was stacking beach stones into something resembling a wall. "Help me carry this stuff into the house?" she called.

She paid Tendai with a tip. "If any of your sisters has more ambition than being someone's wife, she would be welcome at A Casa da Prata. Have a good day, Tendai, see you soon."

She hauled the bags from the cab and waited till the dust from his wheels had settled.

"What's all this?" asked Demi.

"Faith's medical list and replacements for what I overused. Is there a place we can store a few things for emergencies?"

Demi peered into the bags. "Yep. Let's do it now before school is out." She rubbed her eyes. "I think I'm hallucinating. Is that vodka?"

"You said I could buy you a drink sometime," Iris grinned.

"The minute I set eyes on you, I thought to myself, I'm gonna like this girl."

5

____

Almost a week passed in relative peace. Mafalda accepted the replacement groceries with only a mild reminder not to do it again. One of the babies had colic and kept the whole compound awake for two successive nights until Faith relocated the child and her mother to the farmhouse. The weather turned wetter and more humid, with low grey clouds covering the peninsula like a duvet. Days were spent building a dry stone wall along the road as a deterrent, cooking for thirty hungry mouths and trying to coax the muddy ground and treacherous sea to give up its treasures. Every night, Iris fell into bed like a log, always clutching her purifying water bottle.

On market day, Demi cycled through the rain into town and persuaded a few weary market traders to part with damaged fruit and runty vegetables. So far, so normal. Yet on this occasion, she had a specific mission: score ingredients for cocktails. She did not fail.

The clouds dissipated that afternoon and by moonrise, the sky was clear and brilliant with stars. Mafalda, Iris, Faith and Demi walked down to the sea and celebrated a rare treat on the beach. No ice or umbrellas but pulped strained fruit and cheap vodka tasted like luxury. The generator was timed to switch off at ten. When the background hum shut down and the lights flickered off, the four women sat in moonlight, making the most of the silence and a moment to relax.

After the second drink, tongues loosened and conversation flowed, albeit in low voices. Demi won a good-natured debate about mangoes versus pineapples as best cocktail mixer by invoking the Piña Colada. The absence of Jennifer bothered Faith. The younger girl was part of the team, Faith insisted in a fierce whisper almost inaudible under the sound of the waves, therefore she should have been invited. Her argument made sense to Iris until Mafalda spoke. To invite Jennifer would have been unfair. The girl was a people-pleaser to her bones, especially to those she perceived as authority figures. If Faith or Mafalda had offered a casual invitation, she would have been unable to refuse. Despite the fact she was worn out, hated alcohol and found social occasions immensely stressful.

"Jennifer is part of the team and has a vote at our board meetings, where everything is structured in a familiar way. You can't force her to be spontaneous, any more than we can force that damned goat to give milk."

They suppressed a burst of laughter. The goat was a leaving present from the volunteer before Demi. The thought came from the right place, like most good intentions, as a desire to provide the women of A Casa da Prata with a regular source of milk. Or failing that, meat. The animal turned out to be male, aggressive and only useful for attacking people who crossed its stretch of beach. The rest of the time it ate whatever it could access, which was pretty much everything: vegetables, rubbish, drying clothes. Daily, Mafalda threatened to slit its throat and roast it, but it paid her no attention, wandering in and out of the compound at will.

"Ssh, he'll hear us," Faith giggled. "I'm surprised he hasn't already stomped down here to butt us off his patch."

"He makes a damned good guard dog," Iris agreed. "Nothing as stubborn as an old billy goat. The females are supposed to be friendlier. Hey, that reminds me. When I was in Pemba I saw some political posters."

"Yeah, the election's next week," said Mafalda with a shiver. "How come it gets cold so fast when the sun goes down?"

"It doesn't." Demi lifted herself from the beach towel she was sitting on. "You must have bad circulation because there's no other explanation for feeling cold in such a climate. Never come to the Netherlands, you'll die in the first twenty minutes. Here, wrap yourself in this. What were you saying about the election, Iris, and what does it have to do with goats?"

"Not goats, but females. I noticed there's a woman standing for local government. That's an optimistic sign, right?"

Neither Demi nor Faith responded, waiting for Mafalda to answer once she had arranged the towel around her shoulders. The splash of the waves filled the silence.

"You'd think it would be. A woman in power is going to extend a hand to all her sisters, change the law, offer opportunities to those less fortunate and raise the bar for female equality. Amina Mecuande's campaign slogan, believe it not, is 'Everyone Can Prosper'. Uh-huh."

Faith snorted. "That's a pile of shit. She's nothing but a self-serving rich bitch who has pulled up every ladder after she got to the top. Everyone Can Prosper? In brackets, but Me First. I cannot stand Mecuande and will vote for the person most likely to beat the selfish cow."

The heat in her voice gave everyone pause, but Iris needed to know more. "Who is likely to beat her? Are his policies any better?"

Mafalda's laugh was low and husky. "Interested in local

politics, Iris? Maybe you can give us all a lecture one night after dinner. No, I'm not being sarcastic. Many of us have lost hope of change and the rest never believed it was possible. You have fire in your heart. You speak well. If you can convince one of our sisters to use her democratic right, that ..."

An almighty crash came from the compound, accompanied by the screech of an engine, voices roaring and shouting, followed by a growing chorus of female screams. All four women were on their feet and running in the dark, racing each other to the scene. Mafalda yelled orders as she ran.

"I'll check everyone's OK and calm the panic. Demi, switch the lights on and get the gun. Lock the doors, Faith, so they can't get into the house. Iris, go with Demi. NO ONE GETS HURT!"

When they reached the top of the dune, it was clear their booby traps had taken effect. With no more illumination than headlights shining directly into their eyes from the gully, it was impossible to make out any detail. Cries of pain and frustration charged the air and the smell of exhaust fumes was overpowering. Iris could smell blood and alcohol.

The generator ignited with a mechanical clunk and flooded the scene with light. The damage was enormous. The headlights came from a broken Jeep sitting on its haunches in the ditch; a motorcycle rider was attempting to reverse around the stones while his passenger scrambled to his feet. Neither wore a helmet and both had sustained head wounds. Another pick-up had rear-ended the Jeep, tossing its cargo of drunken young men onto the dusty ground or into the gully. Their howls of pain came from falling on broken beer bottles. One guy clambered from the driving seat of the Jeep and advanced on them, jabbing a finger as he yelled something incomprehensible.

A police officer to her bones, Iris assessed the accident as serious, potentially fatal and immediately requiring emergency first-aid. As an automatic reflex, she reached for her knife and secondly, for her torch. To her left, Demi stood, arms folded and feet planted, her jaw jutting like a scythe. Heavy breathing behind them indicated Faith was reporting for duty. They obviously had no intention of helping the intruders. This was a declaration of war.

A flash of inspiration hit Iris and she ran for the kitchen area. The half oil drum retained some cold remnants of coal which she tipped onto the sand. Then she lugged the blackened metal towards the two women who stood side by side, forming a mismatched human barrier. She threw the drum on the ground, open side down and dropped to her knees.

With both palms, she battered the metal in a fierce rhythm and yelled *"Fora daqui!"* (Get out of here!) The noise halted the aggressive man's approach and she saw fear in the others' faces. She drummed her palms once again, an ancient rage fuelling the rhythm. *"Fora daqui! Fora daqui! Fora daqui!"*

Beside her, Demi joined in, pounding her fists on the drum with a more sinister beat, but her voice was a hiss in time with the beat. *"Fora daqui. Fora daqui. Fora daqui."* The Jeep driver pelted through the gate, running as if seven devils were on his tail. All it took was Faith snatching up a stick to thwack the end section and releasing an unholy screech for all the men to abandon their vehicles and run.

They continued drumming, the vodka in their veins encouraging an unusual bravado. Finally, drained by the drama, they fizzled to a halt. The headlights of the stricken Jeep illuminated the performers and Iris almost expected applause. The echoes of their thundering, bellowing and howling evaporated into a shocked silence. Only the throbbing of Iris's palms convinced her it was real.

Footsteps shuffled over the sand from the cowshed. Mafalda gave two thumbs up, breaking the moment. All three released huge sighs.

"We should record that." Demi laughed as she walked to

the Jeep and switched off its lights. "Add a few more lyrics and we can kick Stomp's ass."

Mafalda stared at the destruction. "Faith, take this drum back to the kitchen and knock it into shape. We'll need it for breakfast. Then switch off the generator and leave the clearing up till the morning. I'll go and reassure everyone we're safe. Demi, Iris, can you stand guard? They will come to reclaim their vehicles and that's fine. Just watch to make sure they don't come any closer. When everyone is quiet, I'll call the police and file a report. They never usually do anything about it, but this time some men have been injured, so who knows? My duty is to record these assaults."

"OK, we have it covered," Iris assured her. "Goodnight, Mafalda."

"Goodnight. Thank you for tonight. For all of it." She walked off towards the cowshed, still wearing Demi's beach towel around her shoulders.

The lights went out and Iris was at a sudden loss. "Stand guard how?" she whispered. "Where?"

Demi was nothing more than a silhouette in the bright moonlight. "Outside the farmhouse. Let's light a tiny fire so they know we're watching. You have a torch, I have a gun and we'll collect a pile of rocks to throw at them if they come anywhere near us."

They settled themselves on a wooden bench. Iris lit a fire using pieces of driftwood within a circle of stones. Demi went inside to fetch some water. When she returned, she offered Iris a slice of jerky.

"Thanks. These days I'm always hungry."

"I'm always thirsty. We left the vodka on the beach, I suppose?"

"Yeah, sorry. But the lid was screwed on, so ...?"

"Give me two minutes. If Mafalda asks, I've gone for a pee."

The compound was in complete silence, apart from the small flames crackling at Iris's feet. She rotated her head like an owl, tensed for any signs of movement. The broken Jeep and motorcycle corpse in the black-and-white light made her think of a WWII tableau. No noise came from the road, the cowshed was quiet and the flames at her feet emitted hisses and spits like an angry kitten. Into the silence, sounds of a scuffle and a cry of pain came from the beach.

Iris was on her feet in a second; knife in hand, her pulse deafening. "Demi? You OK?" Her voice was an urgent whisper.

Kicking up sand and muttering curses, the Dutchwoman crested the dune, brandishing a bottle. "Fine, apart from a bruise on my arse. Before I leave, I swear to God, I'm going to turn that bastard into a goat curry."

The triumph of that night was short-lived. The next afternoon Iris was attempting to de-clog the shower with a twisted coat hanger when Jennifer raced inside with a bucket of sardines.

"Iris, police! T-t-t —"

"Breathe, Jenni. The police are here?"

Jennifer held up two fingers.

"Two police officers?"

"Yes, they parked on the road. I s-s-saw them when I came up from fishing. Mafalda is t-t-teaching and we are not allowed to disturb s-s-school unless it's an emergency. What should we do?"

"Let's go ask them what they want."

Iris rinsed her hands in a hurry but by the time she got outside, two uniformed officers were already strolling up the drive, examining the damage and smoking something unpleasant. Somehow, Jennifer had melted into the background. The policemen took in Iris as she approached. It was tempting to shout something along the lines of, 'Finally, you've shown your faces!' but it was not her place.

The farmhouse door opened and Mafalda greeted the officers by name.

"This time I think we can agree it's not just our word against theirs." She indicated all the broken beer bottles, bloodstains, bent wheels of the motorbike, the wreckage of the Jeep and the tyre tracks of the pickup which had taken their would-be attackers away. Out of the blue, she turned to Iris and spoke English. "Could you continue the school lessons while I speak to the officers about last night's incident? Thanks."

Iris played along. "Of course. My pleasure." She headed for the farmhouse with no idea what she was supposed to do. All the camp inhabitants, apart from Demi, Jennifer and Mafalda, were sitting on benches and chatting in a variety of languages. Voices dried to a quiet, expectant murmur as Iris walked up to the whiteboard and turned to face her audience. Above her head, a ceiling fan whisked a faint breeze but did little to alleviate the heat.

Iris clapped her hands once, with a sense of purpose. She addressed them in Portuguese. "Mafalda is speaking to the police. Nothing to worry about. She asked me to talk to you about ... about something very important."

A few heads tilted in confusion and Iris recalled that not everyone could speak Portuguese. The number of languages here were impossible to know, but her audience had one thing in common. They had survived.

Iris started to applaud, her rational mind wondering where the hell this was leading. She clapped all around the room, smiling and nodding, making eye contact and making every gesture she could think of to show appreciation. Some of the kids joined in, bursting into laughter. Their enthusiasm carried their mothers, the younger people and finally the oldest women along with the energy. Some even slapped each other's backs. The only way to finish the round of appreciation was for Iris to raise her arms in the air like a conductor and drop, head bowed.

The effect was instant. Everyone hushed and gave her their full attention. In her head, Iris was willing someone to come in and take over. Seconds ticked past. She had to do something. Mafalda's words from last night on the beach echoed through her head.

'Maybe you can give us all a lecture one night after dinner. No, I'm not being sarcastic. Many of us have lost hope of change and the rest never believed it was possible. You have fire in your heart. You speak well. If you can convince one of our sisters to use her democratic right ...'

"How many of you speak Portuguese?" she demanded, her voice clear and loud.

The majority of the hands rose.

"Very good. For those women who do not, will someone translate?"

A discussion ensued which took longer than necessary, in Iris's view. Eventually, everyone settled down, their faces tilted to hers.

Iris opened her mouth to speak. She had no idea where to begin but the point was to give power to these people, to convince them they were not victims, but heroes. So no pressure whatsoever.

"Thank you for listening to me. I started with applause because I recognise your strength." She paused, waiting for them to pass the message on. The reaction was suspicious overall but they were still listening.

"You are strong. Like rocks in the sea, you are pushed and pummelled and swayed but you still stand. You stand firm. You survive." The conversations relayed her message and several women clutched hands.

"I want to ask you a question. I don't expect an answer.

Please, just take a moment to ask yourself, why am I here? What are you doing here at A Casa da Prata?"

She opened her palms towards them, waiting for the women to silently identify their individual paths to a refuge. After a minute, she continued. "We all agree, I think, that A Casa da Prata is a good place, a safe haven for everyone who needs it, yes? Well, maybe not last night."

Shy laughter rippled around the room and a baby began to grumble. Time to get to the point.

"Can you imagine a time when such a place is not necessary? Where women can make their own decisions? I see your faces. It's impossible, you think. Not true. Next week, yes, only next week, it is possible that you can change your world. And the world of your daughters, sons and grandchildren."

Heads shook and more than one woman shielded her eyes, presumably to roll them at her companions. Iris knew she was doing exactly what all the other job rejections had warned her about. A well-meaning foreigner marching in with no understanding of their circumstances, telling everyone what was best for them. She changed from second-person plural to first.

"If we leave it to the big-mouths who are happy with things the way they are, nothing will ever change for us. Women are stronger when we work together; A Casa da Prata proves it. Every woman in this room can make a difference. Every woman in this room has a superpower. That is a vote. Politicians are our servants, not our bosses. This country belongs to you."

The response was muted and many women began talking amongst themselves. One girl called out, "You want us to vote? Who for?"

Iris flushed for a moment in the understanding she couldn't answer. For once, she had no political axe to grind.

A voice came from the doorway. "Why are you asking her?"

Mafalda stood in the doorway, her hand on her hip. "You always want someone to tell you what to do, don't you?" She stalked around the room. "If she tells you who to vote for, pay no attention. What does she know?"

Heads switched back and forth between the two women as if it was a tennis match.

"Don't look at me!" Mafalda opened her arms in a gesture of exasperation and swept through the room. "I don't know either. You have to make up your own minds. None of us can be sure unless we ask the right questions. What do you want? Tell me what you want from your politicians."

By this time she was standing beside Iris. "If you listened to this woman, and I hope you did, you learned the most important lesson of all today. We have the power to change. This is why we must vote for whoever will best represent our interests. Here's what we're going to do. We make a list, right here on the whiteboard. Then we look at their manifestos. The politician whose promises come closest to our list gets our vote." She pointed at the blank white space. "So come on. What do we want?"

No one spoke.

Iris badly wanted to trigger the debate but bit her lip. As if sensing her temptation, Mafalda turned and once again addressed her in English. "Thanks for stepping in. I'll take it from here. The police towed the Jeep out and took the motorbike away, so can you clear up the drive?"

Iris nodded and with a smile at the women, left the oppressive silence of the room for the oppressive moist air of outside. Just as she was closing the door behind her, an elderly lady spoke.

"No more war?"

Iris walked away, in the shameful realisation that the agencies which rejected her had been right to do so. She hadn't the first clue.

. . .

A few evenings later, Iris was reading a book on her bed after dinner when someone tapped on the half-door of the stable. She sat up, expecting Demi's head to duck around the tacked-up privacy curtain, eager to borrow her book. Reading material was scarce in Pemba.

"I'm not done with it yet!"

Mafalda lifted up the curtain. "When you are, can I buy you a cold beer?"

It was an ordinary suggestion yet completely incongruous in the circumstances, Iris laughed. "A cold beer? We have no beer, not even the warm stuff."

"We haven't, no, but the bar keeps a nice cool fridge full of them. Your book will wait for you. Come on, I'm leaving Demi and Faith in charge."

Iris scrambled to her feet, slipping on her shoes, raincoat and backpack.

"That's not necessary. We're only going to walk along the beach and I'm buying."

Iris hitched the pack up her shoulders. "You never know. What bar are you talking about? There's nothing on the beach between here and Luguni but that bloody goat."

"It's in the other direction. It's cooler at this time of night and a little stroll is always pleasant. Some might say divine."

They left the compound over the dune, keeping an eye out for the goat.

"Dinner was good tonight," said Mafalda. "What did you call those things?"

"Fish fingers. Not quite like the ones I used to eat as a kid, but passable. Mashed sweet potato with prawns and herbs rolled in cashew nuts and fried. We need to change that oil soon. It's getting old."

Mafalda gave a soft laugh through her nose. "Fish fingers.

Funny name. Never tried them before but that dish was a winner."

Her habit of simply ignoring a suggestion or comment she did not like was something Iris had learned to live with. In a few days' time, she might cough up for a new can of oil, or they might continue eating rancid food for the next three months.

"Do you celebrate Christmas?" she asked, throwing Iris a total curveball.

"Christmas? You mean in a religious sense?"

"In any sense. Some people at A Casa da Prata are Christian, some are not, but the festival is symbolic of family. People miss their homes and loved ones so I try to make it an inclusive party. You and Demi have good imaginations. Why don't you think of some things we can do which don't cost much but make the day special?"

"Umm, OK." The beach curved to the right and in the distance, Iris could see the glow of an electric light spilling onto the sand. "How come you didn't tell me you can speak English?"

"How come you didn't tell me you *are* English?" She laughed again. "People's histories are their own business. I never ask or make assumptions, unless it's beneficial or convenient. I spoke English to you in front of the cops because if they think you don't understand Portuguese, that could be both. Oh, looks like Divine's place is lively tonight."

Strains of a rock anthem reached Iris's ears and a string of coloured bulbs came into view. The bar was little more than a wooden shack under a cluster of palm trees with a deck, evidently a locals' watering-hole. Iris slowed, partly nervous of any of A Casa da Prata's neighbours and partly due to a flashback. A few months ago, she'd been walking down the beach towards a hut where a dirty dog slept under the wooden steps and a white heron perched on the roof.

"You don't need to worry." Mafalda clearly sensed her trepidation. "We're always welcome at Divine's place. Especially if you can sing. You want a beer or one of your fancy cocktails?"

She could almost hear Fátima's voice, insisting on a fancy cocktail made from whisky and watermelon.

"Iris?"

"Beer's fine," said Iris, feeling less Iris and more Ann. She noted Mafalda's concern. "If you're sure this place is safe, let's have a drink."

Patrons at the bar were an odd mixture of Africans, Europeans and the occasional American, but everyone welcomed them with smiles. Iris could smell the laid-back attitude in the air. Behind the bar sat a big woman dressed in a green and black *capulana* with matching headdress.

"Hi, Divine. Long time, huh?"

"Good job my trade don't depend on you, Mai Tai. Thank the Lord most of my clientele are far more loyal. Who's your friend?"

"This is Iris, a volunteer from ..."

"Can she sing?" Divine interrupted, assessing the newcomer.

Mafalda looked at Iris for a response.

"After three tequilas, anyone can sing."

That seemed to satisfy their hostess, who held out a hand. "Well, hello, Tequila Sun-Iris and I look forward to you making good on that promise. Now what can I make you ladies tonight? House special is a banana daiquiri."

"Is the beer cold?"

Divine raised a perfectly plucked eyebrow.

"In that case, we'll have a couple of beers and the other house special," Mafalda replied.

Iris took in the deck, with no more than half a dozen tables, a swing chair in one corner and a hammock in the other. The ubiquitous smell of home-grown marijuana and the glow from papery lampshades lent the scene a soft yellowy filter, like footage of another decade. A guy with a man bun picked up a guitar and started strumming something by Elton John.

"It's a pretty mellow place to sit and just be." Mafalda was watching her. "One of Demi's favourite places, as you might have guessed. How about you and me take these onto the beach? It's time we got to know each other."

Mafalda led the way down the steps and brushed some fallen leaves from a wooden bench which had once been painted blue. Light and muted music came from over their heads, the ocean reflected night sky and cool sand trickled over Iris's toes. A tiny jetty with a single boat presented itself like a watercolour waiting to happen.

The echoes of her former existence ebbed and flowed like the waves, although less reliable in consistency.

"Thanks for the beer." Out of habit, Iris wiped the rim of the bottle with her T-shirt. She took a slug of chilled hoppy fizz and closed her eyes in bliss and misery. The taste triggered a slideshow of sea views through sunglasses, hot skin scented with sunscreen, the constant pounding of waves, burnt sausages with mustard, bottles of Grolsch, laughter and the weight of a man's arm over her shoulders. She swallowed again to quell her swollen throat.

"It's weird, isn't it, taking a night off?" Mafalda lit up and took a long drag. "Keeping busy and fighting for survival convinces us we can relax once in a while. We deserve a break. That's exactly when it hits. Do you want some of this? Divine's Holy Grail." She offered Iris the joint.

"Thanks but I'm struggling to keep myself together as it is. What do you mean by 'it'? You said that's exactly when 'it' hits."

"Whatever we're running away from. You're no different to anyone else at A Casa da Prata, Iris. We're all trying to escape something." She blew a long thin line of smoke into the air. "Some of us can name it, for others it's less specific. But one thing we all have to learn is that we bring it with us. Like a shadow, you'll never outrun it. One day, you have to turn around and look it in the face and say '*Basta!*' Enough is enough."

Iris had no answer. The cod philosophy sounded good but dried into meaninglessness when translated into practicality. In any case, she'd been around enough dope smokers to know her opinion was neither required nor valued.

"To my surprise, you got some of them to do exactly that." Mafalda tipped up her beer bottle, drinking like a baby lamb at the teat. "You stood up in front of our women and showed them the driving seat. They heard you, they listened. They want to say enough is enough, so thank you." She thrust her bottle in Iris's direction and they knocked glass against glass. "You'll find this hard to believe, but around of third of them are going to actually vote."

"Only a third?" Iris croaked, the beer prickling her throat.

"Yes, a third. Which is 33% more than planned to pick up a ballot paper last week. Hey, a third is good. Some can't vote because they're too young, others are too fearful to get their papers from their parents' houses and few of them won't leave the compound. One or two don't give a shit and that's unlikely to change. But the remainder are fired up and ready. That's down to you."

The compliment seemed genuine. "Thanks."

They sat gazing out at the sea. The tension that gripped Iris when Mafalda said 'it's time we got to know each other' lessened its hold. If they focused on the day-to-day running of the compound, plans for Christmas, how to get first-time voters into the poll booths and whether whoever got elected was likely to make any difference, they were in safe territory.

"What about the goat?" she asked.

"The goat?" Mafalda looked perplexed. "What about it?"

"You're always saying it's a damn nuisance and we should put it on the grill. Maybe we should. For Christmas. It would give us enough meat for at least two decent meals."

"Maybe. On the other hand, it does a pretty good job of guarding the beach. If we kill it and eat it, we'll have to find another way of protecting ourselves on that side. Anyway, I've grown kind of attached to the ugly great thing."

Iris laughed. "So have I, if I'm honest. The idea of goat curry turns my stomach. I was just trying to be practical."

"Be practical and go get us two more beers. Put them on my tab. Sure you don't want something to smoke?"

"No, beer is enough for me, but thanks for offering." She climbed the steps with their empty bottles, humming along to 'Tiny Dancer' and walked up to the bar. While Mafalda was content to stick to neutral topics, Divine had no such compunction.

"Where's Demi tonight? I like that girl. Takes no shit and what she lacks in ability she makes up for in enthusiasm. You should hear her do Springsteen. What's your party trick, Tequila Sun-Iris?" She cracked open two more bottles of Laurentina Clara, jewels flashing from every finger. "I want to hear your story."

"One of these days, I'll tell you, just as long as you invite Señor Jose Cuervo." She picked up the beers. "You have a nice place here. Relaxed. I like it."

"Most people do. And for those who don't, I have Rusty Nail." She leaned back and pointed at a spot near her feet. Iris stood on tiptoes to peer over and saw a huge tan-coloured dog, asleep on its side. It wore a studded leather collar and its long legs stretched the width of the bar.

"He's beautiful," said Iris, her mind wandering to another beach, another dog.

"Beautiful and fearless. I told Mafalda a hundred times,

your farm needs a dog. Troublemakers think twice when something aggressive with big teeth is on the prowl. A goat's not bad, but men respect a dog. You want anything else? Because it's nearly time for my duet."

"Not tonight. Maybe next time I'll try a cocktail. Thanks, Divine."

"Sure. Then you can provide the entertainment. Say hi to Demi and remind her she owes me 'Thunder Road' before she leaves."

The guitarist had moved on to 'Don't Go Breaking My Heart' and Divine emerged from behind the bar, arms wide as if she were stepping onto the stage in Vegas. Behind her, Rusty Nail loped three paces and sank to the ground, laying his massive head on his paws. The atmosphere crystallised into the high point of the evening. Mafalda was now sitting at a table near the musicians, swaying in time with the beat. They drank their beers, joining in with the ooh-hoos and glorying in a sense of abandonment. Conversation time was over.

At least until the walk home.

Slightly tipsy and buoyed by a sense of community, Iris floated Divine's suggestion – that A Casa da Prata should have a dog. A light rain swept in from the sea, limiting their vision.

"Here's a maxim to live by: only listen to Divine when she's singing. Where has the moon gone? We shoulda got another beer for the walk home. Refreshment and weapon in one handy vessel."

"Three was more than enough for me. Stop ignoring my suggestions. Say no if you want, but at least explain why not."

Mafalda giggled, a sound Iris had never heard her make. "That's the last time I'm buying you beer. Shrinking Iris becomes a Venus Flytrap."

Despite her annoyance at her colleague's evasion and the increasingly heavy rain washing down her face, Iris smiled. "It's a shrinking violet, not iris. My point is this, a dog has ..."

"... to piss and so do I. Down by the shore. Keep me covered." She ran into the darkness, still laughing.

"No, Mafalda, wait!" The patter of feet hitting wet sand faded in the downpour. To add to Iris's confusion, a light swept the beach. It was faster and brighter than a torch, more like the beam from a lighthouse. The light went out and four successive thuds came from the top of the dune.

Not a lighthouse. A vehicle. Four car doors slamming shut and her alone on a beach with no sign of Mafalda. She couldn't risk calling out with a warning. Instead, she grasped her knife and dropped to her haunches. The silver rain jacket was like a flare in the night, so she shrugged it off and balled into her backpack. Everywhere she saw shadows, movements, threats and danger. If the men in the car had seen her jacket, they would aim for more or less the same spot. She had to move and find Mafalda.

She scuttled backwards like a crab, stopping to check every few seconds if anyone was following or had circled around behind her. Once she reached the shoreline, she stopped, squinting up the beach. The rain eased and the ink-black beach took on shades of grey so that Iris could make out four figures heading down the dune. In a second, she could see they were drunk. One lost his footing and fell with a curse, causing the guy beside him to snort with suppressed laughter. The other two hissed at them to be quiet, creating more noise than the first pair combined.

To her right and much closer than the approaching men, someone moved. Mafalda was crouching in a similar pose to Iris, her attention on the unwanted company.

"We need to get out of here," Iris whispered. "If the moon comes out, we're sitting ducks." Four against two was pretty poor odds, even with her combat training. She crabbed her way closer to her colleague and stubbed her foot on a rock, muffling a yelp. That gave her an idea.

"Listen to me. I'm going to send them in the wrong direction. When I say go, you run to the compound as quickly as you can and alert Demi and Faith."

"What about you?" Mafalda had sobered up fast.

"I'll be right behind you. Just take my backpack and don't look back." She curled her hand around the rock, put all her weight on her right foot and hurled it along the shore, in the direction of Divine's bar. It landed with a satisfying splash and the men reacted instantly, thundering towards the sea with a shout of triumph.

"Go now!" she barked, and Mafalda took off, fast and light towards the trees. Iris scrabbled around for another rock, but could only find pebbles the size of skimming stones. Just then, clouds parted to reveal the moon. It took two seconds for the men to see Mafalda's fleeing form and give chase. Iris's blood curdled as she spotted the glint of a machete blade. Her own knife was brutally effective at close range but in defence against a machete, as much use as a paper straw.

Her panicked mind weighed up the situation. If the four men caught up with Mafalda, she stood no chance. Whereas if Iris drew their attention, she could at least split the group and hope to raise the alarm. She took aim with her stones and used all her force to hurl them at the men's heads. A cry of pain told her she had hit at least one target. The group slowed in confusion, searching for the source of the attack. Iris stood up and waved her arms, aware her pale skin would stand out against the night ocean.

"Over here, you bunch of arseholes!" Whether they understood the English taunt was doubtful, but they certainly picked up on the tone. With a mixture of relief for Mafalda and icy terror for herself, she saw all four men turn and fan out into a semi-circle before striding down the beach. There were too many, too close together and one carried a lethal blade. She wasn't going to fight her way out of this one. Her only other hopes were Mafalda rousing a rescue party, Divine hearing her plight and sending Rusty Nail, or maybe the goat would come charging onto the scene to the theme tune from Indiana Jones.

Crazy thoughts were a sign of panic, because she had no idea how to handle four angry drunks looking for revenge. With her back against the wall and no other option, she would have to try diplomacy. Of all her skills, talking her way out of a sticky situation was the most reliable. As if to suggest an alternative, the sea swirled around her ankles, a beckoning caress and seductive invitation.

She didn't need asking twice. Her eyes on her assailants, she backed away, into the waves, allowing the water to carry her out to sea. Once they saw what was happening, the men began running and shouting in protest. Iris struck out in a strong crawl, desperate to gain some distance, blocking out the fears of what else might be in the water. When she came up for air, she saw all four men pacing the beach, yelling at each other or shielding their eyes from the moonlight to try to see where she was. Either they couldn't swim or didn't fancy a fight off dry land. She trod water, only her nose and eyes above the surface and waited for their next move.

Another rain shower battered the beach, creating sufficient cover for Iris to begin swimming a gentle breaststroke parallel to the shore. The men seemed to be arguing and one stormed off towards the road. The others threw several handfuls of stones into the sea, landing 200 metres from where Iris was heading towards the compound. They spat and urinated, yelled curses and finally followed their friend, perhaps afraid of missing their lift.

Only when the vehicle had driven off and any sound of engine noise faded did Iris emerge from the ocean. It must have been close to midnight but the compound lights were still on. She waded out of the sea and splashed her way up the dune, wary of being in the spotlight. Four silhouettes stood at the top. Iris caught her breath until she recognised the tall Netherlander brandishing a gun, Jennifer's excited squeak, Faith's palms pressed together and raised to the heavens, and finally Mafalda still carrying Iris's rucksack. For the first time, relief and delayed fear overwhelmed her. She wiped her face and wrung out her hair, hoping they would mistake her emotional reaction as a natural reaction to a midnight swim.

Faith was the first down the sand, a towel over her shoulder. "Are you OK? They didn't hurt you? Here, dry yourself."

Iris took the thin cloth and buried her face in its stiff fabric. "I'm fine."

Faith patted her sopping shoulder. "Thank God."

Mafalda, Jennifer and Demi joined them, Jennifer weeping with relief. "I was s-so afraid for you, out there, alone. The Lord was watching over you t-t-tonight."

"They didn't follow me into the water. Nowhere near. I don't think they can swim. I waited till they got bored and swam up the beach. You OK?" she asked Mafalda.

"Yes, I am. Without your intervention, I'm not sure I'd have made it. Your backpack."

Iris took it with almost as much relief as getting out of the sea. "No trouble here?"

"Those imbeciles threw a handful of stones and yelled insults as they drove past. But it was pretty feeble. That's when we knew they must have lost you and we came to look."

A snort made them all start and Jennifer gasped.

"That damned goat," Demi laughed. "Come on, we should get to bed. Far too much excitement for one day and I want to rest while it's still rainy and cool. Well done, Iris."

They all chorused the same sentiment. Iris nodded her thanks, suddenly so bereft of energy she had doubts about making it to the cowshed. Her body wanted to curl into a ball right there, goat or no goat. But Mafalda reached for her hand and pulled her up the sandy slope.

"Go to bed. I'm turning the lights off in five minutes. Thank you for what you did. You have courage. Tomorrow, I'll make breakfast. Goodnight."

In the bathroom, Iris peeled off her wet clothes, cleaned her teeth and headed straight for her cot. Her last conscious thought was how she wished she had some cheese.

6

———

December got off to an unhappy start. A major storm hit the coast and for two long days and nights, it wrought havoc on the compound. The cowshed roof ripped open in high winds, but thankfully did not blow off completely. Relentless rain soaked everyone and their belongings, forcing them to relocate to the farmhouse, along with the chickens. Debris such as palm leaves, driftwood and coconut shells battered the buildings, damaging the hen house and the Land Cruiser, and smashing two windows in the farmhouse. For forty-eight hours they huddled in the schoolroom, eating plain rice in shifts, as there was only one pan and one working ring on the hob.

Faith, Demi and Iris made several sorties to the cowshed to recover what they could, but there was no hope of attempting roof repairs in such conditions. Demi went onto the beach to look for the goat, but it was nowhere to be found. They told each other it was bound to be safe, hiding somewhere, because animals had a survival instinct. No one was convinced.

When the weather finally calmed and they went outside to assess the damage, the oil drum they used for cooking had disappeared, as well as the makeshift gate for crossing the gully. Iris was tempted to suspect foul play, but as Mafalda pointed out, people had other things to worry about in such weather. Plus, their own yard was scattered with random objects whipped from who-knows-where. A surfboard, a dented bucket, a torn tarpaulin, children's toys, wooden signs advertising phone repairs or chicken piri-piri while-U-wait, newspapers, clothes, broken glass and several sheets of corrugated tin.

They kept the children inside during the clean-up operation. It was dangerous enough for the adults. Demi and Iris climbed onto the cowshed roof and forced the twisted metal into some semblance of a roof. It was a risky if not impossible task trying to balance on wet surfaces under still drizzly skies. Sharp edges of metal tore their skin and clothes, and twice Iris slipped, once falling off the building. She snatched at a rafter, missing by a millimetre and landed on a pile of sand they had built against the wall to prevent flooding. Unhurt but winded and shaken, she saw she'd had a lucky escape. Beside her was a wheelbarrow filled with all the tools they owned. If she'd fallen a metre to the left, things would have been a great deal worse.

On the fourth day, the sun came out with some force. The women hauled their bedding and mattresses out to the dune to dry under Jennifer's supervision. Faith and Mafalda took some younger ones beachcombing and dragged back something that looked like a garden gate. There was some debate about the best use for it, but Iris persuaded Mafalda to place it over the gully temporarily, so she and Demi could go into town for supplies. Neither of them had a Mozambique driving licence, so Faith took the wheel. They were just wedging the bicycle in the back of the considerably worse-for-wear vehicle when shouts erupted from the top of the dune. The goat had reappeared and, evidently hungry, it was making a meal of somebody's bedclothes.

Amid the laughter and relief, the three women left the

others to deal with the ruminant. Faith drove cautiously over the gate and onto the main road. The storm had not spared any of the properties along the coast road and the extent of the damage was frightening. In Luguni, Demi dragged the bike out and cycled off to trawl the market for whatever fresh produce was available.

Faith continued to Pemba where Iris knew she would have competition for the cement, ironmongery and oilcloths she had on her list. In the city, the effects of the storm were still visible but due to the sturdier nature of most buildings, not as shocking. The women split up. Faith parked between the hardware store and the supermarket, for ease of transporting the heaviest goods. Iris was rather light-headed at having some time alone. After four days eating, sleeping and working in close proximity to other people, it was a wonderful freedom simply to walk down the street.

As expected, the hardware store was busy with people searching for the same things as her. But the place was well stocked, so in under an hour, she had purchased nails, tarpaulins, a set of tools, six cinder blocks, four sacks of cement, a blowtorch and a ladder. A friendly assistant helped her load her trolley and manoeuvre it outside to where Faith was waiting. It took them a while to get everything in the vehicle, but since Demi was cycling home, they filled the back seat and strapped the ladder to the roof. Iris knew Mafalda would disapprove of the amount she had spent, but these counted as exceptional circumstances.

"Faith, we've been pretty efficient this morning. Instead of rushing back, how about we stop for something to eat? You know, as a treat."

"On our own? What about the others?"

"They'll be eating whatever Demi got from the market. There might not be anything left for us. I'm hungry, it's been a tough week and I'm buying. What do you say?"

Faith stared ahead, her expression brightening. "I know just the place."

She stopped at a roadside café and ordered two 2M beers and a *prego* each. It was a bread roll wrapped around a slab of steak. Iris couldn't remember the last time she'd eaten meat. They ate in blissful silence, leaning against the Land Cruiser and savouring every mouthful of the first hot, filling meal in a week.

Faith finished first, swigged the remainder of her beer and let out a massive belch. "That was exactly what I needed. I'll regret it later, sure, but I'm willing to pay the price. Thanks for buying."

Mouth full, Iris could do nothing more than nod.

"Why do you spend your money on us? On the compound? You could be having a lot more fun than living on a refuge in the middle of the rainy season."

Iris swallowed. "I'm a big fan of rainy seasons." She wiped her mouth with her sleeve. "This place was an inspired choice, Faith. Not something I want to eat every day, but right here, right now, it hits the spot." They returned their bottles and got into the car.

They drove along the coast, the silence less comfortable than during their meal. Faith pointed out more storm clouds building on the horizon.

"Oh, shit. That means cement mixing will have to wait till tomorrow," Iris answered.

Faith said nothing.

"Listen, I didn't mean to be evasive just now," said Iris. "I'm spending my time and money here because I can and I want to do something to help those who can't. I've made a lot of mistakes, I know that, but I am learning."

That explanation seemed to satisfy her companion, who grunted and shrugged. Neither made any further conversation until Faith turned the corner to the compound and found the entrance to A Casa da Prata blocked by a truck. She stopped the Land Cruiser and wrenched open the door.

"Wait, Faith, it could be a trap!"

"No trap! I know that truck and I know why it's here." She hitched up her dress, vaulted over the gully and ran up the drive.

Iris looked around, nervous about leaving the vehicle unattended but equally worried about her colleagues. Angry voices and sobs convinced her to defend people above property. She raced towards the farmhouse, where a heavyset man was yelling at a group of tearful women. Mafalda was making pacifying gestures and attempting to speak.

"... against her will. Not us, not you, nobody. She's a grown woman with rights enshrined in law. She has a choice."

"Stuff your 'enshrined in law'! I am her father and MY word is law. Our farm needs all hands to help rebuild or we will starve. Jennifer is coming with me! Come here, girl."

Faith threw herself in front of the sobbing Jennifer. "No! She doesn't want to go with you! This is her home, here with her friends."

The man thrust Faith aside and caught Jennifer's wrist. The women jerked away in fear, some even whimpering.

He dragged his daughter close and glared down at her, his eyes flashing. "This big-mouthed bitch says you have the right to choose where you want to live. So choose! At home, working with your family, or in this pit of perversion! Choose, girl!" He shook her arm with such violence, Iris took a step forward. Demi held out a warning hand.

Jennifer mumbled something through her tears.

"WHAT? I can't hear you! Come home or stay here? Speak up, you whining whelp."

"Home."

"You want to come home?"

Jennifer gasped as his grip clenched around her wrist. "Yes."

"No!" shrieked Faith. "Jennifer, no!"

"You heard her. And if anyone tries to take her away again, I'll have the police close this place down. It's unnatural. Get out of my way!" He yanked Jennifer along, with a wary glance at Demi and Iris as he stomped down the drive.

The urge to jump him and stab him in the ribs was powerful but Iris knew the fallout for the refuge would be disastrous. Jennifer's heartbreaking sobs affected them all. Even Mafalda had tears in her eyes. His truck growled into life and Iris remembered the Land Cruiser was parked directly behind it. She ran down the drive, leapt over the gully and indicated she would move her vehicle. He gave no response other than to gun his accelerator as a warning.

She reversed to the corner, where there was a passing section, and pulled over. By the time he'd completed a ridiculously aggressive three-point turn, she was out of the car and standing in his path. He drove at her, his teeth bared and eyes wide, but she stood her ground. At the last second, Jennifer screamed and he was forced to stamp on the brake.

"You hurt her and I will hurt you ten times worse. I swear you'll regret being born."

He revved the engine and made an obscene gesture, but she knew he'd heard. She stepped aside and caught a glimpse of Jennifer's agonised expression as the truck lurched away.

A rumble of thunder made her turn her eyes to heaven. "Thanks for that. Great timing." She walked to the driveway, hauled the gate over the gully and drove their provisions into the compound. A collective grieving was in full flood, so Demi and Iris unloaded all the day's purchases into the farmhouse. Neither spoke.

· · ·

Dinner was a subdued affair, with outbreaks of emotion wearing Iris down. She cooked and cleared up, even though it was Faith's turn. Although most beds were restored to order in the cowshed, the thought of trying to read her book among all the sniffles and sobs made her reject the idea. The afternoon's threat of a storm had passed without coming to fruition, so the evening was muggy, warm and dry. She went in search of Demi, hoping to make sense of the day's drama. She found her sitting on the bench outside the farmhouse, reading Iris's book.

"So that's where it went."

"Yeah, chickens, goats and children can fend for themselves. Books and passports first. This is good, I have to say. Can we take it in turns? Or I'll never finish it before I leave. Thirty days and counting before I'm out of here."

"And then what?"

"First stop Rotterdam to see my family."

Iris sat beside her, watching the palm trees sway over the beach. "When I said 'then what?' I meant in terms of the refuge. What happens to the women? Do we sit here and wait for those menfolk to reclaim their property?"

Demi closed the book. "You too, huh? Listen, why don't we wander down the beach to see how Divine weathered the storm? Yeah, the other night freaked us all out and today was worse, but I don't think any young guns are willing to fight the pair of us. Not tonight. Come on. I'll stand you a beer, if she's got any left."

The sunset was a cocktail of colours, the sky showing its softer side. Indigo streaks dotted with silvery apricot clouds sank into the sea with a speed that still surprised Iris, even after seeing it scores of times. By the time they reached Divine's place, evening had thrown its glamorous cloak of velvet and diamonds across their corner of the world. Iris noted she and Demi had walked the whole way and watched the entire scene without uttering a word.

Chords of a guitar threaded through the air, lights shone across the sand and Divine's laughter rang out as if the storm had never happened.

"Demi-John! And Tequila Sun-Iris! What a sweet sight for these ageing eyes. I thought you and your girls were gonna get blown away."

They climbed the steps and Demi gave a general greeting to the half-dozen patrons. "Almost did. What's your secret? This place looks untouched."

"I learned from the turtle. Retreat inside. Tell you a secret. After the end of the war in '92, I did a deal with a military man. This whole thing is built inside a tent. You don't see it because it's tucked into the trees but I can tell you it's there. Bad weather comes, me and Rusty Nail batten down the hatches, cover the place with a military-grade tarpaulin and wait it out. So long as we got beef jerky and beer, we can last out Armageddon. Ha, ha! What can I get you classy ladies tonight? Tonight's special is the one and only Dark and Stormy!"

Iris was occupied by the intriguing construction of hut-within-tent so barely paid attention when Demi asked about the contents.

"Dark rum, ginger beer and ice. Fire in your belly, I guarantee."

"I'm ready for some fire in my belly. Iris?"

"What? Oh, yeah, might as well. Divine, where did you get Rusty Nail?"

Divine was pouring and mixing, her hibiscus-coloured lips curling into a smile. "Can't tell you that without incriminating myself. But if you're asking where to buy a good guard dog, I'll ask around. Here you go, two Dark and Stormy specials."

"I'll get these," offered Iris.

Demi shook her head. "On the tab, please." She scooped

up both glasses and sat at the nearest table. "A toast. May we continue to survive the dark and the stormy."

They toasted each other and took a sip of the spicy liquid. Ginger fizzed on Iris's tongue and the rum hit her throat. "Fiery even before it gets to the belly. Demi, I have some questions."

"Ask your questions, then I have some demands."

Iris gave her a quizzical look but Demi's focus was out on the ocean.

"You're leaving in January, right?"

"Right. On the fifth of January, my flight leaves from Pemba. Next?"

This terse, snappy individual was not someone Iris liked. "I get the feeling I'm treading on toes, but no one has taken the time to explain why. Have I done something to offend you?"

"Me personally? Not really. The compound? You'd have to ask them. Iris, our job is to listen, adapt and not try imposing our standards of behaviour on a situation that will continue long after you and I return to our cosy little Western lives. Bags of concrete and a ladder are of short-term use. You must see how the world works here. That ugly great fool that calls himself Jennifer's father even said so. Yes. Women have rights 'enshrined in law'. How much does that mean if no one enforces any those rights or punishes trans-gressions? It's so easy to buy stuff and make a big deal of short-term sticking-plasters. It costs you a fraction of what-ever you hold in your wallet. Then, like me, you'll leave and the cycle starts again. We need to push against the biggest rocks. It's frustrating and we will leave having achieved noth-ing. But that's the only material difference we might ever make."

Two of the beach dudes started singing along with the guitar and their guilt-free spontaneity irritated Iris. What did they contribute to the world? She immediately winced at such an uncharitable and ignorant perspective. "The biggest rocks?" she asked.

Demi side-eyed her and took a mouthful of Dark and Stormy, tapping her feet to a mangled Beach Boys tune. "After her father claimed Jennifer, how much enthusiasm do you think our residents will have for the vote? My guess is zero. They're demoralised and sad, as well cold and wet. If you want to do anything more than put a temporary roof over their heads, you'll light a different fire in their bellies. You'll fail, we all do, but every single drip wears away at the rock face. I'm done. Now it's your turn."

It took a while for Iris to process Demi's words, and the thought of trying to make another tub-thumping speech to a miserable group of women triggered feelings of defeatism. But her colleague was right. They had to keep chipping away.

"Why didn't you let me pay for the drinks? That's not exactly flashing the cash or trying to solve everyone's problems the Western way."

"Because ..." Demi flicked a glance at the bar, where Divine was laughing with another woman, and dropped her voice to a murmur. "We always put drinks on the tab. Then sooner or later, someone pays it off."

"Who?"

"I don't know. I'm not even sure it's the same person. You see, not all the locals are against us. Some are grateful that we take in women and girls who might otherwise starve. Others are relatives who can't afford to look after their daughters or sisters. The bottom line is this: a percentage of the population are in favour of what we do but daren't be seen openly supporting us. So they find ways of helping us out. Anonymous gifts on the doorstep. Envelopes of cash sent to our PO box. Since I've worked here, we haven't received a phone bill. No idea why not. One thing I do know is that we've never had to pay Divine a single met."

"You don't think ...?"

Demi shook her head. "She supports us but she's also a businesswoman. Her profits are tiny, especially in winter, and she can't afford to give booze away. I know one woman who regularly steals from her husband and son when they are passed out drunk. Only a little at a time so they think they spent more than they did at the roadside bar. She saves it up and brings it down here. Funny, because she won't touch alcohol herself. Mafalda told me the guy who runs the wholesale place where Divine buys her beers and spirits often adds a couple of bottles to the order as a gift to us. Even these beach bums have a habit of paying it forward, like buying a round of six and paying for seven. The only area where Divine shows her generosity is the weed. She grows it herself and never charges for that particular special. Have you tried it yet? It's pretty good stuff."

"No, I don't."

"You anti-drugs?"

The part played in Iris's history by illegal substances and those who profited from them was not easy to sum up. She opted for the simple explanation. "No. I just never found a drug I liked. Dope slows me down or makes me paranoid, on coke I talk too much and the only time I took ecstasy, it gave me blisters. From dancing all night," she said in response to Demi's puzzled expression. "But if you want to smoke a joint, it doesn't bother me in the slightest. Shall we have another drink too?"

Demi scanned the sky. "Why don't we get a couple of beers to go and I can get pleasantly stoned back at the compound. I don't feel like getting caught in the rain."

When Iris took their empty glasses to the bar and gave Divine their order, the woman sitting at the bar handed over a piece of paper. "My brother can get you a guard dog. Here's his number. You call him and say Hester sent you."

"That's very kind. Thank you. Thanks, Divine, and I'm glad the storm left you and Rusty Nail alone. See you soon."

They said goodbye to the other patrons, who half-heartedly tried to persuade them to stay for a sing-along, and walked up the beach, Iris carrying the beers and Demi with the joint tucked behind her ear.

"What did that woman give you?" Demi asked.

"A phone number. I asked where to buy a guard dog and she said her brother could help."

"A dog? You checked with Mafalda about that?"

"I suggested it. She didn't exactly say no but ..."

"Ignored you and talked about something else? I know. Sometimes she needs to think things over. But I'm pretty sure she won't come round to the idea. Dogs here are a real symbol of male control. Almost all of our residents are scared to death of them and Mafalda is one of the worst. Divine's probably the only single woman I've seen who keeps a damned great hound."

Iris sighed. "Then how the hell are we supposed to protect ourselves?"

"Hey, don't despair. It took me six months to talk her into getting a gun. Even now, she won't touch it. When I leave, it will gather dust on top of the cupboard, I'm sure. Unless you can handle a weapon?"

Her experience with firearms was another thing she'd rather not talk about. "I'm pretty sure I could learn."

"Good. I'll show you the basics tomorrow. It's only for show, really. We haven't even got any bullets."

7

————

Towards the end of the month, the weather got worse but the atmosphere got better. Mafalda, while still stubbornly resisting the idea of a dog, did relent and allow Iris to teach an hour of school each day. Lessons were mainly about speaking English, but she slipped in a few accounts of women's activism. However, her frame of reference was limited to distant figures such as Rosa Parks, Emmeline Pankhurst, Ruby Bridges, Malala Yousafzai and Chimamanda Ngozie Adichie. The students obviously enjoyed the stories but they might as well have been fairy tales.

Something more immediate and closer to home would have a greater impact. With a little encouragement, Faith was co-opted into talking about the changes in female fortunes during their own country's turbulent history. The collaboration was a success. Not only did Iris learn far more than she had gleaned from the Internet, but Faith was a born storyteller, invoking drama, courage, tragedy and heroism with a pause, a gasp, a change in volume and facial expressions worthy of the best mime artist. Even as Iris watched, she saw the narrator's face and evocative emotions reflected in those of the listeners.

Faith's tales seemed to inspire their audience far more than Iris's simple exhortations to use their vote, and several women approached her over dinner to ask more questions. Discussions had an energy previously lacking and at least half of A Casa da Prata had an opinion on who should serve as their representative in local government.

Mafalda cautioned Iris against getting too optimistic and instead suggested making practical arrangements. Anyone who did want to use her voice on polling day must have the means to do so. That meant organising child care, rearranging work duties, transporting around ten women to an election booth and defending them against interference. Certain groups had tried to disrupt previous elections by setting up camp outside poll stations, threatening women and scaring them away, thereby preventing them from registering their vote. Early morning, as soon as the stations opened, she advised would be the best time to go. So Iris laid her plans.

It took days to gather the correct paperwork for each woman. Two had no ID whatsoever, some had never applied for a voting card and a few had conflicting documents. Iris and Mafalda applied for missing identity cards, requested first-time voter forms and rehearsed what to do in the polling booth. In one case, Mafalda sent Demi and Faith on a one-hour drive north to demand one teenager's birth certificate from her fifty-year-old husband. All because Joana didn't know if she was old enough to vote. The bureaucracy was a tangled jungle that could have defeated Iris but Mafalda spent hours on the phone appealing, cajoling, begging, bribing and even threatening council officials to get her way.

The upshot was that everyone knew the women of A Casa da Prata were planning to vote. This spelled trouble.

On election day, Demi cycled off in the dark to position herself beside the nearest voting booth in Pemba. She took the gun, still empty of bullets. At quarter to eight in the morning,

Faith and Iris coaxed six of the most nervous or elderly women into the Land Cruiser and drove into the town, parking right outside the polling station. As a foreigner, Iris was not allowed to enter, but guided the women right to the gate of the squat little building. It reminded her of a Welsh chapel. Faith ushered them inside, reminding them again what to do. Iris waited in the Toyota. She scanned the scrubby ground but saw no trace of Demi. That, she supposed, was a good thing.

Seven women putting an X in a box should not take forty minutes. Time ticked on and more people breezed in and out of the municipal building. By now, she and Faith should be picking up the next batch of voters and getting some food. She was about to get out of the passenger seat and make enquiries when a police car pulled up at an angle. Three officers emerged and spoke at length to the couple on the gate. One pulled a barrier across the entrance, shaking his head at would-be voters, and stood with his arms folded.

Iris exhaled a snort of frustration which turned into a gasp when the driver's door beside her opened. Demi scrambled inside with Iris's binoculars around her neck.

"They're arguing about Joana. The officials say she needs her husband's permission to vote. Faith insists she's eighteen and an independent woman. The old bastards won't back down and now the police have been called. It's nothing more than intimidation. These rows can go on for hours until someone finds a solution where no one loses face. Meanwhile, gossip goes around and very soon, everyone will rock up here offering an opinion."

Iris groaned. "And six easily intimidated women trying to cast a vote will back down first. Shit. I wish I could go in there and do some intimidation of my own. This is exactly why some kind of NGO involvement is required to guarantee a fair election." She sighed in frustration. "I would kill for a coffee."

"That is an inspired idea! Wait there." Demi jumped out of

the Land Cruiser and sprinted up the road. Her speed hinted at something more urgent than caffeine but Iris held out hope. Another twenty minutes dragged by and rain spattered the windscreen. Most of the people gathered outside the polling station dispersed to gossip elsewhere, presumably not to return. A white van drew up to the gate with a logo Iris recognised: CWI – Child Welfare International. The doors opened and two people jumped out. One was a black man in a suit wearing a lanyard. The other was Demi, carrying two cups of coffee. The man entered the building, waving away the stragglers and pushed his way inside. Demi jerked her head, telling Iris to follow. She jumped out, locked the car and hurried through the gate into the station.

"Just wait here and shut up." Demi thrust a paper cup at her. "Watch this."

The suited man marched across the concrete floor towards the gaggle of women, police officers and elections officials. "Who is in charge here?" His voice was impressively authoritarian. "My name is Nathaniel Nhamirre and I work for Child Welfare International. I understand a minor is being held under suspicion of fraud. My organisation will represent this person against all allegations. I ask you again, who is in charge here?"

The rush to deny responsibility was fascinating. The police were merely there to solve a dispute. The election officials were only doing their job. With a glance at Demi and Iris, Faith gave Joana a nudge. "Show your ID, *filha*. If you are a child, this man will protect you against accusations of crime. If you are an adult, you can cast your vote."

The sight of Joana's frightened face and trembling hand as she held out her identity document scotched Iris's enthusiasm for the showdown. That poor child, sold to a man older than her father, had escaped abuse and slavery only to be harassed while exercising her democratic right.

Nhamirre returned her paperwork with an avuncular smile. "Thank you, *senhora*." Then he focused his contemptuous stare on the officials.

"Can none of you read?" he thundered. "This is not a little girl!" Everyone, including the police officers, dropped their heads as if berated by the headmaster. "This is a young woman who should be encouraged to take up her role in society. Has not our government set quotas for women in political life? Are we not beholden to the females who paid the bloody price of successive civil wars? Who are you to intimidate and block future generations from directing their future? Let this woman cast her vote! Be proud of all these worthy members of society." He included all the inhabitants of A Casa da Prata with one wide gesture. "Ladies, I salute you and your courage. Cabo Delgado needs you." His tone softened and he fixed his attention on Joana. "Please, take your place in the booth and vote."

From the end of the room, Iris could see the girl needed to pee, cry and hide from all the attention. Loud male voices were effective when intimidating men but petrified damaged women.

"Senhor Nhamirre?" Iris called. "Can I ask your advice on a similar issue?"

Her intervention allowed Faith to shield her charge, the cops to shuffle off without embarrassment and the election supervisors to return to their posts. The man came closer and held out a hand.

"Demi's co-worker, no? Your name?"

"Iris Simons. Yes, I'm a volunteer with A Casa da Prata."

"Delighted to meet you. Please call me Nathaniel. I'm happy to help but would you mind if we went outside? I need a cigarette. Are you also from the Netherlands?" In a gracious gesture, he let her and Demi through the exit first. Once outside, he opened a silver case of hand-rolled cigarettes which looked anything but innocent.

"No, thank you. I'm British. I mean, that's my nationality, not the reason I don't smoke. My question was about grants for vulnerable children. We have several at the compound. Is there any money at your organisation to support single mothers?"

He lit up his cigarette and smiled. "As a matter of fact, there is. We should discuss the options. I can see you're busy today. Come by my office next time you're in town and I'll tell you exactly how it works."

The rest of the day Iris spent driving back and forth from Pemba to A Casa da Prata, taking the first set of voters home, bringing the second group to the polling station minus one single mum who lost her confidence, taking the second group home and returning one last time with the under-confident mum plus baby, the last to cast her vote. She collected Demi and her bike from her hideout and drove the final stretch to the compound, singing nursery rhymes to keep the infant sweet. That night, they ate yams and greens and spiced tomatoes with flatbread until the election results were due. Then everyone settled in the schoolroom to listen to the radio, even those who hadn't cast a vote.

Reception wasn't great, but at twenty past ten, over an hour later than promised, the winning candidate was announced as Arnaldo Cantopreto. Iris groaned, sure that the female candidate was the popular favourite. She was stunned to see women leaping up from the benches and applauding. The celebrations woke some of the children but such high spirits and laughter drew everyone into exuberance. Loud women, shy girls, and old cynics made a point of thanking Faith. A few even acknowledged Iris's role. Then Mafalda announced the generator was about to go off and everyone went to bed. As an electoral victory, it was underwhelming.

In bed, Iris switched on her torch and dug out Cantopreto's

election manifesto. For the people (*yawn*). Against extremists (*extreme according to whom?*). Equalising opportunities for everyone (*heard that before*). Arnaldo Cantopreto believes Mozambique should honour its fighters and the women who sacrificed the most (*words into action, mate*). Torch off, she lay in bed and envisaged a conversation with Arnaldo Cantopreto. As if that would ever happen.

8

A succession of good things happened in the run-up to Christmas, all of which the women of A Casa da Prata attributed to the influence of Arnaldo Canto-preto. In reality, he had not even assumed office yet and he had nothing to do with their good fortune. The credit was mainly due to Mafalda, whose tireless applications for grants, permissions and financial assistance had unexpectedly borne fruit. An international organisation founded by an American ex-president awarded A Casa da Prata a small bursary to further the education of women.

Secondly, way back in August, the Ministry for Women and Social Action had sent a representative to evaluate the living conditions and safety standards at the compound. Since then, Mafalda had heard nothing. Now, out of the blue, news arrived that the Ministry would fund an assistant's position for the next two years, so long as the woman was from Mozambique.

It was a bittersweet victory in that Mafalda had applied in the hope of splitting one salary between Faith and Jennifer. But with Jennifer gone, at least Faith could be promoted to an official member of A Casa da Prata staff.

The least significant envelope they collected from the PO box was an official acceptance of Iris's driving licence as legal in Mozambique. Least significant because it only changed one person's life, but Iris was elated. Wheels, even if it meant a clapped-out Toyota, still symbolised freedom.

Iris and Demi finished repairing the roof damage and built a proper cooking area under the shelter. After two weeks of careful planning, they decided to use some of the supplies Iris had hidden away for emergencies to create a Christmas dinner. They involved the children in making paper chain decorations and hanging them on the driftwood and scrap-metal tree Demi had assembled. Privately, Iris thought it looked like something out of *The Blair Witch Project*, but kept her opinions to herself.

On the twenty-second of December, Iris, Demi and Faith took the car into Pemba to find the mechanic recommended by Divine. The vehicle was in dire need of some professional attention as it frequently refused to start and required a push down the drive to get going – always a risky prospect to have five excited teenagers shoving with all their might while Faith tried to steer between the stones and start the engine at the same time. The three women agreed to go their separate ways and perform their respective duties, but there was a certain shiftiness and secrecy in each person's behaviour. Iris understood perfectly. With three days till Christmas, this was the time for present-buying.

It had to be a delicate balance. No one other than Iris possessed anything like a disposable income. Something homemade or a thoughtful item to meet a need, she was thinking. Faith was a practical person and very fond of lists. The whiteboard in the schoolroom always had a little corner filled with her notes. So an exercise book and a pen would be both useful and personal. For Demi, Iris wanted to find a book, ideally in English. In a couple of weeks, the Dutch-woman would be at liberty to wander the bookshops of

Rotterdam, but until then, maybe she'd enjoy one of the classics? The easiest person to buy for was Mafalda, the woman who was constantly cold. Only yesterday Iris had found her wrapped in a blanket as she did the monthly accounting, her lips greyish in the chill. The best solution was a thermal jacket but that was far too ostentatious. A fleece, on the other hand, was cosy and uncomplicated, especially if it had pockets.

She did the essentials first; the pharmacy, the dry goods wholesaler and the PO box before going into the *papeteria/libreria*. She got a plain blue exercise book and refillable pen immediately, but the few English books on the shelves were horribly overpriced. She moved on to the market, the compound's battered wheelie suitcase which substituted as a shopping trolley already full and heavy. In the market, she haggled with the trader of a clothing stall and got a girl's fleece for a bargain price. It wouldn't fit most adult women but Mafalda was so slight and short, it was ideal.

Time was ticking and she chided herself for even looking at sparkly Christmas cookies which would delight the compound children, not to mention the adults. Instead, she negotiated a packet of cinnamon, cloves and nutmeg so they could try coaxing the temperamental farmhouse oven into life and make their own.

Demi's book was still elusive. Across the street was an international school, which was bound to have English novels. Whether they would part with one, Iris was dubious, but she was determined to try. Outside the doorway, a tall man with gingery hair was locking his bike and eating a *pastel de camarão*. The prawn-filled pastry made her mouth water.

"Excuse me? Do you work here?" She spoke English automatically as he looked as British as they come.

"Ah do. How can I help ya?"

"Oh hi, thanks. My name is Iris and I'm wondering if you

have any English books for sale. Not textbooks, I'm looking for works of fiction, classics or similar."

"Ah'm Gary. We gorra couple. Not in the best nick, mind."

"I'm not fussed about what condition they're in. I just want to get a Christmas present for a friend who loves reading and I'm not paying what they charge in the bookshop."

"Don't blame ya, pet. Daylight robbery, tha' is. Come on up and have a look."

Gary showed her into the cramped teachers' room and indicated a half-empty shelf of dog-eared paperbacks. "People donate stuff they've read and we don't say no, even if we can't use most of them. Help yourself and mebbe pop a tip in the pig when ya leave."

She thanked him, wishing he'd stick around and talk a little longer. The Geordie accent was one of her favourites. Instead, she checked the books for something suitable. *Anna Karenina* – too depressing. *Little Dorrit* – thematically awkward. *Pride and Prejudice* – a definite possibility. *The Handmaid's Tale* – not quite the uplifting atmosphere she sought. Then she saw it: Jean Rhys's *Wide Sargasso Sea*. For a woman like Demi, trying to do her part to atone for the horrors of colonialism, this allegory and its connection to Jane Eyre was ideal. The novel would absorb her attention, provoke thoughts and maybe even discussions. She scooped up that and the Austen for herself, even though she'd read it over a dozen times.

She looked around for Gary and recalled his 'mebbe pop a tip in the pig when ya leave'. At reception, which was empty, a pile of the school's business cards fanned out around a ceramic pig wearing a label around its neck: Teachers' Drinking Fund – Give Generously. She put in three hundred mets and hurried off to meet her colleagues. Outside it was raining, so she tucked the books inside her silver jacket and knotted the thin plastic bag to protect Mafalda's fleece and Faith's notebook. A digital clock outside the church said 16.20. She was late but not late-late. Time operated more flexibly here so that four o'clock meant anytime until five. After that was considered late-late.

She ducked from awning to overhanging roof in an attempt to stay dry. A man left a phone box, holding his jacket over his head. Iris stopped. It was almost Christmas and she'd had no contact with the farm in Portugal for months. She was brimming with goodwill and decided a festive call to Lana would be a nice gesture. Firstly to let them know she was alive and secondly to check in with things at the farm. It took a while before she got through. The connection had a delay and audibility was challenging with rain hammering on the roof.

"*Ola?*"

"Hello, Lana! It's Iris calling from Mozambique. How are you? How's Nestor?"

"*Ola?*"

"Lana, can you hear me?"

"*Iris? Where are you?*"

"Mozambique! A tiny place called Pemba. Is everything OK at the farm?"

"*Yes, I can hear you! I am so happy to hear your voice! Are you well? Oh, yes, we're carrying on as usual. Every day I look for a letter from you.*"

"I'm fine too. Letters are difficult but I wanted to say Merry Christmas!"

"*... hear from you and when you're coming home. What?*"

"Merry Christmas!"

"*Yes, Merry Christmas to you. Did you hear what I said?*"

"I don't know when I'm coming home yet. Maybe another couple of months. Do you need money?"

"*... tell anyone where you are. What was the name?*"

The line was a crackling mess and Iris could hear one word in five.

"Mozambique! Pemba. I have to go now. *Boas Festas! Beijinhos!*"

She waited for a response but heard nothing more than electronic soup. She hung up, wishing she could transport herself to that big toasty kitchen and eat some *Bolo Rei* with Lana. She composed herself and moved on.

Under the garage roof, Faith and Demi were drinking coffee with the mechanic. The Land Cruiser looked just as bashed-about as it had before but the one broken window had been replaced with a sheet of Perspex. She waved and saw the boot was full: cans of vegetable oil, catering tins of pulses, trays of canned fruit, a potato sack and cardboard box brimming with veg. She shoved her wheelie case in the back seat and dashed under the roof to get out of the rain.

"Successful day?" she asked, noting the comfortable atmosphere.

"Very." Faith looked like the cat who got the cream. "Mario cleaned up the engine, changed the plugs, fixed the window and repaired the lock on the boot. We got all the shopping for a not-too-bad price and you arrived on time. Did you go to the pharmacy?"

"Of course. First port of call. Great news all round. *Obrigada*, Mario! *Boas Festas!*"

He wished her the same and said a final few words to Faith. Iris squeezed into the back seat beside her case, her plastic bag on her lap, and Demi belted up in the passenger seat.

"Divine is a Machiavellian madam, but this time it worked out for the best. Mario lets slip he has the hots for Faith. We need our vehicle fixed. Divine sends us to Mario's Best Car Shop. Faith chats to Mario, Mario flirts with Faith, we get this heap patched up and those two have a date on New Year's Eve."

Iris burst into laughter. "The Glorious Divine! Bless her on everyone's behalf!"

They teased a blushing Faith all the way out of Pemba until the weather conditions required maximum concentration. The wipers couldn't keep up when sheets of rain hit the windscreen like a hosepipe. They reached Luguni and turned south, away from the worst of the eastern onslaught.

"Good driving, lady," said Demi. "Nearly home now."

Just then a flash of light came from their left. It was brighter than a torch, more like a flare and Faith instinctively touched the brakes. All three glanced towards the beach. Iris was still scanning the late afternoon gloomy horizon for signs of a storm when Faith screeched to a halt, the rear of the vehicle skidding left. A figure was waving his arms in the middle of the road. He was yelling but they couldn't hear his words over the engine and the wipers. He was pointing behind him to another person lying in the mud.

"Don't get out!" Iris barked. "Lock the doors!"

The man rushed closer, banging on Demi's window and shouting for help. She wound down her window by three centimetres.

"What's the problem?"

Faith gasped, her eyes wide in the rear-view mirror. "It's an ambush! Look behind us!"

A gang of men emerged from the bushes, surrounding the car. Most were at the rear, trying to open the boot, but others yanked at the passengers' and driver's door handles. Frustrated by finding all locked, one man smashed a fist through the Perspex and snatched at Iris's hair.

Her temper exploded in a volcanic rush. She punched the man straight in the teeth, flicked open her knife and unlocked the door in one movement. She kicked and slashed, elbowed and punched, felling one assailant with the most obvious duck-and-trip he should have learned in primary school. He hit the ground with a fat splat and dropped his machete. In an instant, it was in Iris's left hand. She brandished it in wild swoops around her head while jabbing at the nearest threats with her own blade.

Seven of them were still on their feet. Another three, including the one she'd smashed in the face, were sufficiently wounded to pose no more threat. The rest crouched in a semi-circle, panting steam clouds into the air, rain pouring into their eyes. Iris took a step forward and whirled the big blade again. They retreated but only by a step.

Behind her, Demi's voice cut through the air. "*Basta*! I said enough! You leave us alone. Go home unless you want to spend Christmas in hospital." She was standing on the running board, holding the gun above her head. "Did you hear what I said? Leave us in peace!"

No one moved. One man moaned from the muddy road. "I'm bleeding, it's bad."

A younger, muscular guy stepped forward, his voice loud and arrogant. "You don't scare us, 'lady'. This bitch has a knife, sure, but seven to one? No chance. And whoo-hoo, you got a gun. The problem is, everyone knows you have no ammo."

The tension grew to snapping point. Iris steeled herself. If one of them took a single step, she would attack with the ferocity of a hellcat.

Demi matched the young bull's volume. "Guess what? I've just been Christmas shopping." A shot tore through the air, a forceful thud shook the earth and just in front of the men's feet, part of the road erupted. A second of shock froze them all. Then the men took off as if the hounds of hell were after them, leaving their injured companions in the mud.

Iris ran to the front of the vehicle and squinted at the 'body' lying in the road.

"Get in, Iris!" Demi yelled. "For fuck's sake, get in and let's go before they come back! Iris! Get in the goddamned car!"

Iris waved her right hand to indicate a negative, trying to think. The men had set up a trap, stopping the Land Cruiser on the way home from the market. They attempted to force the rear door because somehow they knew the lock was faulty. Someone had told them A Casa da Prata's gun had no bullets. They had laid a body on the ground, assuming the women would stop. If the women hadn't stopped, their vehicle would have crushed a body considered disposable.

Iris approached the lump with her nerves on edge. She called out twice as she neared the potato sack, but no sound came from the contents. In the Land Cruiser's headlights, she saw the coarse fabric had been trussed with string. If there was a human body inside, it was tied at the ankles, knees, waist and throat. She stretched out a leg to prod it with a toe, all flight reflexes on high alert. It was heavy and immobile but Iris knew she was dealing with a living thing. What kind, she didn't know. She dropped to her knees, tearing open the ties with her machete blade, ready to spring away if the contents were deadly.

Breath shallow, she bit her lip as the sacking fell away and took a sharp intake of breath when she saw Jennifer's face, gagged, pale and unconscious. With her flick knife, she cut the material away from her mouth and listened for sounds of breath. Impossible under the drumming rain. The girl's skin was cold and her skin clammy, but Iris moaned in relief when she found a pulse. She sliced the crude ties from her limbs and her relief gave way to further concern. The urgency of moving her and the dangers that involved. Not just the risk of aggravating an existing injury, but something that could kill them both.

She stood up and motioned that the vehicle should reverse. "It's Jennifer! She's alive but she could be lying on a land mine! Go back and keep watch!"

The headlights retreated to a safe distance and Iris had no choice but to abandon the sense of sight and rely on her fingertips, her instinct and a reassuring mantra.

The chances of a mine planted beneath Jennifer were

negligible. Explosives had been cleared from the war zone years ago. Even if that ambush party had been hoarding an ex-military explosive device, they were hardly likely to waste it on a bunch of women carrying beans, flour and tinned peaches. The idea of a mine had only occurred as she bent down to see what was inside the sack. Any kind of bomb would have been placed at exactly that point and instantly torn them both to shreds. This road was not exactly a thoroughfare, so no one could place a mine moments before A Casa da Prata's Land Cruiser trundled past. Even as she thought it, she recalled the flare from the beach. Someone had been watching and waiting.

Regardless of the odds, Iris had no intention of falling foul of a booby trap. Detecting mines required technology, sniffer dogs, pouch rats, drones and experts. All Iris had was a machete, a flick knife and patience.

She ran her hands over the surface of the road. Beneath the top layer of moistened dust, now wet mud, the ground was hard packed. Using her fingertips, she explored all around the unconscious girl. The road had not been disturbed. Next, she traced Jennifer's body for injuries. She found nothing obvious but under such conditions, one could miss so much. She was convinced there was no explosive planted but even so, didn't dare endanger the others. Holding her breath, she got a grip of the rough material and dragged her half a metre away from the spot. Nothing happened but more and more rain.

She hailed the vehicle, instructed Faith to keep watch and with Demi clutching the other side of the wet sacking, they lifted the girl off the ground and onto the back seat. For the final couple of kilometres, Iris crouched in the foot well, holding Jennifer's hand and stroking her forehead.

"You're safe now. We'll look after you. Everything will be OK." Only after Jennifer's hair grew stained with red did Iris realise she was bleeding.

. . .

For thirty-six hours, Faith sat by Jennifer's bed, refusing all offers of respite. She held her when she was cold, mopped her sweat when she was hot, fed her water and soup in the times she was conscious and sang her songs when she was not. Early on Christmas Eve, Iris was swearing at wet wood which spat and refused to light when she saw Faith emerge from the cowshed.

"Her fever broke. She's sleeping now. I need a little something then I will lie beside her till she wakes." She tugged a blanket around her shoulders. "Is it cold out here or am I turning into Mafalda?"

"Everything is cold. Except the coffee and leftover flatbread I made in the farmhouse. Here."

Faith gave her a stern look. "Iris, you made this for yourself. I can't take it."

"You've been nursing Jennifer for almost two days. Take it. If you have no strength, how can you look after other people? Eat it or else."

"Or else you'll threaten me with your machete?" Faith smiled and took the plate. "Thank you. Has there been any retaliation after the incident on the road?"

Iris finally got a spark and blew on the wood to fuel the fire. "No, nothing at all. I sustained a few cuts and bruises but nothing worse than I got while fixing the roof. Umm, I need to say something about how we found Jennifer. Just let me get this crappy campfire going."

The flames caught and Iris shielded the nascent glow from the wind. "Burn, you bastard! Burn!" She looked over her shoulder. "Yeah, Demi advised me to play down the ambush a little. She thought it was best to say the men put Jennifer in the road to stop us with the aim of looting our vehicle. We stood up to them and scared them off, picked up Jennifer and came home. I explained this," she indicated the bruise on her forehead and scrapes on her fists and elbows, "as taking a tumble off the Land Cruiser as we scrambled to escape. What I mean to say is that no one mentioned machetes, knives or any other kinds of weapon."

Miniature flickers consolidated into a yellowy-golden mass and the smallest hint of heat came from the pit. Iris rubbed her hands together. "Give me half an hour and I'll be roasting piglets. More coffee?"

"No, I want to get some sleep now. You didn't answer my question. Any retaliation? Did we lose much?"

Iris sat down and poured the rest of the coffee into her own cup. "Thanks to Mario fixing the lock on the boot, almost nothing. I lost a couple of presents – one for you, one for Mafalda. But we gained so much more. Jennifer is home again and those idiots will think twice about fighting the women of A Casa da Prata in future."

The sky lightened and both women watched the sun emerge from the sea, a wonder no one could ever ignore. Wispy clouds the colour of chicks puffed above their heads chased by shimmering shoals of mackerel, and the riotous morning calls of seabirds heralded the day.

"What did you buy me?" Faith murmured, the golden morning reflecting on her skin. After two days of little sleep and constant concern, she still looked as much a part of the country's beauty as a wave or a palm tree.

Iris sighed, still irritated about losing the notebook and fleece. "Something to write with."

"A pen?"

"Yes, and a notebook."

Faith chuckled, tucking the blanket under her chin. "That's funny. I bought you a notebook too. I wanted you to write down your speeches so I can learn. But after what you did with those men, I think you can give me something else."

"A second-hand machete?"

Faith chuckled again. "Why not?" She yawned and blinked

at the sky. "That's what I really want for Christmas. Not something to write with, but something to fight with. Goodnight, Iris."

She shuffled into the cowshed, dragging her blanket behind her, leaving Iris fanning the fire. Once it was properly ablaze, she made a pot of coffee, poured herself a cup and sat on the dune to drink it. The dawn sky, so full of promise, was still blue but a grim bank of cloud was rolling in from the north. Around the foot of a palm tree, the goat was tugging up grass and chewing. He spotted her and let out a bleat. She did occasionally feed him burnt rice or inedible roots because he seemed able to digest the indigestible.

She held up an empty hand and he went back to his grazing. How he defended his territory and survived was a constant source of wonder. Perhaps Faith had a point. *Something to fight with*. With the right amount of aggression and some useful weapons, they could engender a little respect. After all, some cows have horns.

9

Even though they knew it was coming, Demi's departure early in the New Year upset everyone. The tall Netherlander was a reassuring, practical presence around the compound and any change in personnel always caused a disturbance in the group. It was particularly hard coming just after Christmas, where the celebrations had been genuinely joyful. The return of Jennifer acted as a sign of hope and a gift for the whole community. Food was sufficient, if not plentiful, and one group of Makuhwa women explained that as they had nothing to give as a present, they had prepared some music.

They sang a cappella and their voices touched Iris like no music she'd heard before. Even after the applause died down, people were still sniffing and wiping their eyes. Iris was one of them. Demi had never read the book Iris bought her, so was thrilled with her present. In return, she gave Iris a bookmark carved from driftwood – 'because you're always losing your damned place'. Only after they'd all gone to bed did Iris realise how apposite her words were.

On the day Demi left, she threw her pack into the back of

the Land Cruiser, waved a general goodbye to the sad faces and promised to send a postcard. Two of the younger girls began weeping, setting off some of the smallest children, who had no idea what the tears were for. Mafalda clapped her hands. "Good luck! Thank you!"

Demi took her cue and climbed inside, her face hidden by the taped-up Perspex panel. Iris jumped in the passenger seat with Faith behind the wheel and they wove a path down the drive and across the gate bridging the gully. Since the ambush, they drove the long way into town, which was actually more convenient for the airport. No one spoke, all weighed down by their own thoughts. The loss of her friend affected Iris more than she had anticipated and she worried how she could cope with all the work they covered as a team.

"You'll be fine," said Demi from the rear, as if she'd overheard. "Faith isn't as tall as me, but who is? The point is that she's strong and fearless. You two make an impressive pair as defence. With Mafalda attacking on the financial front and Jennifer covering the pastoral side, the place is in great hands. Plus you've got the good and great Cantopreto in charge, so things are looking up. Do you think you'll get an audience today?"

"No," said Faith and Iris in unison.

"Why today?" Faith continued, her tone indignant. "Every day we tried so far, we didn't get close. Too many people, too many requests."

Iris agreed. "He's overwhelmed. No reply to Mafalda's letters, no chance of a personal meeting, nothing from his so-called outreach workers. It's early days, I know that, but I doubt he will fulfil his promises."

Faith turned off and took the road to the tiny airport.

"He's a politician," laughed Demi. "Of *course* he won't fulfil his promises. Weather gods, weather gods, be kind today, send my flight up, up and away."

"We can wait in case there's a problem," Faith offered, indicating and easing the vehicle over to the departures door.

"No, you have better things to do with your time. Drop me here, Faith, thanks." She heaved her massive pack onto the pavement, gave each of them a quick hug and rushed into the terminal.

"That was fast," said Faith, pressing at her eyes.

Iris swallowed. "Some people find saying goodbye too emotional. Especially ..." She didn't finish her sentence because the thought of never seeing Demi again closed her throat. Instead, she got back into the car and belted up, forcing her thoughts in the direction of Arnaldo Cantopreto.

"Ladies and gentlemen, thank you for your patience. I'm sorry but Senhor Cantopreto can see no more constituents today. He has a meeting at four pm. Please come back tomorrow."

Iris was on her feet before the guy in a short-sleeved shirt could retreat behind the magical door containing the man himself. "Thank you for the information, sir. May I make a suggestion? We all have tickets marking our place in the queue. For example, the last person to go inside was 208. Next would be 209, 210 and so on. There are," she counted the remaining individuals, "about a dozen folk here who have waited hours for an audience. Do you think it would be fair to give us tickets number one to twelve for the morning? Meaning those disappointed today are first in the queue tomorrow? You see, not everyone can give up a full day's work to sit in a waiting room."

She'd rehearsed the speech time after time in Portuguese and it came out in a rush. But the other frustrated constituents saw the logic and spoke up in support.

The poor man was harried and overwhelmed, but not stupid. He saw a way of defusing the dissatisfaction and making himself, and therefore his boss, appear reasonable.

With great magnanimity and much over-complication, he issued twelve date-stamped tickets for the morning surgery, warning them if they missed their slot, they would go to the back of the line.

Iris checked the clock above the man's head. 16.55. So where was Cantopreto and why hadn't he left for his meeting? In the noise and confusion, she sidled closer to the office entrance. It wasn't a huge leaden security portal but a basic wooden door muffled by thick curtains. It reminded her of bars in Germany, where heavy brocade kept the cold out. Or brothels in Hungary, where velvet drapes kept the heat in. She checked that the official was still dealing with arguments over running order and slipped through the gap. Hidden from the anteroom but excluded from the great man's inner chamber, she pressed her ear to the gap.

For a second, she heard nothing at all and then jerked away in fright as his stentorian tones, speaking English, boomed out from less than a metre away. "Jonathan, I have to stop you there. You understand my limitations, surely? There's only so much I can do. Please do not interrupt when I am speaking. My only assurance is that I will look at your proposition. You should be aware my campaign had many funders, each with their own wish list. Some of those, as one would expect, are in direct conflict of each other's interests. I understand your predicament but you must give me time to think this over. I have a lot to contend with in my new role."

Before he could come out and catch her eavesdropping, Iris ducked out of the curtain and joined the dwindling group. Faith's worried forehead cleared.

"Where you been?"

"Call of nature. What number did we get?"

"Three. We must be here before nine and our limit is half an hour. Jennifer will have to do the breakfast shift. But thanks to you, we have an appointment!"

.   .   .

The news that two people from A Casa da Prata had an official meeting with a figure whose photograph was still pinned to the schoolroom wall sent a thrill through the entire compound. Dinner for Iris, Mafalda, Jennifer and Faith was a series of interruptions, with everyone promoting their own agenda. Iris got the smallest sense of how Cantopreto must feel.

Many domestic duties were now the responsibility of the inhabitants, since the Ministry money required a system of self-organisation. Instead of housekeeping, Jennifer supervised a team of four washing dishes and tidying the tables. Mafalda asked Iris to join her at the bar for a conversation about her future, and Faith was happy to sit outside the farmhouse as visible security while making notes for the meeting.

The evening was damp and cool after an afternoon storm. Iris returned to her stall to collect her rain jacket and noticed her pillow sat much higher than normal. Under it was Demi's leather jacket and the tattered copy of *Wide Sargasso Sea*. Inside the cover was a note:

Iris, meeting you was one of the highlights of my time in Pemba. You're weird, but in a good way. Another highlight was reading this book. I'll take it with me, in my heart. That's why I leave it with you to share with future volunteers.

I won't forget it. Or you.

Demi xo

PS: I outgrew this jacket, in more ways than one. It's yours. Do whatever you like with it. Keep it, give to Mafalda or feed it to the goat.

Iris washed her face of tears and emerged to see Mafalda waiting by the embers of the firepit. "Sorry to keep you waiting. Demi left you a present." She held up the leather jacket. "This ought to keep you warm."

Just like Iris, Mafalda's face creased with emotion. She took the garment and slipped it on. It swamped her, clearly too heavy for her skinny frame. "What a beautiful gesture. I love it."

"Beautiful gesture, sure, but there's no way you can wear it. Look, why don't we swap? You take my silver coat. It's warm, light, water and windproof, plus I can see you in the dark. In return, I get the whole Matrix vibe and project an image far cooler than reality. Fair trade?"

"I can't. You paid a lot of money for that coat. Demi left me a second-hand gift."

"Yeah, and she also suggested I could feed it to the goat. Mafalda, take the coat, will you? You stay cosy and dry. Meanwhile, I channel Elvis. Now are we having a drink or not?"

They strolled down the beach, trying not to pose, but caught each other's eye and laughed.

"It's been years since I've worn something new," said Mafalda, by way of an excuse.

"And I haven't worn a leather jacket since I was in college."

"It suits you. Although you should probably wear this silver one tomorrow. A leather jacket isn't quite the right look for a meeting with a member of government."

"I'm not sure *I'm* the right look for a meeting with a member of government, whatever I'm wearing. A white woman telling a black official how to run his community? Plus the fact I know far less about the place than you. It should be you who attends with Faith, not me."

"No." Her voice brooked no argument.

Iris struggled with the urge to ask for an explanation and was still trying to find the words when Mafalda continued.

"Anyway, you're not telling him how to run his community. You're asking for his backing. If he stands up in support of us, it will be a huge step forward and open countless doors. The tone is essential. We need his approval and public recognition that we're providing a valuable local service. Female education and participation is one of the government's key talking points and that's all we want. To be talked about in a positive light."

"Which is exactly why you should go. You're ten times more eloquent and better informed than I am."

Without warning, Mafalda stopped. "Here, on the beach, yes. At the farmhouse in the safety of our refuge, yes. But in front of someone like Cantopreto? Iris, why do you think I never leave the compound? Why must someone else always drive the car? Why was I one of the only women who didn't go into town to vote?"

Iris stared at her, running the events of polling day through her mind. It was true. In the mayhem of getting everyone there and back, Mafalda's absence had gone unnoticed.

"You have some kind of agoraphobia, is that it?"

Mafalda started walking again. "If that's the name for being terrified of men. Their loud voices and noisy cars, their massive bodies, nasty dogs and ugly weapons, it all petrifies me. I mean that literally. I freeze and cannot even run away. It took three years without setting foot off our property before a previous volunteer lured me to Divine's bar. Yes, men are there, but they are different, quiet and respectful. Even the dog is well behaved. Can you imagine what would have happened if I'd been in the car when you got ambushed? Yes, I know you and Demi toned down the reality. I made Faith tell me the truth."

"I'm sorry." Iris wasn't sure what exactly she was apologising for, but it seemed the right thing to say.

"You are the opposite. Unafraid, quick-thinking, strong and smart. The night they came in their cars and fell foul of your security precautions, you finished the job and scared them off. Me? I was trembling in the cowshed. That is why you are the person to accompany Faith tomorrow. Otherwise Cantopreto's conversation will be with one assertive woman and a weeping, shivering mess. Now do you understand?"

Abashed, Iris nodded, puzzling at how many signs she had

missed. "Yes. I'll go to the meeting. Of course I'll go. Feel a bit stupid, though, because I never noticed your ..." She fizzled out, unable to find the right word.

"Problem? I hide it pretty well. On the phone, I'll take on anyone. Face to face? Forget it. Last time we were on this beach together, I ran off and left you to deal with those guys alone. That wasn't just cowardice. You couldn't have defended both of us if I seized up. Anyway, I'm sorry."

Chords from a guitar reached them as they stepped into the pool of light from the bar. Iris smiled. "You did the right thing. Come on, we need a drink."

They climbed the wooden steps and said hello to the surfers and the group sitting around the guitarist. By now, a few of their faces were familiar to Iris.

"Ladies! Come to drown your sorrows?" Divine called. "Me too. Heaven knows I will miss that girl. But she gave you her jacket! It's almost as if she's here in spirit."

Mafalda shook her head with a laugh. "Demi's not dead, Divine. She just went back to Europe."

"As far as I'm concerned, that's the same thing. In honour of our dear departed Dutch girl, the House Special tonight is a Snowball. Mai Tai, I had the devil's own job to get hold of some advocaat, so you'd better order at least two."

"Two Snowballs, please," said Mafalda.

"Come sit with us," called the guitar player. "You promised to sing one of these nights."

Divine gave an approving nod. "Go over there and I'll bring the drinks. Edson is a fine-looking man, don't you think? You can't go wrong with a musician. Such dextrous fingers." She let out a delighted cackle at Iris's shocked expression. "Go flirt with him a while. He needs the practice."

Armed with new knowledge after Mafalda's confidences, Iris checked to see if joining a group including men would be acceptable.

Mafalda gave an amused shrug. "Why not? It's good for you to meet more Mozambicans."

Edson, as Divine pointed out, was indeed a fine-looking man. His open face welcomed them as they dragged over some chairs. He had a swimmer's body, Iris noted, his broad shoulders stretching his Rolling Stones T-shirt. The smile he flashed them was vague and general as he strummed the intro to 'Ain't No Sunshine' by Bill Withers, but when he looked up from his fret board, his laughing eyes met hers first.

His repertoire was eclectic. From Aerosmith to Joni Mitchell, he sang stories of absence and loss which could have dampened the mood. Yet his choice of tempo, different accompanying vocalists and gentle chit-chat as he flicked through his song book created a campfire atmosphere.

Aware of her big meeting the following day, Iris refused a second cocktail and sipped at a beer. Edson coaxed Mafalda, Iris and two younger women into a rendition of 'Goodbye, My Friend' by the Spice Girls. They had to squeeze together behind him to read the words and the harmonies came out mangled. Even so, it was a cathartic way to say goodbye to Demi.

She and Mafalda stood up to leave to general groans of disappointment. Then Edson began strumming a melody no one seemed to recognise. Iris did. Her hand began patting against her thigh as her heel thumped on the wooden deck. Without hesitation, she launched into Nickleback's 'How You Remind Me', belting out words she'd forgotten she knew. She sang for Demi and for everyone who had ever pushed her to go further. She danced as she sang the chorus and with an excess of energy, leapt off the steps into the sand for the final chord.

The applause was a mixture of astonishment and admiration. Sweating and buzzing with adrenalin and a hefty dose of self-consciousness, Iris took a bow and jerked her head at

Mafalda to begin their walk home. She waved her goodbyes, noting Divine's whoops and Edson's salute.

Mafalda was still clapping as she descended the steps in the usual fashion. "Wow! I had no idea you could do that."

"Neither did I. Guess I needed to let off some steam," said Iris, wiping her forehead with her palm.

"Either that or her jacket has magical powers. What a performance!"

"Yeah, must be the leather bringing out my inner rocker. It was a lot of fun." Iris was already cringing at her exhibitionism.

Clouds slid over the moon, creating erratic illumination of their path, as if the super trouper operator had drunk one too many Snowballs. Every time the moonlight caught Mafalda's jacket, the silver glinted like snow crystals. For once, she wasn't shivering.

"You impressed everyone," said Mafalda. "Especially Edson. I think he likes you."

"He's a friendly guy and a decent guitarist. But I'm not interested in men."

Mafalda fell silent for a while. "You mean generally, or not right now? Not that it makes any difference if you prefer women."

"Oh, I see what you mean. No, I do like men. One man in particular. It's just that currently any kind of romantic or sexual encounter is the last thing on my mind."

"I understand. I feel that way all the time."

Iris was still processing that non-sequitur when Mafalda spoke again.

"Do you want to stay another year, Iris? Because I think you are a benefit to the refuge. You're good for morale and you're practical. Volunteering is costly, I know, so I am willing to use some of the education grant to pay you a salary. A teaching assistant, for example? It won't be much more than the subsistence money, but you'd be an official employee. The question is, can you stay on for another year? Hiring an assistant for three months is not logical."

"Another year? That's more than I planned."

"I know. But you hadn't met us then." She laughed softly. "It's OK, you don't have to give me an answer now. Think it over. How would a year here fit in with your plans? We'll talk about it again in a few days."

"Right. I'll think it over."

They climbed the dune to the compound. Someone, probably Faith, had left on one of the solar-powered lights. It was a dull glow but enabled Mafalda and Iris to find their respective routes after swapping jackets and saying goodnight.

Teeth cleaned, face washed, she curled under her coverlet and bounced her head six times on the pillow. Six am start for breakfast and preparation for one of the most important meetings of her life. This was no time to start thinking about Mafalda's offer. Another year in Pemba was madness when she had a Portuguese farm waiting for her return. On the other hand, much had changed in her first three months at the compound. What more could she achieve with an official position, determination and the ear of the government? She opened her eyes and stared into the blackness.

10

———

I t seemed she'd been asleep for about twenty minutes when a hand shook her shoulder.

"Iris? Please wake up now. We need you."

Her eyes shot open and her heart raced when she saw Jennifer inside her mosquito net, crouching by her bed.

"What is it? What's the matter?"

"Faith is s-s-ick. She has a fever and she's t-t-talking nonsense. I think it's malaria."

Iris sat up. "Oh, hell, no. What time is it?"

"I don't know. After four, maybe, because it's getting light. I sat with her all night, t-t-trying to keep her cool, but she just got worse. Should we wake Mafalda?"

Iris threw back the cover and sat up. "Wait till I've seen Faith. When did she get sick? She was fine at dinner. Is anyone else showing signs of illness?"

"I'm not sure but I don't think s-so. The compound is quiet. Only me and Joana are up because Faith's s-s-tall is between ours. She was very hot and s-s-sweaty after dinner and said she had a headache. When you and Mafalda left for the bar, she t-t-told me to put a light on for when you came back and she went to bed. I heard her mumbling and writhing around then I checked on her to see if she needed anything. She was shivering and s-s-saying she couldn't get warm. I got in with her for body heat and in a few minutes sh-she was burning up with a fever."

Iris followed Jennifer up the stalls in the weak morning light and even before she reached Faith's place, she could smell vomit. Joana was on her hands and knees clearing up the mess.

"Iris, she's very bad. She needs medicine."

On the bed, Faith was mumbling incomprehensibly interrupted by groans every time she winced with a cramp. Her skin was hot to the touch.

"Jennifer, go wake Mafalda and ask her if we have any anti-malarial drugs. If not, we have to get her to a doctor as soon as we can. Hurry, now."

Jennifer rushed away, her flip-flops slapping on the sandy ground.

"She's cramping which probably means diarrhoea pretty soon. The best place for her is in the farmhouse, where she's near a toilet. There's no chance of her walking, though. Will you find the wheelbarrow, Joana, and line it with bedclothes? Thank you."

No sooner had Joana left the stall than Faith rolled over and threw up again. It was a pathetic attempt, merely an acidic-smelling dribble. Iris sat on the cot to wipe her friend's mouth and cool her forehead. She whispered soothing words of reassurance as she laid her shivery body back on the clammy sheets. This was extremely bad news. Malaria could be deadly, often claiming thousands of lives every year, and Faith's case was clearly serious. Their first priority had to be treating this tough young woman whose wellbeing was essential to the refuge. All thoughts of the meeting with local government had to be pushed to the back of Iris's mind.

At the same time she acknowledged that fact, she was frantically searching for a substitute. Jennifer was like a rabbit in the headlights at the moment even at home in the compound and the more stressed she became, the worse her stutter. Last night, Mafalda had made it clear she was unable to fulfil such a task. Joana was only just eighteen years old. Demi must already be on Dutch soil and probably three beers into her welcome home party. How the hell could Iris, a white volunteer without even a temporary contract, march into Cantopreto's office and argue the case for a local women's refuge?

The sound of the wheelbarrow drew her out of her self-pitying outrage. She heaved a pitiful Faith onto the mound of covers and Joana padded two pillows around her head. By now the noise and activity had woken other residents who came out to help. Iris steered the barrow towards the farmhouse and met Mafalda, who emerged carrying a little white plastic case.

"Good thinking. Let's get her inside. Iris, start the small generator. I'm going to need more light in here."

They set up a sick bed outside the bathroom while Mafalda prepared the medication. "Watch this," she told Iris and Jennifer. "If I'm not here, you need to know what to do. Joana, go get some of the others to help you start breakfast."

She took out a package of individual boxes. "This is artesunate, to be injected intravenously. How heavy is Faith? Fifty kilos?"

"Fifty max. She's short and very light," Iris replied.

"So we need two doses. Good, we can do this in tandem. Wash your hands with sterile soap, Jennifer, and wear gloves. Iris, you disinfect Faith's arm with these wipes."

The women obeyed, conscious of Faith's grunts at every spasm.

"Here's your packet, Jennifer. Take out the chunky bottle. That is the product. Now open a syringe and withdraw the bicarbonate from its vial, that little one there. Inject that into the product. Then we shake it gently and let it rest until it's clear. Next, we extract the air from the bottle because we need room for the saline solution."

The calm reassurance in Mafalda's tone took effect on Jennifer, whose wide-eyed terror had sharpened into intense concentration.

"Now we add enough saline solution to make twelve millilitres of product. Use a new syringe, Jenni, and measure your dose precisely. I'll do the injections this time, but you can administer the second dose, which will be in twelve hours' time. Watch me carefully." She found a vein on Faith's hand. "Can you hold her wrist, Iris? Just in case she pulls away. Now, the essential thing is to press the plunger slowly. It should take over a minute to get all the medication into her bloodstream. Understood?"

"I think s-s-s-so."

Mafalda studied the girl's face. "You're going to make a very good nurse, I can see that."

"Faith t-t-took care of me. I will t-t-take care of her, although I'm s-s-s frightened."

"That's the right attitude, Jenni. I'm proud of you. Iris, you should get ready for your meeting. Can't keep Cantopreto waiting. I prepared all the financial documents."

Iris stood there, waiting for Mafalda to recognise the ridiculousness of the situation. She didn't even look up, busy injecting Faith's other hand. Only when she'd finished did she acknowledge Iris's presence. "Over there, on the table. What is it?"

"I can't do this on my own."

Mafalda's face hardened. "You have no choice. I can't leave the compound unattended, Jennifer is needed here and you could only take Faith if you put her in the wheelbarrow. I'm not sure it would add much if she pukes over his feet. Go, Iris, and do your best." She turned to dispose of the medical detritus. "If you really need moral support, ask Joana to go with you."

Irritated by Mafalda's intransigence, Iris snorted. "Joana? The girl doesn't know how old she is! How articulate is she likely to be in front of a local politician?"

"She might not know how old she is but she can tell him her life story. That's all he needs to hear. While you're in the city, I need you to pick up more medication. I'll make you a list. You get yourself some breakfast and I'll bring it over in a minute."

"How the hell am I supposed to represent an entire compound? This is NOT my problem!" Her voice was louder than necessary and everyone, including Faith, winced.

"We don't shout here, Iris. You know that. I'm afraid it is your problem because you made it so by volunteering to help. Your fear is understandable, but it's a fear of failure, that's all. Do your best. That's all I ask. Take Joana and talk to Canto-preto. Throw everything you've got – facts, passion, finances, pressure, gory details, anything that works. For all our sakes, Iris, this matters."

Grim, bleak, endless rain made the miserable drive feel even more hopeless. Joana stared out of the windscreen as if hypno-tised. This would have been the time to coach the teenager in what to say, but Iris was totally defeated. Faith in danger of death, Mafalda refusing to come out of her shell and now an illiterate teenager as her sidekick, it all seemed completely pointless. What was stopping her booking a flight out of here and going home to the farm? She was on a hiding to nothing and wasting her time. Another year? Forget it.

In her self-indulgence, she allowed herself to open a forbidden portal, her words to Mafalda reverberating around her head. *I do like men. One man in particular. It's just that right now, any kind of romantic or sexual encounter is the last thing on my mind.* It was a lie. Whenever she released the tight grip on her imagination, he was there. Gil Maduro with his stony expression, burnt skin and electric touch, usually wearing his police uniform and a sardonic smile.

"This is the first time I've ever been here," said Joana, her voice cheerful and in wonder. She sounded as if they were on an excursion to Disneyland.

Iris dragged herself back to the moment. "The coast road is much prettier. But we're safer taking the airport road and doubling back into the city. Are you feeling OK about coming with me to this meeting?"

"Yes! I am very lucky. This is my first time in the city, the first time in a car and the first time meeting a politician. What do I call him?"

"Senhor Cantopreto, I suppose. First time in a car, Joana? Aren't you exaggerating just a little bit?"

"Senhor Cantopreto," she murmured. Belted up in the passenger seat, she mimed a little bow. "*Bom dia*, Senhor Cantopreto, *muito prazer.*" She beamed at Iris, smoothing her tight plaits to her head. "I will do exactly what I'm told, don't worry, Iris. You can trust me. I'm eighteen years old and I know how to behave. Yes, first time in the front of a car, like a passenger. It's much nicer than being in the back. You can see where you're going and there's no chicken shit."

Iris thought about her words for a while but chose not to pursue that conversation. "We should rehearse what we're going to say."

Joana didn't respond, her gaze high into the sky.

"What are you looking at?"

"An aeroplane. Just imagine! People are sitting in rows inside that thing, looking down at us and saying how small everything seems. You've been in a plane, no? Of course you have or how could you have got here? Were you terrified? I can't imagine how it must feel."

It didn't seem the right time to share the utter lack of romance and crushing boredom of air travel with this girl. "It's magical. To soar above rainclouds and see pure white fluff below, you feel like you're on another planet. I went scuba-diving a few times and I had the same sense of wonder. There's a world beneath the waves. We only see a tiny slice of life from the ground."

Joana stared at Iris, her blue-green eyes steady and her lips cracking into a delighted smile. "Yes! We only see a tiny slice, but if we look closely, we can see the universe in detail. Can we have the radio on?"

Lost for words, Iris nodded her assent and thought about that comment until they parked outside the municipal building.

The queue was already out the door and Iris hoped the official would stick to his promise of prioritising the people disappointed yesterday. She was impressed to see the first ticket was one of the men who had vocally supported her idea of the previous day. He gave her an appreciative nod as he followed the official to the imposing curtains.

Each appointment overran, so Joana and Iris had been seated in the stuffy anteroom for two hours before their number was called.

They smoothed their clothes and walked through the curtains to meet the man everyone wanted to see.

He stood up as the lackey announced their names and their primary reason for requesting an audience. Cantopreto welcomed them with a smile and gestured to the chairs in front of his desk. He was a huge man whose suit threatened to spilt, Incredible Hulk-style, at any moment. With close-cropped hair and sharp eyes, he radiated an extraordinary presence, like an inactive volcano. With large soft hands, he shook both of theirs.

"Ms Iris Simons and Ms Faith Mbuti, it's a pleasure to receive you. How can I help?"

"Thank you for granting us an audience, Senhor Cantopreto. My name is Iris Simons and this is Ms Joana Zeca. Unfortunately, Ms Mbuti is indisposed with malaria and Ms Zeca is her deputy. We're here to talk to you about A Casa da Prata."

He sat up, clasping the edges of his desk. "I am most sincerely sorry to hear that. Does she have all the necessary medication she requires?"

"I believe so. Thank you for your concern. I know you have many demands on your time and finances. We're here to ask for your support, sir. The Mozambique government has made a commitment to female equality, education and participation in civil society. We run a refuge for women with nowhere else to go. We feed, house and protect them from harm while providing training in agriculture and a general education. Until the most recent election, none of our members had ever exercised their right to vote. This time almost a third went to the polling station. We are not popular, Senhor Cantopreto, because we challenge traditional attitudes. We need money, resources, supplies and staff but above all that, we need acceptance. Half our time and energy is spent defending ourselves from those who resent our existence. The voice of a respected government official validating what we do could transform our lives. Public support, which is nothing more than putting the government's own promises into action, will make our work admired rather than resented. Changing minds is never easy, as you know more than most. It needs leadership from the top. This is why we are here, *senhor*, to ask for your patronage. Your approval will make all the difference. For women fleeing domestic violence, refugees from border skirmishes, young girls thrown out by their families and pregnant women with no opportunities for themselves or their children. Through two civil wars, women have given a great deal to this country. We owe the grandmothers, the mothers, the widows and the children for the sacrifices they have made. All we ask is for your public backing. Thank you for listening."

Cantopreto nodded thoughtfully and then turned his attention to Joana, who had sat spellbound throughout Iris's speech.

"And you, young lady? What have you got to say?"

Joana's eyes lit up at being handed the spotlight. "Without A Casa da Prata, I would be dead."

Her blunt reply took him by surprise and even Iris was wrong-footed.

Joana spoke without sentimentality, her soft voice clear and factual. "When I was fifteen years old, my parents sold me to a farmer. He already had a wife, but she was over thirty and only good for working the land. My job was to deliver him sons. I failed. Three times I fell pregnant and three times I lost the child. He bought a new woman and threw me out. He could not afford to keep three wives. I walked two days and nights to get home but my parents didn't want me either. I was sixteen years old and living on the streets. One day a man offered to pay me for sex. So I did what he told me and when I asked for the money, he laughed. Because of that I got a disease and couldn't even beg for food. I thought I was going to die so I dragged myself to the beach. I wanted to see the ocean for the last time and pray to God for forgiveness. When I woke up, I was in the cowshed at A Casa da Prata. The women fed me, helped me recover, taught me how to cook and how to vote. For the first time in my life, I voted for a politician and I chose you. We all did because you promised you would look after women and girls. That's why I came here today. You will keep your promise, won't you, Senhor Cantopreto?"

Hearing Joana's story came as a shock to Iris, but blindsided Cantopreto. He stood up and turned his back to them, leaning on his chair, staring out of the window. Joana glanced at Iris, her face apologetic. Iris shook her head with a half-smile of reassurance. They waited as the minutes ticked by, both too intimidated to hurry him along.

Finally, he faced them once more, pulling at his nose as if he wanted to make it longer. "Thank you for your honesty. There is much information to take in. Ms Simons, if you would be so kind as to provide me with a concrete proposal in writing, you have my word I will act upon it to the best of my ability. Before you leave, my assistant will take a photograph, if you don't mind. These little things help jog my memory when I come to the relevant paperwork." He pressed a buzzer on his desk which made an absurd noise, a cross between a sheep's bleat and a fart.

The door opened and the lackey Iris had harassed into giving them tickets entered, looking bewildered. "Senhor?"

"The ladies and I have finished our conversation. Now we will take the customary photograph and they can get on with their day."

"The photograph?" The man's face was blank.

"Yes, please. The three of us, against my desk. I will stand in the middle."

The man stared uncomprehending for a moment until Cantopreto said, "Use your phone, man! We don't have all day!"

Iris and Joana got into position and Cantopreto spread his arms behind their backs. Yet his hands did not touch them. The pose was intended to be avuncular and kind, she supposed: a sleep-deprived foreign volunteer and wide-eyed teenage girl either side of a statesman wearing a dignified smile.

"That will be all. Thank you, ladies, and I look forward to hearing from you in due course." He sat at his desk and began making notes.

They whispered their gratitude and received a brief nod of

reply. The assistant chivvied them out the door. Outside, it was sunny and steamy after the morning's rain. A romantic would have seen this break in the clouds as a sign of hope. In Iris's case, the jury was still out.

"What now?" asked Joana, her eyes still shining.

"Pharmacy. More medication for Faith, remember? She'll need a second shot tonight. Why don't we walk seeing as it's not raining? Saves on gas."

It was a suggestion she'd live to regret. No one anywhere would give them an artesunate intravenous shot unless they had official medical ID. Shop after shop, shaking head after regretful grimace, it soon became clear they weren't going to get the medicine Faith needed.

They picked up the post from the PO box and stopped for lunch. At a street stall, Iris bought them both some *bolinhos de bacalhau* with a warning to Joana to eat slowly or she'd give herself stomach ache. "You can always save some for a snack later. Just don't scarf it down, OK?"

"OK." She ate primly, taking tiny bites and chewing thoroughly. Iris smiled, despite her pessimism. In spite of all that had befallen her, Joana's spark continued to burn brightly. With the right guidance this girl could, and probably would, blaze a trail for the future.

"Iris? What are we going to do about Faith's injection? I don't think anyone will give us that *artesinho* stuff, no matter how many places we try."

"Artesunate," Iris corrected. "There must be a way, even if it's under the counter. This is why Cantopreto has to grant us medical status. How the hell did Mafalda do it when she won't even leave the compound?"

"Most likely she knows someone. That's the way to things get done. Connections." Joana swallowed another bite and wrapped the remainder of her cod cakes in their greaseproof paper. "You remember about that time at the polling station when they wouldn't let me vote? There was a man who helped us. He said he was from some children's organisation. Bet you they have plenty of medicines. Can I drink the rest of my Coke?"

Iris stopped eating. Not because her appetite was sated but because the idea was brilliant. "Joana, you can have whatever you like. You are proving to be quite an asset." She flicked through her rucksack until she found his card. Nathaniel Nhamirre, Head of Outreach and Education, Child Welfare International.

Nathaniel Nhamirre not only remembered Joana and Iris, but offered them coffee and cakes on the terrace of the CWI building. He understood the crisis and sent someone to plunder the charity's medical supplies. "You know she will need oral medication after the first forty-eight hours? Do you need help with that also?"

"That's very kind, Senhor Nhamirre, but we were able to get that from the pharmacy. It's only the IV drugs we cannot access. Everyone says we should take our friend to hospital."

He tapped his teeth with a fingernail. "Strictly speaking, they are right. Malaria can be fatal. Your colleagues, I'm sure, are very capable but if she does not improve, I second that advice. And what about you, Ms Zeca, did you eventually cast your vote?"

Joana gave him the same open-faced sincerity as she did everyone else. "*Sim, senhor!* I voted for Arnaldo Cantopreto and he won. Then this morning, I got to meet him!"

Nhamirre sat back in amazement. "You did?"

"We both did," said Iris. "We had half an hour to impress upon him why he should support our project. I don't think I was the best ambassador for A Casa da Prata, but Joana added the personal touch."

Joana shook her head and even put down the *bolo de arroz* she was nibbling. "No, Iris, not true, you were incredible! I was so proud watching you and hearing you speak. Now I know what I want to do when I leave the refuge. I am going to be a politician. I am going to make a difference."

Nhamirre beamed and clapped his hands together. "Joana Zeca, I will not forget your name because I think you will do exactly that. I am going to watch your career with anticipation. You have my full encouragement. Ah, here's Teresa with your medical requirements. I asked her to bring you a funding application at the same time. If I recall correctly, Ms Simons, you were seeking financial support for single mothers. Duty calls but please remember what I said. Hospital is the best place if she shows no signs of recovery. Call me if you need help. You have a friend here, always." With a wide smile, he retreated into the building.

Iris thanked the nurse for the shots and folded the application form carefully in her backpack. Joana pocketed their cakes and they headed back to the Toyota, scurrying to beat the incoming rain. They weren't quite fast enough and got caught in a shower.

Iris smoothed her hair over her forehead, fired up the engine and turned onto the coast road. The long way round was too tiring and if those dickheads tried another ambush, they would regret it. Iris was tired and only too willing to kick someone's arse. She drove carefully and on full alert as Joana hummed happily in the passenger seat. Luguni passed without incident and no one attempted to interfere with their vehicle. At one point, loud music blasted from a cluster of houses, but Iris did not slow down. Getting the medicine to Faith was all that counted.

On arrival at the compound, Joana hopped out to drag the gate across the gully. The place looked deserted and lonely, generating a rising panic in Iris's chest. She waited for Joana and drove a cautious path between the stones. She'd set the rocks herself but in the gloom of the thunderstorm it was easy to make a mistake. A light was on in the farmhouse. The cowshed was in darkness. She parked under the eaves and sprinted into the sick bay. Everything was as she had left it – Faith prone on the camp bed, Jennifer mopping her face, the faint sour tang of vomit and disinfectant from the floor. Mafalda emerged from the office-cum-bedroom with an expectant air.

"How did it go?" she asked in lowered tones.

Iris handed over the CWI bag and everything she'd got from the pharmacies. "A shot for tonight and another for tomorrow. Plus oral remedies. The advice is to take her to hospital."

"Thank you." Mafalda took the bag and examined the contents. "Well done. Did you see Cantopreto?"

"Yeah. I gave my speech, Joana was amazing, but ..."

"But what? Did he listen to you? Did he ask any questions?"

"He wants my suggestions in writing and he'll 'act on it to the best of his ability'. I'm translating that as 'I'll do jack shit', but maybe I'm a cynic." She noted Mafalda's swollen eyes. "Are you OK? Is Faith getting worse?"

She shook her head and beckoned Iris away from the patient and into her office. "No. Faith's getting better. With the shots, she'll recover in three or four days. It's something else. While you were gone, a group of men came on a rampage. Not from the road this time, they used the beach. They tore around the compound, breaking tables, attacking our generator and yelling like creatures possessed. Everyone was terrified."

The hairs stood up on Iris's skin. "Did they hurt anyone? Is the generator broken? What about the goat?"

"None of us got hurt. We ran to safety as soon as they invaded. The generator is still working but will likely need repairs. The goat ... is dead." Her voice broke. "They slit his throat."

Iris clenched her jaw and closed her eyes. "What did they do with him?"

"I have no idea. Left him on the beach, I guess. When they'd finished scaring the life out of every woman, girl and child in the compound, they ran off down the road, roaring like they'd won a football match. The important thing is we are all safe, we have the shots Faith needs and you put our case to the government. A new volunteer is arriving tonight. Can you collect her from the airport? I ..." Her voice petered out.

"Mafalda?" Iris placed an arm around her shoulders and sat her on the bed. "You need a rest. At seven o'clock, you'll have to inject the second shot. Until then, get some sleep. I'll deal with everything else."

She pulled up her hood and marched into the compound, her teeth clenched hard enough to shatter. The damage was far less severe than after the thunderstorm. She righted benches, collected shards of crockery and examined the generator. A few dents and scratches did not concern her. She stomped over the dune and saw the goat's body mere paces away, a dark pool around its head.

"You bastards," she whispered. "He didn't deserve this."

Then she shucked off emotion and turned to pragmatism. Here was enough meat for three if not four meals, if managed efficiently.

"Sorry, my old mate," she said. "You were a great guard dog, until you weren't. Now, you're going to make a great curry." She grabbed the carcass by the horns, dragged it up the sand and over to the oil drum. That was as far as her knowledge of transforming a hairy corpse into succulent flesh went. Inside the cowshed, she called for anyone used to butchering animals. After a show of hands, she went to fetch her machete.

. . .

The practicalities of skinning, jointing, cooking, seasoning and roasting a fully grown billy-goat absorbed everyone's attention. The meal was a great success and even Mafalda overcame her grief at the animal's demise to manage a few mouthfuls of roasted flesh. The novelty of meat lent dinner a carnival atmosphere and the ambience was lively. It astounded Iris how quickly the women bounced back from their shock of the afternoon. She, on the other hand, was smouldering. No one single issue lit the fuse, yet her rage at the injustice and impotence of their situation built into an inferno.

After all his grand promises during the election campaign, Cantopreto had listened for less than half an hour and made no commitment whatsoever to their cause. The self-serving bastard had even squeezed in a photo opportunity. As for those men bursting in here to terrify the women and wreak havoc on their property, how dare they? Who did they think they were to cause wanton destruction and kill an animal out of pure spite? These were people who went to church on Sundays and listened to the pastor preach tolerance and advise loving thy neighbour. They said the Lord's Prayer and wore a crucifix, all pious and holy, until the next time they got drunk. Then the deep-seated hatred for a group of people trying to live their lives in peace resurfaced. Someone should call them out on their hypocrisy.

Had Demi been there, Iris could have shared her thoughts, voiced her anger and let off steam. As it was, Mafalda had returned to the farmhouse with two plates of food for Faith and Jennifer, with the intention of persuading them to eat. So there was no one to stop Iris. She called Joana to help her pull the gate across the gully and told her to drag it back after she had gone.

"Where are you going, Iris?" she asked.

"To the airport for the new volunteer, but there is something I need to do first," Iris replied before getting into the Land Cruiser and driving off into Luguni, looking for trouble.

She wasn't exactly sure where to find them and had certainly not planned what she would do if she did, but that didn't stop her driving with a grim determination to stop the bullying once and for all. The light was beginning to fade and Iris switched on the headlights, only to discover that one head-lamp was out. Exactly what she didn't need – an excuse for the police to pull her over. She slowed, deliberating whether or not to turn around and go back. Up ahead, she saw the lights of a roadside bar and recognised the red Jeep that had come a cropper in their home-made defences. She sped up and parked right behind the vehicle, effectively boxing it in.

She jumped out of the Toyota and stormed over to where a group of men sat drinking around some plastic tables. The laughter and swaggering arrogance fuelled her ire.

"Well, aren't you some big brave boys? You get tanked up on cheap beer, convince yourselves you're some kind of vigilantes, puff up each other's testosterone levels and then take it out on a group of defenceless women. Call yourself Christians? Don't make me laugh. You are cowardly, pathetic bullies and you should be ashamed of yourselves."

Her sudden arrival and furious tirade had initially shocked the men into silence. Now one man who had been leaning against the bar found his voice.

"Get out of here. Nobody likes a woman with a big mouth."

His insult seemed to wake up the others and spur them on to demonstrating their masculinity.

"Yeah, piss off! Don't you come round here telling us what to do! Those half-brained females might tolerate a foreigner interfering in their business, but we won't stand for it," said an older man with a slight slur.

Another guy who Iris recognised as one of the ambush

party joined in. "You and that German think you're pretty clever, don't you? Wrong. You don't know shit about the way things work around here. So take your opinions and shove them up your arse."

The men howled with laughter at this, clapping each other on the back.

Iris waited till the self-congratulation died down. "What is it about a group of women taking care of one another that upsets you so much? Why can't you just leave us alone? We're not causing you any harm, but you persist in making trouble. Frightening vulnerable women with your cars and your dogs and your loud voices must make you feel very powerful. If you had any guts, you would be defending our compound and protecting us. But you don't. Why is that? Because you feel impotent? Our goat had more bollocks than you lot put together. I'm not surprised your women left you. I would do the same. You're nothing but a bunch of sad, weak losers with no balls."

She spun on her heel and got back into the Toyota, the sound of laughter ringing in her ears. Their intent was clearly to ridicule and humiliate, but somehow the derisive laughter did not sound authentic. She wrenched the wheel around and stepped on the gas, driving back the way she came. She did not even glance at the men in the bar, even when one empty beer can banged against the windscreen. Her anger should have subsided since she had vented her spleen, but she was still shaking with temper. She needed a drink. An ice cold beer on a hotel terrace would be just the thing to help her calm down and collect her thoughts. But the hotels were all in the opposite direction, the compound had no booze and she didn't feel like walking down the beach to Divine's place. There was nowhere a single woman would be safe to have a drink. Her single headlight illuminated the turning to the airport and the answer was obvious. Get to the airport early and drink a beer while waiting for the volunteer. She took a right turn, feeling for her backpack to be sure she had her wallet. She shook her head and rolled her eyes at herself. Of course she had her wallet. She kept her essentials on her person every second of the day.

Unlike the night of her arrival, the airport was lit up and bustling with activity. She found a parking spot not far from the entrance and went inside. Her memory had not failed her. There was a coffee shop and bar on the concourse, where people could pass the time while waiting for loved ones to arrive or facing the security measures before departures. Several single travellers, all men, were sitting at the bar and two smart-looking women drank Cokes at one of the tables. Iris ordered a beer and sat near the window to watch the comings and goings. There was something highly charged about airports; reunions and goodbyes, the end of an era or new lives about to start.

The beer worked its magic. The stresses of the day seemed to evaporate along with the bubbles. She breathed deeply and let go of all her tension. At one point, a white guy who looked like a truck driver moved into her line of vision, tilting his head to look into her face.

"What do you want?" she spat through gritted teeth.

He held up his hands in defence. "Whoa! I just wanted to borrow this chair. Is that OK?" His Antipodean accent was soft and his expression sincere. She looked past him to see another four men, dressed similarly, settling themselves at a table.

She waved a hand. "Take it. Sorry, bad day."

"No worries. Hope it gets better." He pronounced it 'bitter'.

Outside, more and more people were gathering outside the arrivals hall and Iris looked up at the electronic announcement boards to see if the flight they were waiting for was the same one bearing their new volunteer. The 18.40 from Johannesburg was due to land at 19.10, delayed by half an hour. Johannesburg. That was the airport where she'd bought her silver rain-coat, a lifetime ago. She imagined boarding one of those planes, travelling to Lisbon via South Africa and finally home to the farm near Viseu. With a flash of insight, she couldn't quite imagine living in that world again. The realisation shocked her because she had been happier in Alcafalche than she had been since losing her husband. Lana and Nestor were like a beloved aunt and uncle, substitutes for the family she no longer had. The thought of family sounded alarm bells in her psyche and she closed that door in a hurry.

Sooner or later she would need to give Mafalda an answer to her offer of a position. In her heart of hearts, Iris didn't want to stay another year. At the same time, she had the sense of a job unfinished. When she'd left Portugal, her intention was to stay a maximum of six months and she was halfway through that period. Where would she go if not back to the farm? What was she doing with her life?

She looked over her shoulder and caught the barman's eye, pointing at her almost empty bottle. He jerked his head in acknowledgement. It was rash to drink another beer, she knew that much. Her rational side listed all of the reasons she was acting irrationally.

If the police stopped her for driving with one headlight and over the alcohol limit, she'd be lucky to escape with a fine. Just after her licence had become official.

Her place was at the compound, protecting its inhabitants, especially after she just prodded the hornets' nest of men at the roadside bar.

She was wasting time and money, hanging out at the airport to consume two beers. What kind of volunteer did she call herself?

The barman placed the bottle on the table and cracked off the cap. She smiled her thanks. On the wall of the bar was a TV screen showing a football match. The image changed to local news and although the sound was inaudible, the images and tickertape feed made it easy to follow. An attack by a terrorist cell in the north displaces more refugees. Verdict in corruption case – businessman gets five years for siphoning off government funds. Arnaldo Cantopreto meets constituents ahead of tomorrow's policy speech.

There he was, smiling, waving and shaking hands with a group of men outside the very same government building where he'd received Iris and Joana that morning. He looked impressive, even Iris would admit that. But appearances mean nothing without action.

The weather forecast predicted more rain. Iris closed her eyes for a moment, wishing she could turn the clock back five years. No explosion at Heathrow, killing her husband. No undercover work, no treachery and therefore no disappearing act. No albatross of guilt around her neck about her deceit and no subsequent shock at moving from betrayer to betrayed. No trail of criminal activity and no falling-out with her only sibling. She missed Katie.

Then again, she thought about all the things she would never have seen, all the people she would never have met ... she was getting sentimental. She opened her eyes and finished her beer. Time to find the volunteer, get into that Toyota and pray they didn't run into any cops.

From the arrivals area, a man emerged, wheeling a suit-case. He looked up at the signs and walked towards the main exit. Iris sat, dumbstruck, for a good thirty seconds then leapt to her feet. She thrust a note at the barman and raced off without waiting for her change. When she got outside, she ran the wrong way, her memory insisting public transport was in the opposite direction to the car park. It was, but that was only for buses. When she realised her mistake and pelted to the other side of the entrance, no one was waiting at the taxi rank. She went inside and scanned the thinning crowd. He wasn't among them. But a round-faced woman standing beside a huge suitcase gave her an optimistic look.

"Hello there! Are you from A Casa da Prata?"

"Yes. You're the volunteer ... sorry, I've forgotten your name."

"Susie Randall. And what do I call you?"

"I'm Iris. Sorry I'm a bit late. Let me take your case. The car's not far."

"I can manage, thank you. You're not late at all. I've just arrived."

They left the building and Susie heaved her enormous case into the car, refusing any help. Iris drove away, scanning every face and making mechanical small talk while trying to recall the details of Susie's CV. Nursing qualifications, midwifery skills, a wealth of VSO experience and paediatric training. On paper, the woman was a godsend. Until Iris met her, she could not have imagined how much.

Susie was sixty-plus and took no prisoners. She rattled off questions from the second she sat down. Her grey curls added a soft focus to a grandmotherly face, and her wrinkles could genuinely be described as laughter lines. She found joy everywhere, saw the funny side of her nightmare journey and gave thanks for Iris's kindness in collecting her from the airport.

By the time they drove into A Casa da Prata, Iris was almost tearful with gratitude. The woman was exactly what they needed. Iris showed her to the stall previously occupied by Demi.

"It's nothing fancy, but it's clean and you have a mosquito net. The bathroom is at the end. Breakfast starts when it's light and I'll come around to introduce you to Mafalda. Do you have water?"

"I wasn't expecting fancy. That's not why I'm here." Susie rammed her suitcase at the end of the stall where it stood like a sentry. "I do have water, tonic and a nip of gin to go with it.

Thank you for fetching me, Iris. I swear I'll do everything I can to be an asset. Goodnight to you and see you in the morning."

Iris washed her face and cleaned her teeth, gradually accepting that a disturbed night, uptight morning and emotionally overwrought afternoon, followed by two beers and wistful memories, had created an apparition. It was nothing more than her subconscious providing a comfort blanket. Because, despite the evidence of her own eyes, there was no way on God's earth she'd just seen Gil Maduro.

11

———————

The first sign that something was not normal happened before anyone was awake. Someone left a cardboard box of coconuts, mangoes, pineapples, bananas and yams on the communal dining table. It was waiting for Iris when she stumbled out of bed to light the fire. The fruits were fresh, not like the normal dregs they got from the market, yet there was no explanation as to their provenance. Wherever it came from, fresh fruit was fresh fruit. Iris lit the fire, still disconcerted from last night's vision at the airport. When the blaze was sufficiently independent she collected Susie, who was already up, dressed and ready for action. They took the box across to the farmhouse, Iris assuming Mafalda would have some kind of explanation.

She didn't. Mafalda was amazed by the generous delivery and Jennifer immediately grabbed three bananas to help with Faith's recovery. While Mafalda took Susie into the office for orientation, Iris sat by Faith's camp bed. The patient was conscious and looked far more aware of her surroundings than the previous day. She understood Iris's questions up and even voiced one of her own.

"Cantopreto?" she whispered. "Any good?"

"Too early to say," Iris shrugged. "The good thing is, he listened and he wants a written report. When you're fit again, we can work on that together. But for now, you just concentrate on getting better."

Faith managed a faint smile and heaved herself onto her elbows when Jennifer returned with some mashed banana.

"S-S-Susie is nice," Jennifer whispered.

"She is," agreed Iris. "She reminds me of Mrs Doubtfire."

Jennifer and Faith gave her a blank look.

"Never mind." Another cultural reference that fell short of its mark.

Mafalda beckoned Iris into the kitchen. "I've checked all of this for toxins. Plus Susie and I ate a piece of everything. It's fine. Why don't we save it for lunch? A big fruity rice dish with cold goat meat leftover, what do you think?"

"That would be a crowd pleaser. The kids love fruit. When you think it came from?"

Mafalda shrugged. "Quite often when we have trouble with the local men, some of their women find a way of making amends. Is the fire lit?"

"Yes, I should go back and tend it, then collect the eggs as Jennifer is busy."

"Thank you. Take coffees for you and Susie and I'll come over with some *xima*. Faith is recovering far faster than I expected. She'll be on her feet by the end of the week. Until then, I hope I can count on you two for all the donkey work."

"Of course you can." Susie poured two cups of coffee and headed to the door. "I can't wait to get stuck in."

Mafalda gave an approving smile and the door closed behind the new volunteer. "She seems perfect. Oh, Iris, did you go somewhere else before the airport?"

There was no point in lying. "Yes. I needed a break. I'll replace the gasoline."

Mafalda's gaze searched her eyes. "I understand the fact you need to get away sometimes. It is risky to go out on the streets on your own, but I know you can take care of yourself. How about a drink at the bar later? Only if you feel like it."

"Let's see how today goes. Right now, I feel the need for a little quiet time, you know, to be alone with my thoughts."

Mafalda nodded as if that was the most natural thing in the world. Privately, Iris wondered if the worst place in the world was inside her own head.

Surprise number two came while Iris was collecting the eggs. They had nine chickens, seven layers and two soon for the pot. Inside the coop, Iris stopped, counted, recounted and still made sixteen adult birds, a bantam rooster among them. Finally, she accepted the evidence as incontrovertible. Someone had broken into the chicken coop but instead of stealing their precious birds, had given them five more and a cockerel. Something very strange was going on. After last night's hallucination, she questioned whether she might have ingested some kind of mind-altering drug. Yet the fruit was real, the chickens were physically present and her body was reacting positively to the caffeine, just like every other day.

Susie stirred the porridge, brewed more coffee and mashed yesterday's fruit into a puree. Mafalda emerged with a bowl of *xima* and the three of them served breakfast for thirty people. Two of the Makuhwa women who knew how to butcher a goat came and stood by the oil drum with their empty bowls. Neither Mafalda nor Iris spoke their language so dispatched one of the kids to fetch Jennifer.

"They're asking if they can clean up, that's all," Jennifer translated. "Cooking the goat yesterday was good for them. They want t-t-to do some work."

Iris burst into a guffaw. "Seriously? Of course! We need all the help we can get. Right, Mafalda?"

The reaction she was expecting was absent. Mafalda gazed at the ground, her expression blank. Everyone waited for her to speak.

"This is a place of education, not a workhouse. Everyone has the right to contribute in whatever way they can. But your place here is not dependent on your contribution. Your obligation is to learn. School starts again today and I expect everyone to attend." Mafalda walked away in the direction of the farmhouse, her shoulders hunched against the wind.

Jennifer translated and one of the women replied with a query, her voice abrupt. Jennifer shrugged and looked at Iris.

"They ask if can they clean up, or not?"

"They certainly can. Thank you, ladies, and help yourselves." She waved at the firepit with an open hand and the two women immediately set to work. Susie was already sitting with some of the Portuguese speakers, making enquiries about one of the children's cough. Iris stood there for a second, feeling the sand shift beneath her feet and assessing whether the blind were leading the blind. She walked across to the farmhouse, trying once again to articulate what bothered her about Mafalda's controlling style of running this place. She got halfway there before spotting a red Jeep at the end of the drive.

Her alarm systems set off an internal klaxon and she took off at speed, trying to remember where Demi had hidden the gun. A half-familiar sound made her hesitate. A bleat, quavering, nervy and far less assertive than their own beach guard used to be, but a goat nevertheless. She dropped to her haunches and watched as two men unloaded a little brown goat from the back of the truck, untied its legs and released it onto their drive with a slap on its rump. The animal, clearly confused, had no idea where to run and turned tail, falling instantly into the gully. One man shouted and ran into the

Jeep. The other dithered, crouching in much a similar position to Iris. The driver fired the ignition and the passenger made up his mind, jumping into the gully and scooping out the goat. He shoved it in the direction of the compound and smacked it on the backside.

The poor confused animal scrambled to escape, running away from the gully, skipping over stones and skidding to a halt in the centre of the refuge. Iris attempted to imitate a goat bleat, to no effect. The Jeep took off in the direction of Luguni, leaving them with a half-grown kid which might easily bolt at any minute.

"Joana!" called Iris. Another pair of hands was essential if this creature was to be corralled. "Joana! Jennifer!" The goat wandered up to the dune, and Iris wondered if all ruminants were drawn to the beach. The girls came running from different directions and stopped short when they saw the new arrival.

"It's a goat!" gasped Jennifer.

"I can see that," Iris replied. "Go around the other side of it and let's drive it towards the kitchen, get it cornered. Grab some rope, Joana, so we can tether the thing. This one is not going to roam wild."

Jennifer cut off the goat's route towards the beach and it skittered in the direction of the cowshed. Some of the children spotted it and came running and shouting with excitement. The animal released the contents of its bowels and leapt sideways, colliding with one of the women cleaning the firepit. She shrieked in fright. The goat reversed, knocking over all the metal plates and cutlery, creating a din fit to raise the dead. In total panic, it bolted away from the approaching women and shot into the cowshed.

"Go round the back!" Iris shouted. "Don't let it escape out the other end." She waved her hands at the children, motioning them to retreat. Half a dozen women and girls came screeching out of the cowshed, naturally alarmed by the arrival of a frantic four-footed creature in the middle of their dormitory.

Iris told everyone to stay outside and closed the door, peering into the darkness for any sign of the animal. "Jennifer?"

"I'm here, Iris. S-s-standing by the bathroom. I can't see the goat anywhere."

Joana's voice called from the other row of stalls. "It's in here."

The two women crept around the corner to see Joana leaning over one of the half doors, pointing at something inside the stall. Sure enough, the goat was nosing around someone's possessions, with every intention of eating them, Iris presumed.

"Whose room is this?" she asked.

"It's mine. I was just going to look for my belt and came face to face with the goat. To get away from me, it ran inside and I shut the door. I thought we could use this as a collar?" Joana held up a thin leather belt.

"A collar?" Jennifer asked. "We can't keep it, it's not ours!"

"Actually, I think it is," said Iris. "A collar is a very good idea, Joana, but I've got no idea how we subdue the thing long enough to attach it."

"Food," said Joana, as if the answer was obvious. "We give it something to eat, keep it calm and put the belt around its neck. They're not wild animals."

She was right. Iris brought some of the fruit and vegetable peelings intended for the compost and placed it on the floor of Joana's stall. The goat immediately began eating, occasionally looking up with its peculiar lozenge-shaped pupils. Joana slipped inside and sat on the bed, waiting until the goat resumed its meal. The girl's instincts were good, Iris had to admit. She reached out and stroked the animal's flank. It jumped and bleated, but soon ignored the intruder in favour of potato peelings. Within a few minutes, Joana was scratching its rump, rubbing the poll between its nascent horns and wrapping her arms around its neck. Whether or not the animal enjoyed the attention, Iris couldn't be sure, but quarter of an hour later, the goat was wearing a thin black collar.

They gathered up its food then led it down the line of stalls to one of the larger sections near the door. Joana filled the trough with water, tied the gate with some wire and went in search of some sea grass to provide it with a bed. Somehow, possibly because the animal had made itself at home in her bedroom, Joana took charge of the goat's welfare. To the extent that when one of the women who had performed her butchery duties the day before offered to do the same again, Joana was horrified.

"No! This one is not for food! She will give us milk for years. We're keeping her."

Iris laughed. "Why do you think it's a she? It's got horns."

"Nanny goats have horns too. It's a she – look underneath."

She was right, the goat was undeniably female.

Iris faced Joana. "You'll be giving her a name next."

"I already have. I'm going to call her Katie." With that, she walked away towards the dunes.

The day was becoming progressively more surreal. A delivery of fresh fruit, a gift of half a dozen chickens, one of their tormentors delivering a goat and now Joana wanted to name the animal after Iris's estranged sister.

"Unusual name for a goat," she called after the girl. "Why Katie?"

Joana stopped at the top of the dune and turned with a smile. "For Princess Kate! She has beautiful dark brown hair and she makes people happy. Our goat will be the same. Our Katie."

Our Katie. To try to process all this weirdness, Iris decided to get on with some of the jobs around the compound which required her to be alone. Unfortunately those were few and far between. The new vegetable patch required no tending, thanks to the rainy season. Climbing the ladder to check the roof was an irresponsible activity without a partner. The dining area and firepit were clean and lunch was nothing more onerous than chopping some fruit and boiling a vast pan of rice. As for the new volunteer, Susie seemed to have set up some kind of surgery at the breakfast table and was surrounded by women with minor health complaints. She certainly didn't require any guidance from Iris.

Antsy and unsettled, she wondered whether to go beach-combing. It was something they usually encouraged the kids to do, because every handful of wood could be burned, every tangle of fishing net utilised. At least once a week, the beach-combers also turned up something they could either sell or eat.

Then she recalled that Joana was scouring the beach for sea grass and changed her mind. Instead, she chose to fill the camp vehicle with gas and collect the post. She hauled the gate over the gully, drove out and returned the metal drawbridge to its hiding-place. The gate wasn't as strong as it had once been and each time she used it, Iris held her breath. It was an accident waiting to happen. She reminded herself to ask Mafalda if they could buy some reinforcement material and a new bulb for the headlight. She held out little hope. The gate, the stones, the goat, the vehicle; a ceaseless, draining battle to keep them-selves safe.

She drove the long way round, in no hurry to encounter any of the men she had berated last night. En route, she ordered her thoughts into formation. The red Jeep took prece-dence. She'd been too far away to see if the goat deliverers were some of the men she shouted at last night, but there was no doubt about that Jeep. Only in Hollywood movies did a heroine unload a passionate speech against her persecutors and through sheer strength of will, make them change their minds. She'd insulted them, told them they were bullies and accused them of having no testicles. The idea that her words would hit the mark was fantastical and the work of her own ego.

So why had two men in a red Jeep brought a replacement goat for the one they killed yesterday? Iris passed the airport and refused to return to last night's delusion. She focused on the matter in hand.

To understand the enemy, one has to put oneself in their shoes. Assuming her injudicious rant had hit the mark, the result was more likely to be an escalation of tensions rather than a peace offering. In which case, any gift they delivered was a possible booby-trap. How the hell does one booby-trap a box of fruit or a live goat?

Presents of food were a problem, in Iris's mind, both welcome and disturbing. Where had they come from, who delivered them and the key question, why? Last night, when everyone was sleeping, someone had crept into the heart of their refuge. For good reasons, it now appeared, but what if the next time was motivated by something other than altruism? Mafalda's explanation of local women making good their husbands' wrongs sounded good in theory. In practice, whatever generosity they usually offered was via a third party. To walk into the compound and leave what amounted to an expensive gift was a departure from the norm. Something had changed and even if it was for the better, Iris needed to understand the reasons behind it.

She parked near the post office, collected the mail – a substantial stack this time – and shoved it into her backpack. Menacing clouds were rolling in from the sea and the wind picked up. The morning light became sooty, and far across the bay thunder threatened another storm. She wished now she hadn't left in such a hurry, forgetting her silver rain jacket.

Then she remembered she'd given the item to Mafalda as a gift and made a mental note to hand it back to its rightful owner.

While Mario was filling up the Toyota at his garage, sheet lightning illuminated patches of sky, intensified by its reflection in the sea. She paid in a hurry, only making the smallest of talk with him.

"Your window didn't last long. You want me to try again?"

"That's very kind. I don't have time today but perhaps Faith will bring it when she's recovered."

"Faith is sick?"

"Malaria. But she's getting better. Definitely over the worst. Thanks, Mario, have a good day."

"Senhora Iris, please tell her I'm thinking about her. If she needs anything at all, I will bring it. Here's my card. OK?"

"I will. Promise. *Até logo!*"

She drove at the speed limit, determined to make good time and get the firepit started before the storm blew in. Even so, she refused to take the coast road. That was asking for trouble. The whole journey she kept asking herself questions she couldn't answer. Who was giving them presents and why?

At the entrance to the compound, she saw a shape she couldn't explain lying on the ground. Until yesterday, something that size squatting in such a place might have been explicable, if unlikely. But this was no awkward, stubborn old goat. It was a package no one was expecting. A memory flickered. Jennifer, wrapped in wet sacking, dumped in the middle of the road. Iris switched off the engine and peered at the object, evaluating its size. She came to the conclusion that unless it was an infant, whatever was in there was not human.

She got out, tracing a wide semicircle around the unidentified object. In the pre-storm gloom, it was impossible to identify any details, although she discerned tentacles looped over the top. A washed-up octopus? From a distance, she scooped up a stone and lobbed it at the lump, hoping it wasn't something a stone might damage, such as a sack of kittens or expensive glassware. Expensive glassware? She really was losing the plot.

The stone fell just short of the lump but there was still no movement. Iris crept closer. The tentacles proved to be handles of a sports bag, the kind that zipped in a tennis racket or gym kit. All the hairs on her arms stood up as she considered the fact this might be the booby-trap she'd anticipated. The fruit, the new poultry and even the goat were designed to penetrate their defences, so that another unexpected delivery would be embraced with open arms. Especially if it was intended for the woman in the Land Cruiser. That big-mouth, interfering white woman gets her comeuppance and goes out with a bang.

She reined in her imagination. There was no reason why an explosive device would be waiting for her on the road. Her history was making her excessively superstitious and she remonstrated with herself.

"This is not Oxford Circus Tube Station. Get a grip."

She picked up another rock, aimed more carefully and threw it right at the centre of the sports bag. Just before it landed, she dropped to the dirt and covered her head with her arms.

The only thing she heard was a metallic clink. She crept forward on her hands and knees, squinting intently at her quarry. Less than a metre away, she could see the bag was open, revealing the dull glint of steel. She stared down at the contents, puzzling as to its meaning. A bag of tools: screwdrivers, a hammer, wire cutters, a box of nails, pliers and a hatchet placed within easy reach and clearly intended for the women of the compound.

She picked up the bag by its handles and lugged it into the Toyota. She repeated the manoeuvre with the gate, adding a little prayer that it would support her one more time. It did, and she took the latest bounty into the refuge.

Just as she hauled the bag from the back seat, a car she didn't recognise trundled past the entrance and tooted its horn. It wasn't the first occasion cars had sounded their horns on passing the refuge. Normally it was one long aggressive blast. This time, the driver tooted five small blasts and a long one. It was a cheerful, positive sound and Iris turned to see a hand wave out of the window. She waved back, more confused than ever.

Faith was sitting at the table, her hands clasped around a bowl of soup. She looked bright and alert, welcoming Iris with a huge smile.

"Where you been, girl, we got news!" She jerked a thumb at the office, where Mafalda was having a telephone conversation.

Iris plonked the bag of tools on the floor and extracted all the envelopes from her backpack. "I went into town to get the post and fill the Toyota. Mario offered to fix the window again and will bring you anything you need. Here's his card. Did you have your third shot? How are you feeling?"

"Fine, fine, don't you worry about me. Sit down and wait for Mafalda."

Iris glanced at the clock. "The rice isn't going to cook itself. I'll come back after lunch and we can talk then."

Mafalda stuck her head around the curtain. "Here she is!" Her face was flushed with excitement and her smile broader than Iris had ever seen. "You worked miracles, lady, and you should be proud!"

"You should, Iris, you really should! Don't you worry about no rice, Jennifer and Susie got that covered. I guess you didn't pick up a newspaper while you were in town?"

The buzzing atmosphere was the final straw in forty-eight hours' worth of bizarre. Iris dropped the keys onto the table and sat down with a grunt. "A paper? What are you talking about? Will somebody please explain what's going on?"

Faith looked at Mafalda, who was flicking through the day's post. She found something that made her eyes widen and used the car key to slit open the envelope. She read the contents, shaking her head and smiling. The two gestures seemed incompatible until she looked up with tearful eyes.

"This is a letter from the office of Arnaldo Cantopreto. He hopes his small gesture goes some way to indicate his gratitude for the intelligence conveyed by Senhoras Simons and Zeca. He was moved deeply by what these brave ladies had to say yesterday morning. He looks forward to a full report detailing the requirements necessary for this organisation to function. Once the report has been read and digested, he would like to invite a delegation from our management to speak to him and his colleagues in more detail. He thanks us once again for offering him an opportunity to execute governmental policy in a meaningful way."

Iris held her hand out for the letter. It wasn't that she disbelieved Mafalda, just that she needed to see such an extraordinary statement with her own eyes. She read it again and then handed it to Faith.

"What does he mean by a small gesture?" Iris asked Mafalda.

She waved a slip of paper. "He enclosed a cheque. You need to bank this as soon as possible. Take Jennifer — it requires two signatories to withdraw or deposit. Then we can spend it on something practical."

"And the fruit, the chickens and a goat? You think those are from him too?"

"Well, I don't suppose he does these things himself. I guess he told his people to bring us some food. Things like that are sustainable. You know, I think it's symbolic. Looks like you and Joana made an impression."

None of it made sense to Iris and she decided to proceed with life as normal. She left the car keys on the table and the tools by the door then walked out to make some food. The second she emerged into the sunshine, she came face to face with Divine. It was such disconcerting experience to see the woman anywhere other than behind her bar that Iris didn't know what to say.

"Where is Rusty Nail?" she asked.

Divine gave her exactly the kind of look such a stupid question deserved. "Guarding the bar, just like a guard dog is supposed to do. I came to give you my congratulations. You moved mountains, Tequila Sun-Iris. Turns out you're not just a pretty voice."

She thrust out a copy of the local newspaper. There on the front page was Arnaldo Cantopreto flanked by rabbit-in-the-headlights Joana on his left and a suspicious-looking Iris on his right. The headline read, 'CANTOPRETO ACTS!'

A hasty skim read of the article was enough. The paper was promoting Cantopreto's message loud and clear. *A man of his word! No time to waste!* Each subheading referred to an item in his manifesto with quotes from farmers, fishermen, law enforcement agencies and the tourist trade, demonstrating how he was already using his mandate for the general good. The fact he had chosen to prioritise women's rights and female education left Iris slack-jawed.

She looked at the photograph in which she appeared almost spectral in her silver raincoat, pale face and sleep-deprived shadowed eyes. Iris had always detested photographs. Long before she had a reason to conceal her identity, as far back as childhood, she would gurn and grimace when a lens pointed in her direction. At eight years old, she told her parents she would only appear in family portraits on condition she could wear the mask of her choice. They indulged her, assuming it was a phase, and initially found her inventiveness entertaining. She graduated quickly from sequinned eye masks through Miss Piggy snouts to a Hannibal Lecter mouth guard. The novelty factor wore off and her parents threatened that unless she posed as herself, she could no longer appear in family photographs. Mission accomplished.

Normally, family albums are imbalanced in favour of the firstborn. By the time the second or third has come along, the obsessive desire to record every detail of their progression has grown stale. The Joneses were different. Very little of their eldest daughter's childhood was preserved. Instead the pages were filled with the photogenic, amenable, people-pleasing second child – Katie.

Twice in one day her sister had invaded her headspace. It was not healthy. She handed the newspaper back to Divine.

"Wow. I don't know what to say. Show Mafalda and Faith, they're inside. Are you staying for lunch? The menu today is cold roast goat and fruity rice."

"In that case, I am staying for lunch. Iris, are you cool with all this? You look shook."

Iris nodded with an attempt at a reassuring smile. "I'm shook, yeah. Pleased, of course, but it's unexpected. When you hammer and hammer at an immovable object and it suddenly gives way, it takes a while to come out of battle mode."

"I'm with you. Nobody is ready to believe this. Then again, everyone is ready to celebrate. Come down to the bar tonight. The drinks are on me."

Iris laughed. "You mean on the tab?"

"Nope." Divine broke into one of her huge smiles. "I mean the drinks are on me."

12

Divine was the first but not the last to deliver a copy of the newspaper. By the time lunch was over and Iris was clearing out the firepit, they had three well-thumbed, grease-stained copies and two perfectly pristine issues to be kept in the office.

Jennifer translated for those who did not read Portuguese and Mafalda recited the article verbatim for those who couldn't read at all. Joana and Iris were the objects of much praise, and in Iris's case, a good deal of total amazement. Such a complete contrast in the usual level of attention was disconcerting and made Iris thoroughly uncomfortable. Thankfully, the afternoon was devoted to schoolwork, and the Sunday picnic atmosphere deflated to normal life. Mafalda was teaching, Susie took the chance to sleep off some jet lag, Faith had already started on the CWI application, Jennifer collected her fishing gear and Joana took some vegetable peelings to the goat.

When the compound was clear of people, Iris was at a loss. There were a dozen minor jobs to be completed, including a drive to the bank, but the sun was out and the sea beckoned. That yearning to be alone had not left her.

Since arriving in Mozambique, Iris had been in the sea twice but used her swimming costume only once. There was always something more urgent requiring her attention than having a leisurely swim. She took a towel and her backpack and flip-flopped her way over the dune and down to the beach. Not a single person was visible from either right or left. She rejected the false sense of security, dropped her towel over her backpack and planned to swim lengths up and down the same section of water. *Never let down your guard.*

At first, the water seemed bracing and chill. It only took a couple of strokes before the warmth embraced her, chasing the goose bumps from her skin. The thrill of being at one with the ocean exhilarated her and sparked the urge to swim hard and fast, using all her muscles and her breath. She wanted to exhaust herself, to obliterate thoughts and hypotheses. Up and down, front crawl, backstroke, competition-speed breaststroke and the occasional glance at the sand to reassure herself her backpack was exactly where it should be. She couldn't shake the sense of being watched, but no one was visible anywhere along the beach.

The sea was boisterous and she had to work hard against the current, something she relished. Intense concentration and physical effort shut out her brain. At least for a short time. Out of breath and with her skin buzzing from the exfoliating nature of the sand, she emerged to dry off in the sun.

Her thinking seemed clearer now and the answer seemed obvious. She would build a fence. The fruit, the chickens and the goat were all amends made for what had been stolen. Somebody somewhere had whispered in the right ears. So the thieves returned their spoils, or rather, found some replacements. The intention was good and everyone was grateful, but people creeping around while they slept gave rise to an uneasy feeling. A fence was what the compound needed. Something practical, Mafalda had said. All they needed were the materials, and between them they could erect a fence to keep the goat in and intruders out. It was such a good idea she was impatient to get started.

On her way up the dune, she saw a man coming along the shoreline. She wrapped her towel around herself and shielded her eyes from the sun. The man waved and called out.

"Hi, Iris! Remember me? Edson, the best guitarist from here to Luguni."

Iris relaxed a little. "Edson, hi, how are you?"

He waited till he got close enough for a conversation before replying. "Impressed is how I am. You certainly know how to shake things up. I just came from the village and it's all anyone can talk about. You're full of surprises." He gave her a charming smile. "Been swimming?"

"Yeah. It's a little rough out there."

"This is not a great place for a swim. Wimbe beach is better but it gets crowded. I know a couple of spots over the other side. Peaceful in every sense. You should come with me one of these days."

"Thanks. That's a generous offer, but to be honest, I don't get a lot of free time. What with the Cantopreto thing, I'm probably going to get a whole lot busier."

Edison lifted his sunglasses to look into her eyes. "How do you mean? Are you expecting more … I don't know what you call them. Guests? Residents?"

"We call them women," answered Iris truthfully. "I don't know if more people in need will seek us out. Maybe. What I meant by getting busier is setting up some kind of security around our compound. I want to build a fence."

Edson whistled through his teeth. "That's a job for a professional. I have a cousin who is in the building trade. I can ask him how much it would cost, if you like?"

"We can't afford to pay a professional, Edson. We have to

do it ourselves. Although you could ask your cousin if he'd offer us a good price for the materials."

"I'll ask him, for sure. Are you coming down to the bar tonight? I can get you an approximate quotation by then."

Iris sighed, unable to think of any good reason why she should not celebrate with her friends, other than the fact she just didn't feel like being sociable. "Yeah, I'll be at Divine's place later. I must get on. See you."

He gave her a salute and another one of his brilliant smiles before walking away. He was a looker, she couldn't deny that. Strong and capable, not to mention well connected. Plus a genuinely nice guy. She scolded herself as she powered up the dune. Now was not the time to even think about men. Her duty was to get dressed, find Jennifer, drive into town, bank that cheque and start dinner before school ended for the day. She took a detour around the dark patch of blood on the sand, hoping the rain would soon wash it all away.

Thanks to Jennifer's catch that afternoon, dinner was fish stew with yams. In an unusual gesture, Mafalda invited anyone who felt like celebrating to join them down at the bar for a drink. Nobody accepted, to Iris's enormous relief. Trying to keep everyone safe in the compound was challenge enough. On the beach? Her worst nightmare. She assumed Mafalda knew they would refuse and was merely making a point. Freedom? Independence? Who the hell knew how that woman's mind worked?

The spotlight should have been on Joana but she was more interested in minding the goat. Faith was still weak and taking her oral anti-malaria medication. She thanked Mafalda for the invitation, but stated her preference: she was happiest keeping watch outside the farmhouse with Jennifer.

That Susie showed no interest surprised Iris. A drink with

one's colleagues was a time-honoured British tradition, a way of getting to know each other. But the older woman dismissed the idea with as much distaste as if Mafalda had suggested skinny-dipping.

"Not for me, thank you. I'll turn in early. It's been quite a day."

Iris willed Mafalda to give up the bar excursion, so she could retire to her stable and read some Jean Rhys. She should have known better.

"Pity. I guess it's just you and me, Iris."

The two women strolled along the sand, listening to the sea and saying nothing although there was plenty to say. All day long had been nothing but chatter. A few minutes of silence was like a massage because they both knew the bar would be bubbling with conversation.

Even though she was enjoying the peace, Iris had to broach the fencing project, in case Edson mentioned an offer from his cousin. Three months had taught Iris to understand Mafalda's sensibility. All decisions went through the boss. If not, she was liable to reject any suggestion out of hand. Worse, she might refuse Iris any kind of authority.

A breeze blew in from the ocean and the moon hung milky in the night sky. Iris found herself staring intently at it as if trying to take strength from its pearlescent light. Moon-gazing was not a practical activity when walking along an uneven and occasionally stony beach. She stubbed her toe and because she was only wearing flip-flops, swore colourfully.

"I didn't know a lady like you knew such wicked words," Mafalda snickered.

"Then you should have heard us when Demi and I were repairing the roof. We ran out of curses and had to invent a few of our own." This was her opportunity to segue into further home repairs. "I meant to ask you, have you decided how to spend Cantopreto's cheque?"

"That's funny because Cantopreto's cheque and your future are kind of one and the same question. By the way, did you bank it?

"Yeah. Jennifer and I went in before lunch. I explained how she could get a bank account of her own now she's going to be a salaried employee. She was too nervous to do it there and then, but I think when Faith is fully recovered, it's on the cards. What did you mean about my future and Cantopreto's cheque being connected?

Mafalda's face was half hidden by Iris's own shadow. When she answered, her voice was quiet as if she suspected eavesdroppers. "I have three beneficial donations and I have to choose how to spend them. Yes, of course I want to pay Faith and Jennifer and train them to become managers of the refuge. Susie has her own means of support and is only volunteering for three months. I also need a Jill-of-all-trades, if you like. You're a good example. When we spoke before, I suggested a year. If that's too much, we can negotiate."

Before she'd even put her brain in gear, Iris responded. "A year is definitely too much. My plan is to leave at the end of April. I want to be home on my farm for planting season and I think this place could run perfectly well without outside influence. There are two main things I'd like to do before I go. One of those is to mentor Joana. The girl is bright, capable and an excellent spokesperson for A Casa da Prata. The second thing is that I'd like to build a fence all around the compound, with gates at the end of the drive and an exit onto the beach."

"A fence? Won't that need mean having men on the property?"

"Not necessarily. Hand over the project to me and I will oversee the purchase of materials, training of labourers, by which I mean some of the women in the compound, and the physical construction of the thing. We can do this ourselves and it will make everyone proud. You'd just better be prepared for plenty of swear words."

Mafalda didn't laugh. "Do you really think we need a fence now? Cantopreto has thrown his weight behind us. People see A Casa da Prata far more positively. A signal like building a fence could be seen as hostile."

"Not if you spin it right. We spread the word that it's to keep things in, like children, goats and chickens, rather than keeping people out. That way it will be more palatable. Anyway, Cantopreto is supportive today but in a week's time or maybe a month when he's being lobbied by other interests, public opinion could turn. While we've got the money, I really think we should invest in infrastructure."

Further along the beach, Divine's bar was lively. Recorded music indicated more of a party than the usual sing-along. This both enticed and repelled Iris. On one hand, she was open to drinking cocktails, letting her hair down and forgetting the dramas of the last few days. On the other, she knew she was likely to be the centre of attention, a position she had never enjoyed.

"Let me think the fence idea over," said Mafalda. "I can see your reasoning but I really hoped you'd stay for a little bit longer. Hey, look at that! Divine has pulled out the big guns."

The bar glittered and sparkled in a way Iris had never seen before. A disco ball reflected tiny lights from half a dozen lanterns hanging from the roof. Across the entrance, silver bunting caught the moonlight and a white banner stretched across the railings saying *PARABÉNS – A CASA DA PRATA!* in black lettering. Mafalda and Iris stopped in their tracks and stared. Divine spotted them and began a round of applause. Everyone joined in so that when they climbed the steps and accepted their first cocktail they felt like conquering heroes.

The surfer gang were there, with Edson in the middle. Hester, the woman who had offered to arrange Iris a dog, was standing at the bar wrapped in a silver and white gown with matching headdress. Half a dozen local women Iris had seen before but never offered anything more than smiles got to their feet to join in the ovation. Divine's voice boomed over the applause. "Welcome to the women we've all been waiting for! Tonight's cocktail, in honour of A Casa da Prata, is the Silver Bullet. Enjoy, ladies!"

She handed over two wineglasses filled with a cloudy, whitish liquid garnished with lemon peel. "A toast, everyone! To all the ladies at A Casa da Prata, we wish you every success."

Everyone raised their glasses and Iris soaked in all the smiling faces, including Mafalda's before she took a sip of her drink. It had a kick like a goat and she spluttered a cough after she swallowed.

"What the hell is in this?"

Divine, resplendent in something that looked like baking foil, lifted a bottle. "Gin base, Sambuca, lemon juice and ice. The original has Kümmel liqueur but there's no way I could lay my hands on that at such short notice."

"At such short notice, you did an incredible job," Mafalda marvelled, pointing at the glitter ball and the silver bunting.

Divine tapped her nose. "Just something I had stashed away for a special occasion, thanks to my friend in the military. Now Tequila Sun-Iris, I want you to tell us everything about Cantopreto. You're the only one of us who has met him or is ever likely to meet him. What did he smell like?"

Once again Iris spluttered at the unexpected question, leaving her speechless. Fortunately, she was not expected to answer as everyone offered their opinions as to Cantopreto's suit, scent, body shape, wife and choice of tie. The group of women beckoned her over to join them, which was another first. They were a strange mixture of friendly, curious and shy. One girl admired her leather jacket.

"Thank you. It was a present from our previous volunteer."

"What about the silver coat you were wearing in the photo-graph? That's so pretty."

"It's very practical. Waterproof and highly visible, plus it keeps you warm. That's why I gave it to Mafalda. She's always cold."

All of them had questions – why Pemba? Why A Casa da Prata? How come she spoke Portuguese? Where did she usually live? Iris answered as honestly as she could and turned the spotlight on them. What did they do for a living? Why did they come to Divine's bar? Was it because they were all good singers?

That question elicited a round of giggles and everyone pushed and pointed towards one of the youngest in the group. "Alba can sing; she could be famous. Maybe later, Edson will play and Alba will perform. She knows all the songs."

"I'll look forward to that. It was nice to meet you, everyone. I must find Mafalda." Finding Mafalda was not much of a challenge. She wasn't at any of the tables inside the bar so she had to be on the beach, probably smoking another house special. Iris was about to descend the steps and join her when she saw her boss was already in conversation, sharing her joint with Edson. It was the first time she'd ever seen Mafalda talking to a man. Instinctively, Iris retreated, leaving them to a moment alone.

She had another cocktail and chewed the fat with Divine, sat with the surfers for a while and began to feel the effects of the alcohol. Edson came up the steps and suggested they turn the music off and sing along with the guitar. He sat beside Iris and began strumming some kind of ballad. Iris looked across to Alba and beckoned her to come and join them. After much shoving and pushing from her friends, Alba eventually got to her feet and was just walking across the bar when a furious deep barking made everyone gasp. Alba screamed and leapt backwards, knocking over all her friends' drinks. Mafalda, who was leaning at the top of the porch, cleared the steps in one leap, scrambled behind the shack and melted into the darkness. Rusty Nail stalked down the centre of the bar, his hackles one coarse line from his tail to his neck and his growl menacing. Divine strutted behind the dog, her feet creaking across the boards, and placed a hand on his collar. Everyone else peered into the blackness, holding their breath.

Divine called out. "Who's there?"

"A friend." The shadow of man approached from the beach. When he stepped into the light so everyone could see his face, Iris had the shock of her life. Right there, on a far-flung beach in Mozambique, stood Gil Maduro.

13

___

"Friend? Whose friend? My dog doesn't like you and I trust his instincts more than I trust my own."

Gil's eyes found Iris and she clutched the back of a chair to steady herself.

"He's a friend of mine," she said, attempting to keep her voice calm. "Everyone, I'd like you to meet my old mate, Gil. Come up and have a drink. It's OK, Divine, I can vouch for this guy. Edson? Could you go and find Mafalda? I think the dog scared her."

"Sure thing. Did you see which way she went?"

"Around the back, I think. With the dog in front and a stranger coming up the beach behind, she probably ran into the dunes."

Edson put down his guitar, vaulted over the railings and disappeared into the night.

Gil climbed the wooden steps with great caution, nodding his acknowledgement of the other patrons in the bar. No one spoke until he met Divine's eyes.

"That's a handsome dog. It's all right to let him go. Like

you, I trust a dog's instinct." He crouched to his haunches and held out a hand, palm face down, for the dog to sniff.

Rusty Nail had stopped growling and his hackles settled to his normal smooth-haired coat. Divine glanced at Iris, who gave a shrug.

Released from Divine's guiding hand, the Rhodesian Ridgeback paced cautiously towards Gil. It wasn't the ideal situation in which to earn an animal's trust as Alba was still whimpering with fear amongst her friends. Everyone else watched intently as Rusty Nail sniffed Gil's outstretched hand. Iris tensed her whole body. If the dog attacked, Gil was in an incredibly vulnerable position. She would have to pull the animal off and subdue it. Such a scene would traumatise not only Alba but everyone else in the bar.

"There's a good dog. See, nothing to worry about." The tone of Gil's voice was warm and reassuring. Rusty Nail raised his eyes to look at Gil's face and wagged his tail once.

"*Está bem, Senhor.* If he thinks it's OK, you can come in. Rusty?"

The dog turned around, accepted something from Divine's hand and loped off behind the bar. There was an audible release of breath and people restarted their conversations. Instead of facing Gil and asking the millions of questions bubbling inside her, she helped Alba and her friends right their table and clear up the spilt drinks. Her mind was racing with how best to play this. She was alternately thrilled to the core of her being and terrified he had led her pursuers to her door.

She called over to Divine. "Can we have another round of beers, please? I'll pay for this."

"Coming up, Tequila Sun-Iris. What about your friend?"

"Gil, what would you like to drink? There's a house special cocktail called Silver Bullet, if you're interested."

He stood there, relaxed and comfortable as if he hung out

at this bar on this beach every night of the week. "Thanks, Iris. A beer's just fine."

She looked at him directly for the first time. "It's good to see you," she smiled.

"I was thinking the same thing." He took a step forward and she met him halfway for the greeting, kisses on both cheeks. He smelt exactly as she remembered and her body responded. She turned away, embarrassed. Part of her wanted to rush off and help Edson find Mafalda. Another part wanted to introduce her friend to Divine, so that she could control the narrative. All of her wanted to wrap her arms around Gil Maduro and hold him as close as she could.

"Seven ice-cold beers! A-ha, Edson found her! Mai Tai, how many times I got to tell you the dog won't hurt you? He's only aggressive with strangers. Otherwise, he's a big baby."

Mafalda gave a tight, embarrassed smile, then noticed Gil. Edson appeared equally curious and they both came over to say hello.

"Divine, Mafalda, Edson, I'd like you to meet my friend Gil, from Brazil. Gil, this is Divine, who owns this bar. Mafalda is my boss and Edson is the greatest guitarist on this beach."

"Pleased to meet you all." He offered his hand to each one for a brief shake. "I'm sorry for alarming you this evening. I just wanted to surprise Iris. We haven't seen each other for a while."

"Good to meet you, Gil." Edson grinned. "There's one important thing we need to know. Can you sing?"

Gil shook his head. "If I did, I would set the dog off again."

While Edson and Divine laughed, Iris glanced at Mafalda, who gave her a quick nod. Permission, she assumed.

"Why don't you and I go and sit on the beach?" Iris asked Gil. "We've got a lot of catching up to do." She led the way down the steps and to a rough wooden bench in a pool of light spilling from the bar. They sat side by side, staring out at the moon.

The seconds passed before they both spoke at once.

"How are you?" he asked.

"What you doing here?" she said over him. "I'm fine, apart from being shocked to see you walk into this bar. How the hell did you find me?"

He took a swig of his beer. "That's a long story. I had to find you because I couldn't wait any longer. It's been quite an adventure." He dropped his voice. "Do I call you Iris now? Even when we're alone?"

"Yes, please. I no longer have another name."

He was silent for a moment, revolving his beer bottle between his fingers. "I missed you."

His voice melted her resistance. "I missed you too." She reached out and took his hand. Their fingers interlinked but Iris didn't dare look at him. The pressure of his grasp sufficed. They sat together, drinking occasionally and saying nothing at all.

"Iris?" Mafalda's voice was timid. "I'm sorry to interrupt."

Iris dropped Gil's hand and stood up. "You want to go home?"

"Yeah. It's nearly ten and the generator will go off soon. You can stay here, it's no problem."

"I'm not letting you walk up the beach on your own. I'll come too."

Gil stayed seated but swung around to face Mafalda. "If you like, I can give you a ride. I hired a Jeep for the duration of my stay. It's just up the steps and I'm driving past your place towards Pemba city."

Convinced Mafalda would refuse, Iris already prepared her excuses, but she was surprised.

"Thanks. It would be quicker than walking. That's very kind."

They said their goodbyes to the patrons of the bar with an extra thank you to Divine, then made their way up the wooden steps towards the road above the beach. Gil went first, Mafalda behind him and Iris brought up the rear. The steps were steep and illuminated by nothing more than moonlight, so their pace was slow. Conversation had to wait until they reached the road and the Jeep. Shiny and new, it represented the complete opposite to their clapped-out Land Cruiser.

"Nice car," observed Iris.

"I thought a four-wheel-drive would be best as I had no idea what kind of roads were like outside the city. Judging by the journey here, I made the right decision. Mafalda, would you like the passenger seat?"

In the semi-darkness, Iris smiled at his gallantry. She sat in the back, quite pleased to be able to observe him as he drove.

"You said you rented this Jeep for the duration of your stay," asked Mafalda. "How long is that?"

Gil flicked his eyes to the rear view mirror. "It depends. I'm flexible. But I've come a long way to see Iris so it would be nice to spend a while in Pemba. I promise you, ladies, I won't get under your feet." He started the engine and the road rearranged itself from scary amorphous shapes to sharp distinction in the headlights.

The Jeep rumbled along the road and Mafalda had to raise her voice for the next question. "And what do you think of Pemba so far?"

"It's the bluest place I've ever seen and I come from an island. Have you lived here all your life?"

"No. I come from the south, outside Maputo."

"What brought you up here?"

"I was training as a schoolteacher and trying to get into university. It's not easy in this country. Then the law changed and for the first time women were allowed to own land. I took all my savings and travelled north. Many women were fleeing extremists and had nowhere to go. I bought an abandoned cattle farm and called it A Casa da Prata, after the moon. There it is, right over the road."

Gil pulled over and Mafalda jumped out with a wave and a smile. "It was nice to meet you, Gil, and thank you for the lift. Hope to see you again sometime. Take your time, Iris."

It seemed the night for unexpected revelations. She'd known Mafalda since November and Gil had got more information out of her in a two-minute drive than Iris had managed in four months.

He swivelled in his seat to face her. "What now?"

"I can't invite you in or offer accommodation here. We have a strict no-men policy. Where are you staying?" The temptation to touch him, kiss him and devour him was all consuming.

"A tourist hotel on Praia de Wimbe. Do you ever get a night off? For example, tomorrow? I'd like to invite you to dinner." He exhaled an ironic laugh through his nostrils. "Is that the best I can manage after tracking you through four countries? 'I'd like to invite you to dinner'. Ann, Olivia, Iris, whatever you choose to call yourself, I want to be with you. We need to talk."

She nodded, filled with emotion and confused as to where to start. "Yes, we need to talk. Gil, I am overjoyed to see you, but you must understand that anyone turning up out of the blue makes me nervous. I want to be with you too and I will ask Mafalda if I can have a night to myself tomorrow. How can I contact you?"

He took out his wallet and extracted a card. "This is my hotel. Tell them to put you through to Room 16 or ask for me by name." As she took the card, he grasped her wrist, pulling her towards him. His kiss, a mixture of tenderness and passion, awoke so many long suppressed desires, she thought she might faint. He broke the kiss and held her chin.

"Promise me you won't run away. Not again."

Iris's breathing was unsteady. "I won't run away, I promise. We'll see each other tomorrow evening and if I can't make it, I'll call you to tell you when I can. Thank you for finding me." She kissed him lightly and opened the Jeep door. When she was safely across the gully and halfway up the drive, she looked back and waved. Instead of tooting his horn, he flashed his hazard lights just as he had done the last time they said good-bye. Once, twice, three times. Then he drove away.

In a daze, Iris washed her face and cleaned her teeth then fell into her cot, convinced she would never sleep. Gil Maduro, the man who haunted her dreams, was here in Pemba. The implications toppled like dominoes in her mind. In one flight of fancy, he would stay and they would work together to strengthen and defend A Casa da Prata. For convenience's sake, she forgot the strictly-no-men rule. In another, they would return to Brazil where he would pick up his role as detective and she would operate in the intelligence services. In another fantasy, she wondered if the role of a farmer might appeal and they could live a peaceful existence at A Quinta do Douro.

She rolled her eyes, even though they were closed. She was getting ahead of herself, as usual. First, he had to tell her the truth. Even though he was a police officer, there should have been no trail since she left Hong Kong. In order to track her from the Far East through Europe and to East Africa, he must have access to extraordinary information. Therefore, he could be very useful to certain people. Yes, she was crazy about the guy and could see he felt the same way about her. Even so, she had learned not to trust those she loved. Because a whole lot worse than heartbreak might lie in store.

14

Maybe it was a full moon or Mercury turned retrograde because the very next morning, positive events in the domestic life of A Casa da Prata came to a sudden end. Iris woke to thunderous rain pounding on the roof of the cowshed. Even though it was still dark, she got up and dressed ready for breakfast. Crossing the compound, with the wind sharp and brutal, she had a moment's selfish regret and wished for her silver raincoat with its protective hood.

The lights in the farmhouse were on, which was unusual. Of course it had its own generator for Mafalda's late-night office work. Other than that, it was only used for an emergency. Iris dithered about whether to start lighting the fire, a likely hopeless task, or going to offer assistance. Her knowledge of the compound told her that if Mafalda was dealing with one crisis, the rest of them needed to get on with daily life.

The first to emerge from the cowshed were Joana and Jennifer. It was still dark and Iris was still alternately coaxing and threatening the firepit into a convincing blaze.

"We might need to prepare the first round of coffees, by

which I mean ours, in the farmhouse. This stubborn piece of crap will not burn. Don't we have any dry wood at the cowshed?"

Jennifer pulled a piece of corrugated tin from behind the old half oil drum. "Let me t-t-try, Iris. There's s-s-some dry wood in the stall next to the goat, I think. We can't go into the farmhouse this morning because Mafalda and Susie are tending two sick babies. Susie said she doesn't think it's colic."

"Not malaria?" said Iris, silently adding a prayer.

Jennifer dropped her eyes. "I don't know. No one knows. Shall I find some dry wood?"

With a sinking feeling, Iris understood. Several of the women refugees who had fled extremist activity in the north were HIV positive. Of course, they'd passed this on to their children. It was not as if they had a choice. Therefore, if either of the babies succumbed to any assault on their immune system, it was a course for extreme concern.

"Joana can collect the wood and say good morning to the goat at the same time. You work your magic on this fire while I talk to Mafalda. Don't worry, I'll stay outside." She ran through the rain and arrived on the doorstep with her hair plastered to her face. "Shitty weather!" she swore.

Before knocking, she circled the farmhouse under the eaves to ascertain what was going on inside by peering through the windows. In the schoolroom, she saw a huddle of bodies but due to the rain sliding down the windows, she couldn't make out who was who. She rapped on the window to attract attention and Mafalda's face, furrowed with concern, turned to meet her eyes. She shook her head vigorously and pointed to the back of the building.

Iris made her way around to the rear, unsure if she'd understood the direction correctly. Wind and rain blasted the back wall of the farmhouse with a ferocity not even a goat could stand. Iris ducked behind the side wall and waited. She had no idea what else to do. Water dripped from the roof down her neck and she moved away just in time before the window shutters opened and Faith stuck her head outside.

"Iris! Do whatever you can with these for breakfast. Be prepared, you might have to drive these children to the hospital later. *Ai*, this weather!" She dropped two bags into Iris's arms and slammed the shutters closed.

Thunderclaps and forked lightning added to the nervous atmosphere, making all the residents skittish and easily upset. The bags Faith had dropped from the window contained tins of fruit and short-grain rice. By the look on Jennifer's face, what to do with these items was a complete mystery.

"Rice pudding!" said Iris, rubbing her hands together. "My favourite!" To her credit, Jennifer had managed to create a solid fire in the pit. Iris filled a large pan with some pre-boiled water and tipped in half the quantity of rice. There was no controlling the amount of heat from the fire so she and Jennifer lifted the pan and threaded the metal spit through its handles. Between them, they boiled some coffee, split a dozen coconuts and opened the cans of fruit.

Within half an hour, twenty-four women sat down to bowls of rice, fruit and coconut with a cup of coffee. The atmosphere was still jumpy and the only topic of conversation concerned the two infants in the farmhouse, but a warm bowl of rice and each other's companionship made a world of difference.

There was no hope of doing any farm work until the storm blew out so Iris suggested a clean-up of the cowshed. Jennifer allocated duties while Iris stacked half a dozen tiffin tins and returned to the farmhouse. This time she knocked on the door.

It opened after several minutes and Susie stood in the doorway looking as sweaty and relieved as if she had just given birth.

"You brought us breakfast! Aren't you a dear?" Her smile was weary but content.

"How are they? Everyone's worried."

"They will survive. Some kind of virus, I guess, but nothing life-threatening. Their temperatures are now normal, they are feeding and will probably sleep the rest of the day. God knows, I wish I could do the same."

Iris handed over the tiffin stacks. "You can. There's nothing happening out here, not in this weather."

The older woman lifted the lid from one of the tins and inhaled. "You're a miracle worker! This smells delicious and exactly what we need. Thank you. I'll feed everyone and then I might just have a little nap."

Mafalda took Susie's place in the doorway.

"Thanks for breakfast. Last night was exhausting."

"So I hear. How's Faith?"

"Annoying. She wants to get back to work. She is driving me crazy, pacing up and down, in and out. Why don't you give her something to do? Just nothing too strenuous. She's weaker than she thinks she is. If you're going into the city to collect the post, maybe she could go with you and get a few essentials?"

Iris didn't answer, wondering how to broach the subject of a day off.

"Tell me, what about your friend?"

"Oh, yes, I wanted to ask you about that. He's staying in a hotel in Pemba and wants to invite me for dinner. I wondered, unless this is a stupid question, if I could have a day off? Not a problem at all if it's a bad time. This can wait."

"Let me think about it. These people are hungry and I could eat a goat. Just don't tell Joana. I'll come and find you before lunch. He's very handsome."

Iris couldn't find the words to respond. "Enjoy your breakfast!" She battled her way back to the cowshed, enduring her third shower of the morning.

· · ·

Faith arrived while Joana and Iris were pounding cassava for lunch. Anyone seeing this bright, lively woman for the first time would never have believed she was the same sickly creature of several nights ago. She updated them on the ailing children and suggested a meeting with Child Welfare International. "You have connections, Iris, and we all know you're a good speaker. Don't be modest, we all saw what happened with Cantopreto. Yes, Joana, I know you were there too but who is he going to listen to? What I mean is that we should stockpile some medicine for these children because they're susceptible to every disease going. Where is Jennifer?"

Iris couldn't let that go. "Let me tell you something. I made my speech by rote, remembered my words and emphasised the key points. Cantopreto listened politely but with no real interest. I can't blame him, it was as exciting as reciting my times table. Then Joana spoke. She talked about her personal experience and what it means to be a woman without a safety net. Only then did he show any emotion. Joana broke the seal, not me."

Joana continued pounding the cassava without any reaction. There was no modesty, neither was there arrogance. As usual, she simply accepted other people's version of events.

"Here's Jennifer," was all she said.

Iris looked up. "I thought you were supervising the clean-up of the cowshed?"

"Finished." She brushed an affectionate hand over Faith's hair. "Your plaits are loose. Want me to fix them?"

The two women straddled the bench, Faith in front of Jennifer, as if they were in a rowing boat and Jennifer started work, unplaiting and re-plaiting her friend's braids.

Faith squinted up at the sky. "I hate the rainy season. Can I come with you into town to collect the post? I'm desperate to get out of the compound, even if it's only for one hour."

"Sure, if Mafalda thinks it's OK. You look so much better, Faith, I'm relieved."

Faith looked from her to Joana with a shy grin. "I know who to thank for that. Mafalda told me what you did, which is why I know you have connections with that hospital guy. No one should get greedy, I understand that, but making the most of connections is the lubrication of life."

Iris laughed, her mouth wide open in delight. "You will never cease to surprise me."

"She's right though," said Mafalda, who had appeared to stand behind them. "Nhamirre has extended the hand of friendship twice on our behalf. Faith, you finished the application, right? When we're done with lunch, why don't you, Jenni and Iris deliver it in person? Then you can pick up the post, see what you can get at the market, maybe get the car window fixed and drop Iris at her friend's hotel. She's having a night off."

Joana stopped pounding, Faith's mouth fell open and Jennifer's busy fingers stopped weaving.

"A night off?" Faith was incredulous, as if she'd never heard of such a thing.

"You have a friend here?" asked Jennifer. "What's her name?"

"Are you going to stay in a hotel too?" Once again, Joana's eyes were enormous.

Mafalda looked amused as she waited for Iris to answer.

"Yes, I asked Mafalda for a night off to have dinner with my friend. His name is Gil and he comes from Brazil. No, I'm not going to stay in the hotel, I'll come home."

Faith widened her eyes. "A Brazilian man! Is he handsome?"

"Yes, he is," Mafalda answered. "I can vouch for that because I met him last night. He gave us a lift home in his jeep."

Joana gasped, Faith whistled and Jennifer clapped her hands over her mouth. The first one to speak was Joana. "Is he a good man? Will he be kind to you?"

The tension in the air as they waited for an answer made Iris uncomfortable. Not because she was under the spotlight but she had no idea how to articulate her feelings amongst a group of women whose own experiences with men had been so scarring.

"He was very kind to me when we knew each other before, in Brazil. In my opinion, he is a very good man. I like him very much and hope he still likes me. Right, unless we finish this cassava, we have nothing for lunch. Faith, even if you are having your hair done, your hands are free enough to peel some yams."

How to prepare for a date with a 'very good man' when you haven't looked in the mirror for four months? The only clothes she owned were combat shorts, jeans, T-shirts and a rock 'n' roll leather jacket. Her hair had long since returned to its natural dirty blonde, her skin was tanned but dry, and her normal curves had all but disappeared due to outdoor work and a modest diet.

She needn't have worried. Word got around and the women of A Casa da Prata sprang into action. Joana insisted she have a shower while the team cleaned up the kitchen after lunch. Faith gave her a simple printed caftan, the only dress she had. With her finger pressed to her lips, Jennifer turned up at her stall with a necklace made from pieces of glass washed up on the sand. Iris understood. This wasn't a present but a loan. The gift was intended for someone else. She wrapped it in a towel and tucked it in her backpack.

"I'll return it tomorrow. I promise."

Jennifer smiled and clutched her hands together in excitement.

Freshly showered and slathered in the only moisturiser she had left, Iris was on her way out of the cowshed when the goat butcher appeared. She held half a dozen wooden bracelets. Neither woman spoke a common language, but it was clear that the jewellery was an offering. Iris initially tried the British way and modestly chose just one, which did not go down well. The woman caught Iris's hand and stacked the bracelets at her arm. Then she patted Iris's cheek and said something soft. Using every form of sign language at her disposal, Iris expressed her thanks.

It occurred to her that a visit to CWI should include Susie, as the child welfare expert of the compound. She went to her stall, whistling to announce her approach.

Susie appeared over the half door with a smile of greeting. "I feel much better after a bit of shut-eye. How are the babies?"

"Still sleeping, as far as I know. We're about to head into town to do some errands, including a visit to CWI. We thought they might let us have some medicine for the kids."

"CWI?"

"Child Welfare International. You know, the NGO? It supports children all over the world."

"Oh, yes, of course. Good idea."

"Would you like to come with us? Your medical knowledge would be a bonus."

A frown crossed Susie's face. "I won't, if you don't mind. My tummy is taking a while to adjust to the local food, so I'd feel more comfortable staying here. You look very glamorous. Do you always dress up to go into town?"

"No, never. But tonight I'm meeting an old friend for dinner, so I thought I'd make an effort. What do you think?" She gave a twirl.

"You look very pretty. I'm sure you'll knock his socks off. Where do you know him from?"

"He's Brazilian. We met a while ago. Do you need anything from the city?"

"No, thank you very kindly. Ah, Brazil is a wonderful country. I spent a year working for the Red Cross in Brasilia, Rio and São Paulo. Is your friend a city boy?"

Iris was awkward about sharing information about Gil. "No, he's as rural as it gets. I'd better get a shift on, they're waiting for me."

When she and Susie walked into the courtyard, every woman, girl and infant had formed a small crowd around the Land Cruiser. They first applauded and then some kind of lively disagreement erupted. Mafalda was doubled over with laughter and Iris simply couldn't understand the problem. Finally Jennifer ran towards her and whispered in her ear.

"Your shoes! You can't meet a man wearing those shoes."

Iris looked down at her working boots and had to admit they did look incongruous underneath Faith's caftan. She smiled at the crowd around her, swung her backpack over her shoulder and pulled out a pair of flip-flops. The result was instant relief and approving smiles. Eventually, after many little rituals of luck and blessing, she was allowed to get into the Toyota. It reminded her of a holiday in Switzerland, where she and Sal had watched a cow parade. The dun cattle, having grazed all summer on the high pastures, were garlanded, decorated and beautified for the long march downhill, their cowbells practically deafening as they strolled through the Alpine villages. Prize cow as she was in the circumstances, she was decorated, blessed and sent forth into the world of men.

"Hellfire," she said as she got into the back seat. "What a song and dance! I'm only meeting an ex-boyfriend for dinner." Then she shut her mouth, counting the number of crass assumptions and ingratitudes she had expressed in one sentence.

Nathaniel Nhamirre received them with the same affability as previous occasions and after extensive enquiries as to Faith's health, spent twenty minutes with her, poring over the single-mother funding application form. Jennifer, as always, was nervy and eager to return to the compound. Coffee, cakes and the secure environment had no effect. Iris gave up on any attempt at chit-chat because Jennifer's stutter had become less of an impediment and more of a block. Instead, the two of them sat at a window seat, observing Praia do Wimbe. It was a stunning view, an apparently endless stretch of sand around the bay, sending wave after rolling wave onto the shore. In a way, it acted as a kind of meditation.

She took several deep breaths, inhaling the sea air and trying to calm her nerves. Obviously, she was filled with antici-pation at the thought of seeing Gil Maduro later that day. At the same time, her radar was sending some kind of alert. She sat as still as a spider and threw a sensory web across this small, clean terrace. To her left, as she had expected, there was a high-pitched sense of tension emanating from Jennifer. Two tables away, Nhamirre bent his head over the documentation Faith had provided, his concentration intense. The only pulse she got from that partnership was energy, but in a benign way. Not a single individual on the terrace even raised a blip in her subconscious.

Alerts, as she had learned, were not always danger signals. Something she had seen, heard or possibly even smelt had trig-gered something in her lizard brain. Inside, she smiled at her own analogies, having transformed from a prize heifer into an arachnid and now a reptile in under an hour. What next, a seagull?

Footsteps disturbed her reverie and she looked up with a smile as Faith and Nathaniel came towards them. She could tell by their faces the meeting had been positive.

"Sorry to keep you waiting. Senhora Mbuti and I can see a lot of common ground and potential for future collaboration. Recent political developments indicate that the doors are open. I very much hope our organisations will become solid allies. But for now, I will submit your application for funding and revert as soon I am able. Thank you for coming to CWI. On behalf of the entire organisation, I can tell you that we are grateful. Have a very good afternoon."

The three women left the beachside building and walked towards the market. Two streets passed before anyone spoke.

"Is it my imagination or is Nathaniel Nhamirre hopelessly in love with you?" asked Iris, to irrepressible giggles from Jennifer.

Sashaying ahead, Faith smoothed her plaits with her palm. "If he is, he'll have to join the queue. Come on, ladies, to market."

It took a while before Iris noticed the stares. Once again her radar twitched and she became aware of an unusual level of interest in herself and her companions. Under normal circumstances, she would be tense and prepared for fight or flight. However, on this occasion, the curious glances and overt observation did not seem threatening. In fact, the trio received an unusual amount of nods, smiles and polite greetings. Market prices too were not ludicrously inflated and with a little haggling, fell into the region of quite reasonable. Not all the traders were of a mind to treat them like any other customer. The miserable old git selling cashew nuts was as abusive and disrespectful as ever. One snotty-looking woman rushed her teenage daughter away from them as if they were diseased. Twice someone accidentally on purpose bumped into Iris, which was par for the course when navigating the crowded aisles. Her reaction was the same now as it had been before – a sharp elbow in the ribs and good wishes for a nice day.

They were almost finished when a couple stopped to congratulate them on making the headlines. An older couple with distinguished hair, they were pleasant and friendly, but Iris could sense Jennifer's tension and kept the conversation brief. She suggested Faith take the vehicle to Mario's garage while she and Jennifer went to the post office. That would give Faith a little longer to flirt with the mechanic and achieve two tasks at the same time. Jennifer and Iris got out of the car at the football stadium and waved goodbye to Faith. The PO queue that day was quite short so they managed to complete their business in quarter of an hour. Iris was in no hurry to get to the garage so persuaded Jennifer to do a little window shopping en route.

"Thank you for loaning me that necklace, Jenni. It's very pretty and I promise to take good care of it. It's for Faith, isn't it?"

Jennifer nodded, with a shy smile which couldn't quite hide how proud she was. "Faith is like a big s-s-sister to me. She t-t-takes care of me and t-t-teaches me things I don't know. I wanted to give her the necklace at Christmas but it wasn't ready. Now I'm s-s-saving it for her birthday. I hope she likes it."

"Of course she'll like it, it's beautiful. I'm honoured that you trust me with such a precious gift. When is Faith's birthday?"

Jennifer held up two fingers.

"In two days? Oh, you mean in two weeks?"

The girl shook her head. "S-s-s ..." She scrunched up her face in frustration.

"Sorry, I'm being slow. You mean the second of March?"

Jennifer nodded, with a grateful sigh. "Mafalda is going to let me make a cake. Only a s-little one."

"Well, you know what they say, good things come in little packages." Up ahead was a row of stalls where women were selling handmade jewellery. "Shall we stop and have a look at these?"

Jennifer nodded her agreement, as if there was any likelihood she would do otherwise. The women greeted them optimistically and Iris engaged them in conversation, asking how long a pair of earrings took to make and where they sourced their materials. While she was talking, she cast surreptitious glances at Jennifer to check whether her ears were pierced. The girl moved away to look at some items on the adjoining store and Iris caught a glimpse of silver sleepers. She took the opportunity of a moment when Jennifer's back was turned to buy two pairs of earrings – spiral shells for herself and gold stars for her friend. Then she thanked the women and caught up.

"Pretty, aren't they?" she said, indicating a necklace of wooden beads. "But not as pretty as the one you made. Just think what you could make if you sold your jewellery. We'd better stop dawdling like a pair of ladies who lunch. Faith will be waiting."

They walked the rest of the way to the garage without making any further chat. Jennifer never initiated conversation, unless it was an emergency. Iris was preoccupied with her imminent reunion and wondering whether Gill's arrival would in some way or another hasten her own departure. Her heightened radar could have been initiated by him, just turning up out of the blue.

"Iris?" Jennifer's head was bent, her gaze on the ground.

Her voice pulled Iris from her own introspection and made her immediately tense. "Yes? What's wrong?" She scanned the street for any potential threat.

"Where would I sell it?"

Iris's mind rewound her most recent throwaway remarks

and understood the context. "Any place you can find a buyer. Like those women, you could set up a stall by the side of the road." By Jennifer's reaction, she could see that option was unappealing. "Or not. It could be a viable work-from-home business. For the sake of argument, you let people know you're open for commissions. Someone places an order, you give them a quotation as to how long it will take and how much it will cost. You contact them when it's ready and they pay you. It's not complicated really, plus I can help with the logistics. Have we gone the wrong way? I thought the garage was on this corner."

"No, Mario's is the next one. Thank you, Iris, I'll think about that." Her voice was calm, fluent and assured.

Iris actually did a double take. "You're welcome."

Faith and Mario were sharing an ice cream. Iris and Jennifer shared a significant look.

"There you are!" called Faith. "I've been waiting for you for ages."

"I'm sure you didn't get bored," Iris grinned. "Anyway, there was a big queue at the post office. Hi, Mario, how did you get on with the Toyota?"

He stood up and wiped his sticky fingers on his overalls. It was less of a cliché than diesel oil, Iris acknowledged. She shook his hand and prevented any awkwardness by stepping in front of Jennifer and pointing to the vehicle.

"All fixed, *senhora*. I found some old Land Cruiser parts down at Tito's scrapheap and saved them for you. No more Perspex, I replaced the whole door." His pride was irrepressible and deservedly so.

"Wow!" Iris stepped around the vehicle and admired his handiwork. The new door was green, not yellow like the rest of the Toyota, but it was functional and even the window-winder worked. "This is really impressive. Thank you, Mario. From now on, I'm going to call you Super Mario!"

He beamed with satisfaction but didn't seem to get the joke. Faith was finishing her ice cream and Jennifer was picking at her nails. It occurred to Iris that a Nintendo character might not quite hit the cultural reference mark, less to do with their video game experience and more to do with her age.

"Right, how much do we owe you?"

"Faith already paid me. I gave her a receipt." He hesitated. "Senhora Simons, can I make a photograph with you? I told my cousins you are one of my customers but they won't believe me."

Her automatic response would have been to refuse, as she always did when people requested a photograph. But something about Mario's enthusiasm made her discard her principles like a worn-out dishrag.

"Sure. Shall we have Faith in the picture too?" Instantly, she realised by including Faith she had placed Jennifer under pressure. "Jenni, would you like to join us or do you want to check out the repair work on the car?"

Jennifer nodded and ducked quickly behind the Toyota. Iris and Faith flanked Mario, their arms around his shoulders as he took a selfie. He showed them the results. Iris was unimpressed. She barely recognised herself. Her vain streak took hold momentarily as she envisaged her dinner date with Gil Maduro.

"I hope that convinces your cousins," she smiled at Mario. "Thanks again for a great job, we need to get back to the compound and start dinner. Have a lovely afternoon!"

When Iris read out the address of Hotel Escudo, Faith boggled her eyes. "You know where that is?" she laughed. "Right next to the place we were this morning. It's next door to CWI. You sure you're meeting some Brazilian friend or have you got a hot date with Nathaniel Nhamirre?"

"If I had, I'd be on a hiding to nothing. He only has eyes for you." She was unlacing her work boots. "We probably drove past it this morning. Of course a tourist hotel is bound to be on Praia do Wimbe."

"It's very posh. Good job we got you all dressed up. You're so lucky!"

Iris gave her a sassy look. "I think you'll find he's the lucky one."

Faith hooted with laughter and parked on the opposite side of the road to Hotel Escudo. It did look impressive and Iris tried to look nonchalant as she closed the brand-new/second-hand backdoor. She blew kisses and waved until the Toyota had driven around the corner then turned to face the beach. This was it.

Somehow, she was unprepared and in need of a moment's contemplation. She crossed the beach road and sat on a café terrace. Under a Lipton Ice Tea umbrella, she ordered a coffee and sparkling water. Surfers surfed, tourists sunbathed and waiters waited. Teenagers whooped while viewing a Tik-Tok on their friend's phone. A mother separated two squabbling toddlers and snapped in half the donut they were fighting over. A pineapple seller strolled up and down the beach, calling '*Ananas, ananas, ananas*, good price!' and the treble notes of some American pop song filled the seconds when he took a breath.

This was why she was unprepared. Everyone in her eye-line knew who they were: surfer, mother, sunbather, waitress, vendor, consumer. And what about Iris? If she was indeed Iris.

The man she was about to meet knew her as Ann, a poet from a small village in England. Not that he had believed that for long. He'd unearthed her police background, her under-cover role and the reason why she had run and hidden. God knows, if he hadn't shot a hitman in the back, she would no longer be here. His parting gift, before she fled Brazil in a blind panic, was to call her by her real name. He knew who she was.

Except that name was consigned to history, another identity she'd shed. He had no hope of knowing who she was. Because neither did she.

She looped Jennifer's necklace over her head and put in her new earrings. Which mask should she wear tonight?

"Good evening. I have a dinner appointment with Senhor Maduro. He's expecting me, I believe."

"Your name, *senhora*?"

"Iris Simons."

The clerk lifted his head from his screen. "The lady in the newspaper! Now I recognise you. You look different today. Better, in my opinion. Take a seat in the bar, *senhora*, and I will inform Senhor Maduro that you are here. Have a very nice evening."

The bar was a narrow corridor overlooking the pool, with stools and cubes in random arrangements on the deck outside. Iris took her tonic water and walked to the furthest point for some privacy. Not that the terrace was crowded, but she planned ahead for when the crowds arrived. She perched in the corner, so anyone approaching would be visible from a distance.

It was too early for a spectacular sunset. People ran in and out of the sea, delighted at stealing a summery afternoon from the rainy season. It wasn't the same view as they had enjoyed at Pousada Figueira, but the pool and sense of a haven elicited memories of the first night she and Gil drank cocktails on a balmy evening.

Even as she recreated the image of him in uniform, the man himself emerged from the hotel and walked in her direction. He wore light trousers and a white short-sleeved shirt, showing off his natural tan and *moreno* colouring, his sunglasses thrust on top of his head. Something about that confident, contained posture made her poise collapse and she ran to him, throwing her arms around his neck. They held one another for several seconds, Iris squeezing tight to ensure this was no figment of her imagination. He kissed her, one hand slipping into her hair and another around her waist. She forgot everything apart from the moment. She was home.

They both took a step backwards to catch their breath.

"I found you," he said, with a profound sigh.

"And therein lies a tale. Do you want to discuss it over a cocktail?"

He glanced over his shoulder at the bar. "Not yet. Let's walk along the beach." He took in her flip-flops. "You came prepared."

She smiled up at him, the temptation irresistible. "I'm prepared for anything."

He took her hand, she whisked up her backpack and they descended the ramp to the white sands of Praia do Wimbe. Both put on their sunglasses rather than wince at the brilliance. For a couple with so much to say, they were unusually silent, exchanging nothing but looks, smiles and the occasional squeeze.

Iris made the first move. "When some people ask, 'how did you find me?' they actually mean 'why did you find me?' The answer is meant to be a demonstration of the seeker's loyalty and love. Not so here. There's a difference. I am not a giddy fiancée with cold feet or an old schoolmate who took off to the Silk Road to find herself. When I ask 'how did you find me?' I want to know the practical steps you took to track me down. Because if you can do it, so can anyone else."

"I know. That's why I wanted to walk and talk. This is a conversation I don't want overheard."

They walked a little longer but talking was yet to make an appearance.

"Gil?"

"Yes, I'm sorry. You're waiting for an explanation. I'm trying to get everything in order and start at the beginning."

"Start wherever you like. Believe me, if I have questions, I will ask them."

He squeezed her hand and let it go. "OK, here goes."

"No. I don't want to stroll in the sand with you hiding behind your Ray-Bans. This is one of those occasions I need to see your eyes." She looked up at the road running parallel to the beach. Under the palm trees was a concrete bench where one could sit and soak in the view. Graffiti either decorated or disfigured the seat, depending on one's point of view.

Iris couldn't have cared less. "This way."

15

———

"I let you go." Gil's voice was muted. His gaze remained on the waves. "It was the most painful thing I've ever done, but it was a simple choice. Keep you and see you killed, or let you go and hope you would return. Remember what my mother said? 'In order to be happy, you will have to work harder than you ever imagined for someone extraordinary'. She was right. The Soure police force would get sick if they saw how hard I worked to find you. I never put that amount of effort into my job." He gave a rueful laugh.

"Months went by with no word or sign or message from you. I was so sure you'd come back to me, I learned English. It was a way of feeling closer to you. One morning I awoke with my mother's voice in my ear. Life, she said, doesn't come looking while you hide under a stone. You have to go out and find it. Then she kicked my bed. That woman had a very short temper."

His evocation of his mother struck Iris as natural and unaffected. "Unlike the subconscious."

Gil's eyes softened. "You're right. The subconscious takes its time and chooses its moment. Next morning, I applied for three months' leave." He rubbed his face with his palms. "What a load of bullshit. I'm making this all about me."

"Your story is all about you. We can unpack the emotional side later over cocktails. Please can I have the executive summary? Gil, how did you find me?"

"Yes. Of course." He snapped into professional mode, even to the point of straightening his spine. "You left Brazil to seek your ex-colleague in Hong Kong. Oceans, rivers and endless tributaries where one could sink without trace. It was a fool's errand to dive in after you. My plan was to wait for you to surface. That's why I found your family, your sister."

"Katie."

"Yes, Katie. Are you OK?"

"Does Katie know where I am?"

"Wait, what I was going to say ..."

"DOES SHE KNOW WHERE I AM?" Her bark echoed across the beach and ricocheted from the street.

"No! No, nobody knows where you are." Gil's face blanched in alarm. "Katie is your sister. The one person you can trust."

Iris had heard enough. "You know nothing about my sister." She stood up, ready to run.

"Listen to me, please. I know more than you do because you didn't let her explain."

She clenched her fists and her jaw, rage building. "I'm sorry?" Her voice was cold as a blade.

"How can I explain when you're standing there like a hand grenade? You think Katie informed on you and in a way, you're right. But you're wrong about why. Sit, Iris, please. I don't want to shout this story across the whole of Cabo Delgado."

She sat, brittle as a brandy snap, refusing to meet his eyes.

"I'll begin again. Listen to me with an open mind, that's all I ask."

"For crying out loud, Gil, will you ever spit it out?"

He cleared his throat. "Chasing you to Hong Kong was foolish and hopeless. Instead, I went digging for your roots. Nothing ever made more impact on you than that man saying he'd taken care of your sister. Your loyalty to her was absolute."

"More fool me."

Gil let that one go. "It wasn't complicated to find your family through police records. When I was sure I had the right woman, I travelled to Yorkshire. I visited the practice and persuaded Katie to meet me for a coffee. She was very suspicious on the first occasion and gave almost nothing away. Over a period of three or four weeks, we spoke several times and she began to trust me. I shared a lot about how we met, what I had learned of your personality and why I had fallen in love. She understood and told me stories of your childhood. How she looked up to you and admired your courage, how much she missed you and feared for your safety."

Iris snorted, but said nothing.

"When you disappeared the first time, Katie suspected you had been killed. She refused to believe the police line that you had gone AWOL. So when an associate of the Osman-Vargas organisation got in touch, she was in a very vulnerable position, willing to believe anything so long as it gave her hope. She was struggling. It was down to her to look after your father, face her own breast cancer while still not over your mother's death, raise a family and worry about you. That's why the man's offer seemed like a gift from God. He told Katie that you were alive, in serious danger, but alive. According to him, the police and the bad guys were after you and the only people able to protect you from harm were Milo Vargas and his brothers."

"How stupid and naïve can you get?" gasped Iris, incredulous. "The most deadly and ruthless collection of black-hearted bastards were offering me protection?"

Gil paused for a moment. "You forget Katie knew nothing about those guys. All she knew about your job was what you had told her and that amounted to very little. Then a charming, concerned individual in a suit offered her everything she wanted: top-level private healthcare for her mastectomy paid for by your 'concerned friends'; protection for her runaway sister; and a phone number to call if she needed anything else. The only thing he asked in return…"

"… was to rat on me the second I poked my head out of a hole."

"That's not how she saw it. She believed you were being stubborn and headstrong by hiding from the only people who could help you. In her own words, she knew you wouldn't be happy with her but at least you'd be alive. She loves you and wants to keep you safe. There's no way she could have known what they are capable of."

His words made sense. Katie always believed the best of people, making excuses for bad behaviour and giving people the benefit of the doubt. The Osman-Vargas operatives could be incredibly charming and the added generosity of her healthcare must have tilted the balance. At the same time, Iris was not yet ready to sympathise with her sister's predicament, and far from able to forgive. "Yes, well, her sisterly concern almost got me killed."

"Look at it from her point of view. The guy who spoke to Katie knew you very well. He convinced your sister that you were your own worst enemy and could not survive on your wits and luck in a hostile world. Your life, he said, was at risk by staying off the radar. All he needed was to find you and take you under his wing. She accepted and promised to call him the minute she heard anything from you."

Iris was impatient to get on with the trail that led Gil to Divine's bar, but there was something she needed to know. "What was his name? The guy in the suit."

Gil reached into his jacket and pulled out the same kind of police notebook he had used in Brazil. He flicked through the pages until he found what he was looking for. Even before he spoke, Iris knew what he was going to say.

"Chris Randall. Does that mean anything to you?"

Iris nodded once. Baby-faced Chris Randall, the epitome of suave, smooth-talking charm. Popular with women and useful to men, he was the respectable face of the organisation. He was also a vicious sociopath, who could be relied upon to oversee the worst kinds of punishment, so long as he didn't get his own hands dirty. Wherever they employed him, supervising the casinos, arranging girls for lavish parties, organising drug deliveries or property dealing, there were always complaints. But the Vargas brothers only shrugged. 'Randall gets the job done'. He got the job done but he was unpredictable, violent and predatory with no understanding of the word 'consent'.

Iris had seen him watching her when he thought no one was looking. He would never dare make a move on Milo's girl, but he was thinking about it, she was sure. The idea of him within five miles of her sister made Iris's flesh crawl. Then she realised how narrow her own escape had been. The 'taxi driver' was meant to collect her and deliver her to Randall. Of course the Vargas brothers wanted the most sadistic brute in their organisation to administer her punishment. Her toes curled and wingbeats of panic fluttered in her chest.

"Katie called Chris Randall to come and get me," she said, her voice flat.

Gil gave her a searching look. "But he didn't come and get you, did he?"

"No. We must have just missed each other. Please carry on. You found my sister who had no idea where I was. So it seems a bit of a leap for you to turn up here." She could hear the tightness and anger in her throat but seemed unable to hide it.

Gil seemed to sense her mood and continued. "Katie had

the idea of putting an advertisement on the vet website. We worded it together and she promised me if you called or emailed or even read that ad, she would let me know. I left Yorkshire to travel south. I wanted to learn more about the Osman-Vargas empire and your time with the Metropolitan Police. By February, Katie heard nothing, I'd learned very little and my time had run out. I returned to Brazil, empty-handed. I gave up." The sky accompanied his bleak tone by turning grey, and a cool wind whipped the palm trees. He scanned the sky with a frown. "Shall we head to the hotel?"

"Is there any chance of you ending this story if we do?" She smiled to soften her words.

"I'll finish it before we get there." He reached for her hand and they walked along the beach, as if it was nothing special.

"In September, out of the blue, Katie called me. She hadn't given up. Instead, she hired a computer analytics specialist to assess the practice's website. It was a genius move because she could see someone had clicked on the advertisement we wrote. Statistics showed that in April, a person in Aveiro, Portugal had read our words. It probably meant nothing, she said, but your husband was from Porto. It was where you had hoped to retire. That was all I had to go on."

She must have looked sceptical because he hurried on with great eagerness.

"A Japanese restaurant in a Portuguese town. What are the odds that someone would be searching a Dewsbury vets' announcements board? It was six months ago and you might have just been passing through. It could have been a computer error or a holidaymaker checking up on whether their pet had been found. It was the slimmest of chances but I left Brazil the next week."

"I have questions."

Gil sped up as rain spattered the pavement. "I'm sure you do and I'll answer every single one when we're in my room.

Just let me finish. It was obvious you would have changed your appearance but I had a selection of photographs to show the restaurant staff in Aveiro. One waiter recalled a woman who ate two mouthfuls of her food and left. He couldn't be sure from the photographs it was the same person but said it was a definite possibility. I pressed him on details. The woman, he remembered, was wearing a pink T-shirt with the words A Pantera Rosa on the back."

Iris groaned. "And you found Alonso."

"I found Alonso, who introduced me to Nestor and Lana and A Quinta Douro. Quite rightly, they were cagey and defensive, refusing me any information on your whereabouts. I spent two months working on your farm, trying to earn their trust."

Working on the farm? Her mind was operating in slow motion.

"They told me you would be back by planting season. Even if I couldn't persuade them into sharing your location, I could wait for your return. Then you called to wish them Merry Christmas. I was right there, sitting in the kitchen, listening to Lana's end of the conversation. How I managed not to snatch the receiver from her hand is a mystery. The line was awful and crackling but it was your voice, shouting Merry Christmas. When the line went dead, Lana sat at the table and shed a few tears. So did I. Quick, inside now, it's going to throw it down."

Gil's tale had absorbed her attention so completely the hotel's sudden appearance came as a surprise. They rushed inside just in time. Iris stared out at the downpour while Gil retrieved his key from the reception desk. They took the stairs up one floor. He unlocked his room, guided her inside and handed her a towel.

She patted her face and hair but could not wait for the final chapter.

"So that's how you knew I was here? You overheard me yelling over the phone?"

He waggled his head. "Sort of. After we stopped crying,

Lana told me you had always wanted to volunteer at a women's refuge. She didn't know where you'd gone, but she knew why. Your phone call helped us work it out. Three flights later, I arrived at Pemba Airport. The first thing I saw was your face on the front page of the newspaper."

"Oh, yeah, that."

"I knew where you were. I also knew a man striding into A Casa da Prata would not be welcome, so I made a few enquiries. A one-legged beggar outside the supermarket said he could help. For a price. I had to buy him a *francesinha* and listen to his life story over a couple of beers. Then he told me about Divine's bar and its clientele. I hired a jeep, drove along the coast road and braved the guard dog. It took four countries and almost eighteen months, but I found you. And here we are."

Everything he said added up but Iris was well trained enough to know that one never accepts a story at face value. There were so many points in his narrative she wanted to pick at and question until she would feel satisfied he was telling the truth.

On the other hand, the man she'd been dreaming about, the object of her fantasies was standing right in front of her, a towel around his neck and a lustful glint in his eye. The interrogation could wait.

"Maybe we should close the blinds."

The stumbles and trips of verbal interaction were understandable after such a brief relationship and long separation. The physical nature of their relationship, however, had no such social awkwardness. For far too long, this man had existed solely in Iris's imagination. Now she craved proof he was real. She explored his body, offering hard evidence to each of her senses. Feverish kisses recalled the taste of his skin, so irresistible she had to bite. His scent triggered an urge to rub her neck and jaw over his damp hair, as if she was a cat. Their breathing, trembling and heavy, excited her to a pitch of intensity she could not control. She wanted to clutch him, wrap her legs around him and devour him, like a spider with her prey. She absorbed Gil Maduro as if he were a drug.

The fluency of their love-making broke any remaining barriers and they lay spent in the darkness, touching one another on the shoulder, on the cheek, on the hip, on the wrist as if they could not believe the other was real. Each kiss was precious until it turned passionate and communication reverted to lustful greed. Without stating the words, they were making up for lost time. The sun set, filling the bedroom with silvery-pink light.

Iris propped herself up on an elbow. "Word on the street is you're going to buy me a cocktail and answer my questions."

"Room service, madam?"

"If we get room service, we'll end up doing this all over again."

Gil traced a finger over her eyebrow. "And that would be bad?"

"It would be very good, judging by recent performance, but there's a time and a place for everything. Cocktails and food and questions deserve our full concentration"

Gil stretched his arms above his head with a yawn, giving her a full view of his armpit hair and burn scars.

She touched them with her fingertips. "Do you remember that night ...?"

"In that village up Rio Negro? Our first time, in total blackout. The sexiest experience of my life. Even if you were out of your mind on *masato*."

She flicked his shoulder. "I had long since sobered up. I knew exactly what I was doing."

"I can't disagree with that."

She dodged his arm and hopped out of bed. "Can I have a shower? Proper hot water and shampoo is a special treat."

"Feel free. Call me if you need help soaping your back."

She didn't need help soaping her back. What she did need was a few minutes alone to block out the sensory overload of Gil's presence. Under the hot, fragrant water, Iris replayed Gil's explanation of how he'd tracked her down, and identified several points which required elaboration. She availed herself of all the miniature toiletries, luxuriating in the warm water. Then she dried off, wrapped herself in a towel, tied her hair into a knot and pocketed the hotel's beauty kit. She would share each element among her friends at A Casa da Prata. Outside in the bedroom, Gil was sitting on the bed wearing only his boxer shorts.

"Feel better?"

"I do. That was bliss. Sorry to hog the bathroom for so long."

"No problem. I'm only going to wash my face, get dressed and we can go downstairs. I'll have a shower before we go to bed."

Iris stopped in the act of picking up her underwear. "Gil, I can't stay the night. I have to go back to A Casa de Prata. It's my job."

He hid his disappointment well. "Sorry, I was making assumptions. I'll drive you home after dinner. You will stay for dinner?"

She paced across the room and drew him to his feet. "Yes, please, Prince Charming. I want cocktails, dinner, wine and dessert but Cinderella must be home by ten o'clock." She wrapped her arms around his back and kissed him deeply. "I missed you like you wouldn't believe."

He held her tightly against his chest. "Good job I found you, in that case. You smell nice."

"Don't start that again, or we'll never get out of here. Get dressed and let's go."

The sun was setting by the time they took their martinis to the deck. Conversation seemed superfluous as the sky and sea performed its nightly spectacle. Iris rested her shoulder against Gil's and tried to imagine this scene as her future. But the needle skipped off the record and her daydream crashed against reality.

Gil drew her closer, planting a kiss on her shoulder. "Her eyes roam the horizon but her head is filled with doubts. Ask your questions. I've told you the whole story, but we're both still detectives. The witness's version of events must be tested. So test me."

She didn't hesitate, turning to face him and breaking the embrace. "You left Yorkshire for London to discover more about my time with the Met and the Osman-Vargas operation. How the hell did you do that without setting off alarm bells from here to Melbourne?"

More people came out of the hotel onto the terrace, chatting, drinking and admiring the evening. Before long, it would be too dangerous to have any kind of confidential conversation.

"I have some friends in London," Gil answered. "A couple who work for the Met and another journalist who has run more than one exposé on undercover operations. I posed as the country cousin, a wide-eyed buffalo rider enthralled by the way British law enforcement works. It didn't take long before I realised they knew nothing. Your operation had a far higher level of security clearance and anything my friends knew was little more than gossip."

It sounded plausible but she couldn't give an inch. "Right. So having gained my sister's trust and finding nothing from your mates in London, you returned to your job in Brazil after a three-month sabbatical. Correct so far?"

"That is correct so far." He took a sip of his cocktail, his eyes never leaving hers. The air he projected was confident, relaxed, even amused. He knew, or at least he thought he knew, his story was watertight. In his white shirt and black jeans, he leaned on the terrace railing, giving her his full attention.

"A three-month sabbatical you had to apply for in advance, apparently. Then my sister calls you with a faint, outdated trace on my location then you get a flight to Portugal the following week. There's no way you got permission from the Soure police for another random goose chase. Do I look like I was born yesterday?"

A shadow crossed his face. "You're right. I didn't get permission from the police force. I quit my position, offered my apartment to a friend, put my stuff into storage and left Soure for good."

Iris stared at him, consciously searching his expression for a liar's tic. "On the strength of one computer click, you dropped everything to come after me? You're insane."

He laughed softly. "When you put it like that, it does sound a little rash. But you were the only thing that mattered. Your sister's description of me as a bloodhound hit home. Dogged, stubborn and impossible to deflect. Not forgetting the sad face."

A waiter bustled along the terrace in the direction. "Senhor Maduro, your table is ready. Come this way."

They followed him into the dining room, carrying their drinks and holding hands. Even though they did present the image of a classic honeymooning couple, Iris maintained her guard. Under the pretence of admiring her environment, she clocked every other diner with a focused attention to detail. Meanwhile, she allowed her subconscious to spread out, alert to anything out of the ordinary. There was something out of the ordinary – a familiar face with the party of people sitting near the window. In an instant, Iris recognised Nathaniel Nhamirre, listening intently to the man on his left. Iris bent her head and leaned forward to Gil.

"If you don't mind, could we change places?"

A frown tensed his brow but he rose and switched seats. Whether or not he worked for the Soure police was irrelevant. He still had a detective's radar. From behind the menu, his eyes took in the room from right to left. He said nothing but expressed his concern with a look.

"It's fine, just someone I met earlier and I'm not in the mood for small talk, that's all."

"OK, if you say so. I'm hungry. Let's have starters and a main course with a bottle of good wine. We deserve it."

The little lamp on the table was supposed to emulate candlelight and in Iris's view, did a very good job. Gil's skin glowed and the reflection of fake flames danced in his eyes. His happiness radiated like a sunburst.

"You know what, I worked up quite an appetite after this afternoon's activities." She gave him a look from under her lashes, unashamedly flirtatious. "I'd like the seasonal salad as an appetiser with a club sandwich and fries for my main meal. As for wine, I'll leave that up to you."

Rather than engage in her banter, he stiffened and looked over her shoulder. Iris sensed a presence and looked up.

"Senhora Simons? I thought it was you. Sorry to interrupt your dinner." He smiled at Gil. "Good evening, my name is Nathaniel Nhamirre and I work for CWI – Child Welfare International." He held out a hand towards Gil.

With only a second's hesitation, Gil rose to his feet and shook it. "Good evening. My name is Gil Maduro and I'm here to offer assistance to Senhora Simons. It's a pleasure to meet you."

Nhamirre gave an approving smile. "I'm very happy to

hear that. What a difference Senhor Cantopreto's support and patronage has already made! Senhora, I just came over to tell you that your application is approved already. I will be travelling south next month to receive the various cheques and collect donations. If anyone from your organisation would like to join me, there is a seat available on our coach. We leave on the morning of the twentieth for one week. I will detain you no longer, enjoy your meal and I look forward to hearing if anyone is interested in taking up my offer. Good evening, Senhor Maduro, Senhora Simons."

They wished him a good evening; he bowed and made a retreat.

"Another admirer?" asked Gil, his lips twitching into a smile.

"An admirer, most certainly, but not one of mine. Faith, who is on the management team at A Casa da Prata, seems to hold every man she meets in some kind of thrall. That invitation was definitely not for me. In any case, I have everything I need right here."

The look in his eyes was vulpine. "You are absolutely sure you can't stay the night?"

She shook her head with finality. "I am absolutely sure. Not tonight. As for tomorrow, let's see how it goes. Now please can we order some food?"

On the drive along Avenida da Marginal, Iris opened the window and inhaled the night air. Not since her arrival in Pemba had she felt so sated, comfortable and fizzing with hope. The future was still unclear and none of her problems solved, but she was reunited with Gil Maduro and that meant everything.

"Can I see you tomorrow?" he asked. "Or the day after? I

know you have commitments and I respect that. Whenever you can fit me in, I'll be there."

Iris gazed out at the beach as if she were on tiptoes at the edge of a precipice. Whichever way she leapt, her life would change irrevocably. How could she stay on the run, disappearing at will or confronting her enemies when every step endangered this beautiful, determined and loyal man? For the first time in her life, Iris had no plan.

"The simple answer is that I don't know. Mafalda has offered me a job for another six months. My farm in Portugal is approaching planting season. The people who are trying to kill me will not give up. My past is a mess, Gil, and the future is a blank. All I can do is get through tomorrow. Can we talk about this over the next couple of days? The last thing I want to do is make a hasty decision. How long did you book your hotel for?"

"A week. I can always extend it. I don't want to rush you into anything, I swear. So long as we want to be together, we'll find a way. My priority is keeping you safe. I love you and that's all that matters."

She swallowed her emotions and reached for his hand. "I love you too but that is not all that matters. If I really wanted you to be happy, safe and freed from the impetus to run around the world, I would tell you to go home. I'm an albatross, Gil, and I will curse you with bad luck for the rest of your life. But I'm greedy and selfish and I want to keep you with me. How the hell we do that, I have no idea. It's up here on the left."

"I know where it is."

Gil pulled over to the drive of A Casa da Prata and switched off the engine. The lights at the generator still shone and Iris could see Faith and Jennifer sitting outside the farmhouse, their necks stretched to peer like meerkats.

Iris called out of the jeep window. "Hi! It's me. My friend

gave me a lift. See you in a minute." She turned to Gil to say goodnight.

His head was bowed and his breathing almost bullish.

"Gil? What is it?"

"This place is not safe. You are not safe. I think I understand your intentions but this is not the right way to help other women." He took her hands in his. "Iris, Ann, Olivia, you say you endanger me by our being together. Maybe that's true but I'm a police officer and I can handle myself. These women are already vulnerable and at risk. The last thing they need is a fugitive from the police or various other interested parties looking for vengeance. Together, we can help, but only from a safe distance. Promise me this: think about what these women need. Then let's talk about how you and I can cooperate to deliver their requirements. Perhaps that can be achieved from somewhere else, where you are not quite so exposed. Just consider it, for your sake and for theirs." He released her hands. "I plan to have a drink at Divine's bar tomorrow evening. I'm hoping to meet a beautiful woman, drink a cocktail and stroll along the sand, talking about our future."

Iris leaned across to kiss him, her head so full of questions she could not articulate a single one. "Thank you for dinner and everything else. I'll be at the bar tomorrow and I will think about what you said. Goodnight."

He held her close, his breath hot on her neck. She squeezed him again, slipped out of the jeep, hopped over the gully and picked her way up the drive. When the engine started up, she turned with a wave, slipped off her jewellery and walked up to face the interrogation committee.

16

———————

Although written nowhere in the constitution of A Casa da Prata, a night off required double the effort on the following day. Iris had not finished batting away her colleagues' questions by midnight but still rose at six to begin the morning's fire. The practicalities of feeding the compound were now so automatic that Iris's mind was free to wander at will. She lit the fire, boiled water, made coffee, peeled fruit and stirred grains, recalling every detail of her afternoon in the arms of Gil Maduro.

Joana was the first rise, her sleepy smile and extraordinary blue-green eyes a welcome sight in the doorway of the cowshed. "It's cold, no? Maybe that's why Katie gives no milk."

"That goat isn't old enough to give milk and neither has she been impregnated. Joana, you understand why she will or won't produce milk, don't you?"

"Of course!" she laughed. "Somebody has to make it happen, just like you make the coffee. My mother taught me how to milk a cow and a goat's not that different. Katie trusts me. She will give me milk when she is ready. What happened with your friend? Does he want you or not?"

"Why don't you go and collect the eggs? If we have enough, I might make pancakes."

Joana squealed. "I love pancakes! Good morning, Susie!"

Susie waved, her face creasing into an easy smile. "Good morning, Joana, Iris! Another lovely day, if a touch on the nippy side. Let me do the rice pudding, Iris, you must be worn to a frazzle after your late night. Did you enjoy your date?"

"Not exactly a date, but yes, it was nice to eat posh food for a change. How's your stomach?"

"Settling down slowly. Your water filter bottle was an inspired idea. I should have thought of that. No matter how old I get, there's always more to learn."

From the cowshed, indications of the community rising and shining grew louder. Iris knew she and Susie were likely to be on their own for the breakfast service as Faith and Jennifer had fallen into bed even later than her. It crossed Iris's mind that she was letting standards slip. Her primary focus should be the security of A Casa da Prata. Wouldn't it be reassuring to have a trained security professional on the premises? Someone practical and physically useful in whom everyone in the compound could trust?

One of the toddlers came racing out of the cowshed, aiming directly for Susie's legs. Iris dropped the metal spoon she was using to stir the rice pudding and caught the little guy around the chest before he knocked the older woman into the fire. She scooped him up to head height and kissed him on the cheek.

"Will you be careful, Nuno? Or you'll fall into that firepit and I will roast you and eat you for dinner." She pinched his arms. "Lots of succulent, meaty flesh on this little piglet."

He shrieked with laughter and wriggled until she put him down.

"Good morning." Mafalda carried a mug of coffee across the yard. "Something smells appetising. Did you have a pleasant evening?"

"It was perfect. Thanks for giving me the time."

"You deserved it. I thought perhaps this morning we could start measuring for a fence. At least get an idea of how much material we're going to need. What do you think?"

Iris played down her surprise. "Sure. Great idea. I can start right after breakfast, just as soon as Faith is ready."

"No, you and I can manage it together. It will give us a chance to talk. Good morning, Susie. Just a word to the wise, the beach can be dangerous at night. Better to take a stroll in daylight. Hello, Joana. Did we get many eggs?"

Iris set to making pancake batter, wondering what exactly Mafalda wanted to discuss.

Other than a few short-lived showers, the weather stayed fine enough for Mafalda and Iris to stake out the site of a fence by mid-morning. The kids scoured the beach for bits of string, which they tied together to make one long colourful ribbon. Iris strung it between the mismatched pieces of wood standing in for fence posts before she and Mafalda paced the perimeter.

"It's big," Mafalda observed.

"Yes, very big." The scale of the task was daunting. "We're going to need almost 300 metres of fencing and thirty posts, not to mention the tools to do the job."

"It's going to take months. Are we up to this?"

Iris didn't answer, balancing realism with ambition.

"Unless ...?" Mafalda left the word hanging.

"Unless what?"

"Unless we get some help."

"Can we afford help?"

"I don't know. First we need to cost the materials. Can I

leave that to you? Take the Land Cruiser and check with a few different building merchants. I've used the one in Luguni before, but you might get a better deal elsewhere. What about your friend?"

Iris struggled to see the connection. "What about him?"

"Would he be interested in some labouring work for a couple of months? He's looks pretty capable."

"He's very capable, but he's a man."

"I had noticed that," Mafalda smiled. They reached the top of the dune and gazed out over the beach at the deepening layers of ocean blue.

"You said you didn't want men on the compound. We have a no-men rule."

"We make our own rules. If we want a fence, we need help building it. I will talk to the women and ask them to vote. If they are in favour of having a trusted man to handle the fence construction, we change the rule. He would only be permitted on site during the day and always in the company of a member of management."

Iris looked at her, intrigued. "You've got it all worked out, haven't you?"

"Just looking for solutions that make everyone happy."

"Do you want me to ask him? We're meeting tonight at Divine's place."

"I'll ask him myself, unless you have any objections."

"None whatsoever. I would be ecstatic to have him around."

"Good. The other thing is that a new volunteer is arriving at the end of March. She speaks at least two of the local languages so can help integrate the non-Portuguese speakers. Will you show her the ropes?" She turned to continue their walk around the makeshift fence.

"Of course. Another volunteer? Wow."

Mafalda stopped and looked back at her. "Wow what?"

"All this change. Nothing happens for months and now everything is going on at once."

"Yeah, that's normal. Except this time, some of the things are positive. Susie is so good with the kids and the women trusted her immediately. What's your impression?"

Iris agreed. "Yeah, she fits right in. Right where we're standing is where we should put the gate, I think."

"Maybe we should consult our fence-builder first. He's in love with you, isn't he?"

Iris shrugged and fell into step with Mafalda as they walked back to the farmhouse. "I guess he must be to come all this way."

"You can see it in his face. Yours too, even though you think you can hide it. Ah, how romantic! You and Gil, Faith and Mario, love is in the air."

"Mario has competition. The guy from CWI has offered us a seat on their coach to collect some of the sponsorship money. He wants Faith to go."

"Maybe she should. It's time she saw a bit of life outside the compound. Sometimes these girls can grow up too sheltered from the world."

"Yeah, that's something else I meant to mention. Joana said something about the goat which makes me think she's rather naive about the birds and the bees. Do you think some sex education would be a good idea?"

Mafalda considered the question. "Sex education usually happens organically, with older women passing on what they know to the next generation. But there's no reason we can't teach something more general, like biology. It might make some of our grant applications stronger. Good idea, Iris. Why don't you come up with some sort of outline for what we should cover? Yes, biology as part of our agricultural education, why not? Knowledge is power."

They continued walking toward the kitchen area. While

they were still alone, Iris took a chance. "Talking of romance, what about you and Edson?"

Mafalda did not, as Iris expected, dismiss the idea or scoff. Instead she gave her an inscrutable smile. "Why do you think I want to change the no-men rule?"

Iris gasped and Mafalda laughed at her dropped jaw.

"Even I deserve a little fun once in a while. 'Feel the fear and do it anyway', right? Come on, let's finish this and get started on lunch."

Six different builders' merchants, including Edson's cousin, gave vastly different quotations for the wire and fence posts. Two were aggressive and hostile, one eager to please and the other three indifferent. She drove home through a wet and windy afternoon, willing the weather to clear before the evening. All the residents were in school, leaving the bathroom free, so Iris did some hand washing, including Faith's caftan. She hung everything on the line over the showers and pondered how best to use her time. Outside work was impossible in such conditions and the lull was a perfect opportunity for Iris to curl up in her stall and get some sleep. Instead, she read the new volunteer's CV, made calculations based on the various suppliers' estimates and scribbled a mind-map of what should go onto a biology syllabus. She was writing notes on menstrual cycles, her eyes beginning to droop, when she sat up with a jolt. Who the hell was she to offer reproductive advice?

Her own cycle was rarely predictable but she knew more or less when her period was due. Approximately two weeks from today. Which meant she had indulged in unprotected sex during her most fertile stage. Trying to stay off the grid alone was one thing, but hauling a child around the world, hiding from a team of psychos determined to make it an orphan? She must be out of her mind. If Gil accepted the job and their relationship was to continue, birth control was a necessary point on the agenda. She lay on her cot and dozed, dreaming of bouncy little goats jumping over a half-erected fence.

Cooking smells woke her. She gathered up her borrowed finery and went in search of their owners. Jennifer was relieved to regain her precious necklace and overwhelmed to the point of tears with the little gold star earrings. The goat butcher accepted the returned bangles but selected one and handed it back. Iris acknowledged the gift with a squeeze of her hand. In the kitchen area, Faith was making *xima* and giggling with Joana.

"I washed your caftan. It should be dry by morning. Thank you for letting me borrow it."

"Why shouldn't my dress get out? I can't wear it because I never go anywhere. On the coach with Senhor Nhamirre, though, that would be an occasion for a caftan. Do you think I should, Iris? Joana thinks I'm crazy to leave the compound and travel the road with complete strangers."

"Joana, you're talking about the man who helped you cast your vote. He's hardly a complete stranger. The trip is to meet CWI donors, show your gratitude on behalf of A Casa da Prata, do some networking and spread the word about the changes we're trying to make. There is no question whether you should go, Faith. We're lucky to have the invitation. Without Cantopreto and Joana's natural charm, it wouldn't have happened. Someone from here must represent us and you're our secret weapon. Is someone going to turn that flatbread? It's burning."

Because Joana was staring at Iris as if hypnotised, Faith flipped the bread.

"That's what I think. You're going to have to teach me some of your pretty speeches, Iris, because I don't talk like that."

"No, pretty speeches are not what they want to hear. What

Joana said in front of Cantopreto swung the balance. None of my well-rehearsed patter but a sincere statement of fact. Now, listen. We're starting a new project. Who are the fittest and strongest of our residents?"

By the end of the evening meal, Iris had a list of four potential labourers, one of whom was the goat butcher. None of the four spoke either Portuguese or English. Jennifer assured her it was no big deal. She would translate and act as go-between. The team were excited to contribute to the good of the compound. Iris wondered if that enthusiasm would last once they saw they would be working alongside a man.

"Iris, are you ready? Faith, Jennifer, we're going to the bar to conduct some business. Can you keep watch? I'm sorry to ask you again."

The young women assured Mafalda there was nothing they would rather do and settled themselves on the bench outside the farmhouse with Joana sitting on a stone by their feet, whittling at a piece of driftwood. The three of them sang a few lines of a song before stopping to bicker over the lyrics. The scene was peaceful and relaxed.

Iris and Mafalda ducked under their makeshift string barrier and strolled along the beach, both looking slightly more polished than usual. The sand was wet from the afternoon storm but the sky stayed clear and moonlight reflected from the sea. Iris absorbed it all, in the knowledge she would soon leave it behind.

"Joana is smart. We should give her a role." Mafalda's voice jerked Iris from her introspection.

"Communications." Iris responded without a second thought. "She and Faith would make the most extraordinary team. Articulate, appealing, with no need to fake facts because they have lived them, they are the best public-facing duo I can imagine."

"Hmm. But what about domestic care? That is Faith's role,

along with Susie and Jennifer. And mine, of course. We don't just feed and house these women, we look after all their needs."

Iris stuck her toe under a piece of wood and flicked it up to the shoreline, with every intention of collecting it in the daylight. Nothing goes to waste.

"Forgive me if I'm out of line, but a lot of these women can look after themselves. They wanted to get involved in the cooking, the maintenance, in every detail of camp life. Education is vital to arm them for the outside world. The fact is they already have a lot of skills they can contribute to our daily routine. Some of them might take longer, but others are ready to participate and re-engage. By protecting and distancing them from reality, we might be doing them a disservice."

Mafalda said nothing.

A sense of an old wound flared in Iris's subconscious. Just one afternoon in a comfortable bed with a committed man was all it took to convince her she was an icon for all womanhood. She knew best for women whose lives she couldn't imagine, she knew better than the people providing refuge and she had yet to learn to keep her mouth shut.

"I'm sorry. You are the founder of A Casa da Prata and I respect your judgement. I apologise for being a ..." she reverted to English "... a gobshite."

Unexpectedly, Mafalda burst into genuine laughter. When she'd recovered, she repeated Iris's words and spoke English. "A gobshite? Where did you learn that expression?"

"I don't know but I've worked with plenty of Irish people in my career. The question is, where did you learn it?"

"That's a story for another day. Divine's place looks lively tonight. Come on, a cocktail is exactly what I need!" She took off at a run, her silver raincoat flashing in the moonlight.

Iris let her go. It would take a decade to decode Mafalda and she had fewer than three months. In any case, her boss wanted to make an offer to Gil Maduro. Better to linger along the beach and let them negotiate terms. Iris crossed her fingers. Two prickly and standoffish individuals might clash and set fire to any hope of cooperation. She recognised the urge to run, mediate, soothe and broker the deal.

No. What will be, will be.

She sat cross-legged in the sand and stared at the moon. The night air was warm, the sky remained clear, and mellow music from the bar lifted her spirits. Once upon a time, she used to be the director, the narrator, the fixer and the connector. No more. Her only obligation was to stay alive. She had money and means. A donation could transform A Casa da Prata without the need for three months bashing posts into the ground. She could take Gil Maduro to somewhere so remote nobody had ever heard of it. A place they could be safe.

"Iris?" Mafalda's voice threaded through the air. "Where are you?"

"Just watching the moon. Be there in a moment."

The bar was full and the music eclectic. Iris climbed the steps, greeting Divine, Mafalda, Edson, the surfers and Hester the barfly woman, tonight wearing yellow. But she couldn't stop her eyes drifting to Gil Maduro. He leant on the bar beside two glasses, his smile broad.

Divine yelled, drowning out his voice. "Tequila Sun-Iris, come over here and drink your Caipirinha like a boss! We got ourselves a Brazilian!"

It seemed the most natural thing in the world to greet Gil with a kiss on the lips, so Iris was unprepared for the whoops and howls which followed the gesture. She was mortified, blushing as if she were in sixth form again. The attention didn't seem to bother Gil, who pulled her into an embrace and handed her a Caipirinha.

"Here's to my new career! Cheers!"

She grinned at him and flashed a glance at Mafalda, who grinned and nodded.

"Your new career as a fence builder?" she laughed.

"I prefer to call myself a security consultant. I've made an agreement with Mafalda. Providing the residents vote to accept a man working on the premises, I will work at A Casa da Prata for the next two months."

"Two months! That is brilliant news! But surely you can't stay in a hotel for the next eight or nine weeks? Where are you going to live?"

"I can help you there," said Divine. "See this parcel of land?"

They couldn't because it was pitch black.

"It stretches from here to A Casa da Prata and I own every metre. A couple of farmers use it to graze their cattle for a small fee. Other than that, it's empty. A business in Luguni rents out Portakabins. Hire yourself one of those, Gil and Tonic, and park it at the other end. Then you can get up in the morning, walk along the road and up the drive to the refuge. I'll only charge you a few mets for the privilege and if you don't mind cows as neighbours, everybody's happy."

Gil stared at her, an expression of amazement on his face. "That sounds like a brilliant solution. Thank you very much, Divine."

Hester the barfly lady chipped in with some advice about haggling with the Portakabin owner, and Edson came over to talk to Iris about his cousin. It appeared they might get a significant discount on the price he had been quoted earlier that afternoon. He offered to accompany Iris and Gil on their next visit to guarantee the maximum amount of materials for the lowest possible price.

The atmosphere was enthusiastic and positive, a combination which went to Iris's head far quicker than the cachaça in her cocktail. She looked around the bar; taking in groups of people laughing, singing or having intense conversations, before bringing her focus back to the man in front of her.

"Happy?" Gil asked.

Iris nodded. "So happy I can't believe this is real. It's like one of my craziest fantasies with added fireworks." She searched his face. "But what about you? I doubt you lie awake at night, dreaming of living in a Portakabin and banging in fence posts."

He laughed. "You'd be surprised by what I lie awake at night dreaming of. The point is, you and I can be together. Our positions here are not permanent, but we have time to think about the next steps. That's worth celebrating, don't you think?"

They lifted the glasses in a toast and turned to gaze out at the moon's reflection on the sea. Not normally a touchy-feely person, Iris couldn't resist holding Gil's hand, stroking his thigh, resting her head on his shoulder, constantly reassuring herself of his presence. She watched him as he explained variations on the carioca cocktail to Divine, his hands expressive and his laughter warm. Gil Maduro. Iris made herself a sincere promise.

Now that he had found her, she would never leave him again.

17

———————

The vote from the residents of A Casa da Prata was not the shoo-in Iris expected. At least four women were visibly upset at the idea of a masculine presence in their safe space. Word got around that the man in question was Iris's boyfriend, provoking accusations of her abusing her position. Under the circumstances, Iris could not attempt to negotiate or reassure the objectors and left it to her boss. Over three days, Mafalda discussed the issue, made offers and counter-offers, added elements of persuasion and press-ganged those with favourable opinions into speaking their minds.

Meanwhile, Iris and Gil were involved in a similar protracted negotiations; one with Edson's building-merchant cousin and another with the owner of the Portakabin company. The former ended well, with a very good deal on materials and mates' rates on the hire of equipment. The latter collapsed and as Gil had arranged to check out of his hotel by the end of February, they had an accommodation problem. Iris was yet to explain her true financial situation, which gave her the means to pick up the tab for his hotel stay for the rest of the year if necessary. Instead, she sought a creative solution.

Leaving Gil to work out logistics with the builders, she drove to a specific supermarket. Stupidly, she assumed Berto the voluble beggar was there every day. She assumed wrong. After she'd hung about until lunchtime, he still hadn't shown up. A guy in his position was likely to rotate his days at different supermarkets, to catch the widest possible audience. She found a phone box and called Tendai's number.

"Hi, this is Iris from A Casa da Prata."

"Hi, Iris! Saw you in the paper last week! Congratulations! You need a ride somewhere?"

"Not today, thanks, Tendai. I'm looking for information. Remember when you collected me from the supermarket, I was talking to an older guy by the name of Berto? He has only one leg, the victim of a land mine. You said everyone knows him."

"Sure, everyone knows Berto. Everyone's heard his stories, most of us more than once," he chuckled. "What do you want with him?"

"He told me he lived in a mobile home, a gift from some benefactor."

"Yeah, that's right. Samuel Albino gave him an old caravan that used to belong a *fartura* vendor and stuck it behind the GALP garage on the N1. Albino is a generous man, but with pockets as deep as his, he can afford it."

"How does Samuel Albino make his money?"

"Bit of everything. Cars, land, hotels and I think he's on the board of a few charities. What do you want with that guy, Iris?"

"Cars, land, hotels and caravans?"

"Caravans? Sure. Just south of the airport there's an import warehouse. Always a couple of conversions, ex-food stalls, that kind of thing. Be careful, some of them are falling apart, but you can't argue with the price. Iris, I have a fare, call me later if you need more."

"Thank you, Tendai!"

The site was huge. Iris parked near the main building, searching for some sort of reception desk to orient herself. She was breaking all the rules: driving alone, deviating from the plan and not updating Mafalda on her location. Although, Mafalda would be in school at the moment, talking to her students about caprine reproductive systems, so it would be rude to interrupt.

A car pulled in beside hers. She steeled herself and prepared for a battle of wills with used-car salesmen. The vehicle beside her was enormous, a gleaming tank of an SUV with tinted windows and a kangaroo grille. The door opened and a dapper man wearing sunglasses and a panama hat stepped out with a welcoming smile. Iris registered it all in slow motion.

It was not just a surname. The man had albinism. He was just as physically imposing as Arnaldo Cantopreto, but had white skin, blond eyebrows and a starburst of boot-polish freckles across his jaw line.

"*Bom dia!* English? American? Hello and good morning!"

His voice was disarming. "Good morning. You must be ... the owner?"

"Samuel Albino, yes." He clasped her hand in both of his. "Ah ha! I recognise you! The women's refuge spokesperson from the newspaper, no? Very clever, getting Cantopreto on your side. What is your name and do you have time for a coffee?"

Iris trusted her instinct. "My name is Iris Simons and a coffee sounds like a great idea."

"Follow me, Iris Simons, I have an Italian machine in my office. An indulgence, because no one other than my wife wants to drink coffee with me. You can lead a horse to water, but you can't make it appreciate a decent lungo. An English-woman in Pemba – not a tourist, not a teacher, what a curiosity you are."

"I'm a volunteer," said Iris, hurrying to keep up with the man's long strides. "Your English is extremely good. Sorry, that sounds patronising. It's just you're one of the few English speakers I've met in Mozambique."

"Not patronising at all. I take my compliments where I can get them. What do you think of my accent? Can you tell where I learned the language? I do hope so because it cost me a great deal of money." He unlocked a door in the huge slab of ware-house and invited Iris to go in first.

The interior was like an airport hangar with an odd assort-ment of items standing around in no particular order: an ice-cream truck, two military Jeeps, pallets of cement sacks, a rail of overalls, an articulated lorry, an Art Deco style bar, half a dozen mattresses wrapped in cellophane and a claw-footed bathtub. Three men manoeuvred a grand piano from one side of the space to the other, where a woman attached a shipping label to one of its legs.

Samuel Albino greeted everyone with a wave and indicated a glass box in the corner. That, Iris assumed, was his office. Inside the room was much quieter than the noisy hangar and Iris accepted the offer of a seat.

"Well? You don't have to pinpoint the exact town, but the county would be good. Cream and sugar?"

"I prefer mine black, thanks."

"You prefer black? You got something against white?"

Iris froze, with no idea how to respond.

"Hey, I'm only teasing. I get the jokes in first before anyone else has the chance. One way to break the ice, you see. Here we are. The finest espresso outside Rome."

"Thank you. Um, I can't really detect a specific accent. You speak a very neutral kind of British English, just like a classic BBC newsreader."

"I'll take that! Cambridge, my dear, about as neutral as it gets. Whereas you have a faint touch of Yorkshire in your vowels. I hear it in the way you said 'just' and 'can't'. York is a charming city. Indeed, the whole region is an exquisite part of the world."

The coffee smelt incredible and Iris took a deep inhalation. "Yes, I come from Yorkshire but I thought my accent had faded. Obviously not."

"It probably has. Only the keenest ear would pick up those nuances." He sat back in his chair, cradling his little cup. He was immaculately turned out, in a well-cut navy suit with polished brogues, a white shirt and what appeared to be a silk tie. "Tell me, what does a lady from Yorkshire want with Albino Export/Import Operations Unlimited?"

Iris explained her encounter with Berto and why she was sourcing a caravan. "It's just that we have a no-men policy on the compound, Mr ..."

"Call me Samuel, Iris. We're friends now."

"Thank you, Samuel. As I was saying, we have a space for a Portakabin or static caravan right next door, but the prices the guy in Luguni is charging are obscene."

Samuel shook his head as if in disapproval. "He deals with building contractors who can afford his inflated terms. For you and your cause, he should have made an exception. Ah, well, his loss is my gain. I have two possibilities in mind. Do drink your coffee while it's hot, my dear. I agree that the aroma is quite extraordinary, but the taste is sublime."

Iris drank. He was absolutely right.

• • •

Outside the rear of the hangar stood a row of vehicles; tractors, forklift trucks, camper vans, a mish-mash of farm machinery and at a distance, a helicopter bearing the SA logo.

He followed her gaze. "I know. A terrible indulgence, but some of my business interests are at a significant distance and the roads, well, need I say more? I took my pilot's licence three years ago. You should come for a ride sometime."

"But you're so close to the airport! Isn't it dangerous?"

"Not at all. I pay ATC the courtesy of filing flight plans and obtaining permission. Air traffic controllers, in my opinion, have levels of intelligence and responsibility which would daunt normal human beings. Like a gigantic game of chess but each piece is filled with human beings. To our quest. Here's the first option."

Samuel unlocked the largest of the camper vans and showed her the interior. It was perfectly spacious enough for a person to eat, sleep and live comfortably, but it smelt of damp, and black stains were spreading from the window frames.

"It needs a little cleaning up, as you can see, and the tyres are all flat. It hasn't been used in two years. With a little TLC, it could be quite cosy. But before you decide, come and see my other suggestion."

They left the neglected camper and entered a second hangar, about half the size of the first. Iris saw it instantly. "A shed!"

In a similar layout to the first building, the space was filled with various objects or piles of goods, with a small unit in the corner. The difference was that Samuel's office in the other hangar was a glass box, while this was a sizeable wooden garden shed.

"Correct. Isn't it whimsical? A long time ago, I had dreams of becoming an artist. Watercolour painting, crafting poetry or playing the lyre, something along those lines. To that end, I commissioned an artist's shed. Windows in every wall for the best light, a desk, bookshelves, enough room for a chaise longue, an easel or music stand and a door which allows me to close out the world. I adored it and had my wife not objected, I might have moved in permanently."

The man was so very unusual in his mannerisms, speech and utter absence of self-consciousness, Iris couldn't help but like him.

"What happened?" she asked.

"The worst imaginable fate to befall any artist – my muse deserted me. That is presuming she was ever there in the first place. I had no talent, no fire, no imagination and no ideas. My heart is that of a grasping merchant, a capitalist whose only desire is amassing filthy lucre, without an artistic bone in his body."

A laugh escaped Iris and his cheeks lifted in appreciation.

"The artist's not-quite-garret became my first office, a Swiss chalet tucked in the corner of my ever-expanding empire. Then I noticed that all the bosses on television dramas about police or journalists have offices made of glass." He tapped his nose. "Smart. A boss should be visible, a physical presence, not a closed door. When we built the new place, I commissioned something similar and bade farewell to my shed and my artistic ambitions."

Iris grinned. "You may not be a poet, musician or painter, Samuel, but I think you would make a wonderful actor."

For the first time, he took off his sunglasses. He widened his blue eyes, their radiance enhanced by a frame of white eyelashes, and beamed. "Do you know, I think you might be right."

The shed was everything Iris wanted. One room, big enough for a bed, a table and chair, with a lockable door. She could already imagine Gil standing in the doorway, holding a cup of coffee, or better still, a bottle of wine and two glasses.

"OK, Samuel, for this shed, a small generator and fridge,

plus a chemical latrine and transportation to A Casa da Prata, what kind of deal can you offer me?"

Changes in daily life over the past week confused Iris so much she couldn't process everything. Like pedalling up the steepest mountain, she had crested a peak and was speeding downhill so fast she couldn't take in the scenery. Samuel Albino gave her an unbelievable bargain: they could have the shed on a two-month trial basis. After that time, it was returnable, free of charge. The only costs were the appliances and transport.

A canny businessman, he naturally wanted something in return.

"Once a month, my wife and I host a lunch at one of the quieter hotels. We invite four guests to discuss a classic work of literature. In order to expand all our horizons, we take turns in choosing the novel. My personal preference is for the nineteenth century but I am open to suggestions. I would like you to be a regular guest. It's always the last Friday of the month. Too late to include you in February, I'm sad to say, as the thoughts of a Yorkshire lass on *Wuthering Heights* would add gravitas. Would you be willing to select a book for March?"

Iris thought about it while Samuel donned a panama hat and supervised the loading of her purchases into the Land Cruiser. He shook her hand and promised delivery of the shed by tomorrow afternoon.

"And your choice of book, Iris?"

"I have a feeling *Wuthering Heights* is not your first Brontë. Have you read *Jane Eyre*?"

He inclined his head. "One of my wife's favourites."

"In that case, on the last Friday of March, I'd like to discuss *Wide Sargasso Sea* by Jean Rhys. It was a pleasure doing business with you, Samuel."

"The pleasure was mine. I look forward to March. Here's

my personal card, in case of emergencies. I must go inside. The sun is cruel to someone with my complexion. Goodbye and good luck."

Under the glare of that same sun on the drive home, Iris pondered why a man would name himself after his own condition. The answer was as clear as the blue skies above. *I get the jokes in first.* Samuel Albino, she decided, was a class act. Roll on March, because she couldn't wait to meet that man's wife.

A Casa da Prata was quiet, since school was still in session. The only movement was the bright strings marking the fence and the chickens scratting the earth within their coop. Iris unloaded her goods outside the back door of the farmhouse and saw a figure sitting on the beach.

"Jennifer?"

The girl jumped up, grabbed her fishing-rod and bucket then ran off the beach. "Iris! I didn't hear the car. Mafalda did it! Your man can start work t-t-tomorrow! What about the fence and the cabin? Were you s-s-successful?"

"Very. What about you? Good catch?"

"Yes, look!" She lifted the lid of her bucket to reveal at least a dozen decent-sized fish, glassy eyed and fresh.

"You are so good at this, Jenni. Now we can make a stew for dinner. You want to start cleaning them now and I'll prepare the vegetables? Where's Susie?"

"Walking. I s-saw her going up the beach in the direction of Luguni. I don't know why she wants to walk when it's s-s-so hot but she does, every day."

"A little time for herself, I guess. She works hard during the mornings. Now, tell me about how Mafalda got everyone on board with the fence project."

Jennifer gutted and scaled while Iris peeled and chopped.

The practical activity absorbed Jennifer's focus and her speech became almost natural.

"She made a t-timetable so that people who don't want to see him don't have to. He's allowed to come into the compound during school hours. The rest of the time he works on the boundary. Every morning, Mafalda will tell us where he is working. He leaves before dinner and arrives after breakfast. This is for us and for him. Mothers must keep their children away from the construction site so they don't get in his way. Women willing to help must give their names to Mafalda. One of us from the management must watch him every day. He will not come here at weekends."

Iris bit her lip, the injustice of Gil's treatment stinging her eyes as much as the onions.

The doors of the farmhouse opened and kids raced out ahead of their mothers. Mafalda wandered across with the women, a look of pride on her face.

"Our hunters-gatherers-fishers had a good day?" she asked.

"Fish s-stew with peppers for dinner!" Jennifer announced.

"Sounds delicious! Go get some yams from the store so we can add bulk." After Jennifer dashed off to wash her hands under the pump, Mafalda sat opposite Iris and switched to English. "What about you? Is the project practical?"

"Yeah. Materials due Wednesday and the labourer's hut will be delivered tomorrow. I hear you've convinced them."

"More like a trial run." Mafalda waggled her head and sneaked a slice of carrot. "Three of the women are still resisting the concept but if we can keep them away from any building activity, we can maintain the peace. They're still 'on the fence', if you know what I mean."

Iris was in no mood for jokes. "Gil wants to help us, Mafalda. He's not some fox in the hen house, but a professional with skills we can use. I know him and I trust him. Gil would never hurt a woman."

Mafalda took another penny-sized piece of carrot. "If I had a dollar for every woman who swore by her man, I could buy the next election. I know, I know, this one is different. So are they all. Here comes Jennifer. I have to make a few calls before dinner. Well done on getting the fence wire and everything." She strolled in the direction of the farmhouse, leaving Iris with no opportunity to retort.

18

Day by day, life at the compound changed. Susie held a morning surgery, encouraging the women to make preventative healthcare a priority. She usually disappeared in the afternoon for what she called her 'afternoon constitutional', but showed up to help with the evening meal. Responsibilities shifted from Mafalda, Faith, Jennifer and Iris to the whole community. Mafalda never once acknowledged the idea had come from Iris, but implemented it as if it had been her plan all along.

Food preparation was now on rotational duty, mainly involving the Makuhwa speakers and supervised by Tawona, otherwise known as the goat butcher. Team A cooked the meals one day while Team B cleaned, then they switched. It worked smoothly, other than occasional debates about the 'best' way to prepare almost every local dish.

The goat had her first season and it was time for her to make a contribution. Joana and Jennifer walked the animal down the road to a farm where the owner had a whole herd, including a billy goat. They paid a flat fee to get Katie serviced and observed a practical lesson in reproductive systems. Now the whole compound kept their fingers crossed the goat would conceive.

The construction workers changed too often for practical purposes, so Iris and Gil made an executive decision. The regular team comprised four people: one paid labourer – Gil – and three willing volunteers. Iris was impressed to see Jenni was one of them. The other two were displaced twins from Moçímboa, both tall and muscular enough to carry buckets of water on their heads. They only worked morning shifts, because school took precedence over everything.

While they learned literacy and numeracy skills in the farmhouse, Iris stepped up to hammer and twist and dig alongside Gil. The school hours were also an opportunity to show him the camp and explain some of her ideas for improvement. He listened. His observations were helpful but somehow distant. She put it down to a fear of mansplaining.

He set her right. "No, I'm not afraid of telling you what to do. Hit that post, hand me that mallet, that's not the problem. Along with Jenni, Ni and Maria, I can take care of the practical stuff. Someone has to act as the ambassador for A Casa da Prata. You've become the spokesperson for this place, whether you like it or not. You should teach some of the younger ones to get out there and talk to the press, the TV people, visit communities and get their faces known. Play to your strengths, Iris, because that's where you make the real difference. If you do your job well, the fence won't be half as important."

She consulted with Mafalda, who had an opinion on sound bites, media angles and image appeal; to the extent she insisted Iris wore the same silver raincoat for every picture. "A Casa da Prata, Iris, come on. The word *prata* means silver. You and your silver tongue, you stand for us!"

With wide-eyed and enthusiastic Joana, plus practical, determined Faith, Iris went on a charm offensive, posing for pictures, talking to journalists, having their photos taken and sharing the story of A Casa da Prata with anyone who would listen. Local government opened doors and invited them to a conference on furthering female agency. Results weren't quite as instantaneous as battering down wooden posts, but it felt more like sowing seeds.

Meanwhile the fence progressed, an impressive barrier along two sides of the compound, including a gate onto the beach. Mumbles and grumbles about the 'man' fizzled into nothing and no one complained about their new security measures. A Casa da Prata was changing for the better.

So was Iris.

Most evenings after dinner, she and Gil walked along the beach, sometimes to Divine's bar with company, sometimes without a destination and alone. Two or three nights a week, she spent the night in his shed, a privilege she had earned after making the place as welcoming and comfortable as a bijou hotel room. Physical work at A Casa da Prata exhausted them both but their passion for each other was inexhaustible.

One morning, patterns of golden sunshine refracted by palm leaves poured through the mosquito net and roused her from sleep. She rolled onto her side. Gil slept on, his eyelashes resting on his cheeks. The sun and exercise had given him an uneven tan and a powerful musculature. A swell of love washed over her, binding her to his side come what may. The journey he had undertaken left her breathless. It was time to be honest with this man, who had given up his life and career simply to find her. She was uncomfortable with living a lie. The longer she kept her wealth a secret, the harder it would be to make plans. She made a vow to tell him before the end of the week. He deserved to know who she really was.

The other obligation she had before the end of the month was a lunch with Samuel Albino and his wife to discuss a novel. It seemed such a remove from her daily existence, she almost dismissed it as a throwaway remark until a card arrived in the PO box, addressed to her.

Senhor & Senhora Albarinho cordially invite you to our monthly literary salon

Where: Hotel Quirimbas for a three-course luncheon

When: 31 March, 13.00

Book under discussion: Wide Sargasso Sea, *by Jean Rhys, chosen by Iris Simons*

Dress code: Smart casual, no sports shoes or flip-flops

Sitting in the Land Cruiser outside the post office, she read the card and laughed aloud. Now she understood the provenance of his name. The last comment, she had no doubt, was aimed at her. She showed Joana, her constant companion these days, and read the message aloud.

Joana didn't see the funny side. "What can you do, Iris? You can't go barefoot!"

"No, but the next best thing. Ballet flats. We saw some stall at the market earlier, no? Buy two, get one free? A pair for me, a present for Faith and you get the freebie. You can wear them for the interview on Saturday morning."

Iris bought the shoes – red for herself, green for Faith and green for Joana – and a couple of metres of brightly coloured material to make new clothes. Her T-shirts were threadbare and she had not a single dress to her name.

When you are invited to a luncheon, Iris, it behoves you to dress the part.

In the event, it was one of the most enjoyable meals Iris had eaten since arriving in Mozambique. Samuel and his wife were gracious, thanking her for such an intriguing choice of book. The other guests, two prominent businesswomen and a South African journalist reporting on Cabo Delgado, were excellent company, well read, opinionated and ready to laugh. Iris ate well, challenged her companions on their interpretations of the novel and drank one too many glasses of red wine.

They posed for a picture for Senhora Albarinho's album, an awkward moment in which Iris did not know whether to look like a critic or a grateful nobody. She thanked them all for a stimulating afternoon and prepared to leave. Kabo, the journalist, invited her for another drink but her literary analysis extended to reading his intentions. She declined. Next salon was scheduled for 28 April and books proposed included *Sons and Lovers*, by DH Lawrence, or Fitzgerald's *The Great Gatsby*. Iris expressed no preference. By the end of next month, she might be on a plane to Portugal.

Iris used the bathroom to wash her face and clean her teeth. She noted a light coming from Susie's stall and hesitated. Surely she wouldn't be so careless as to risk a candle? The glow was steady and Iris assumed it was a torch. Why shouldn't the woman have some illumination to read before bed? She chose not to interrupt, ducked around the temporary fence and headed for the shed. Another light shone from the window.

Gil was lying in bed, watching local TV. He switched it off as she closed the door.

"You're awake. Wasting electricity on entertainment?"

"Gripped by the latest interviews with Faith Mbuti and Joana Zeca. The inside story of female empowerment. A Casa da Prata, the face of change. How's the volunteer working out?"

Iris dropped her clothes on the floor, slipped under the net and wrapped her limbs around Gil Maduro. "Susie's the best! Practical, skilled, capable and everything I'd like to be."

Gil kissed her. "You're everything I want you to be. Seriously, your media blitz is getting all the right attention. I honestly don't know what more you can do for A Casa da Prata."

"I can do so much more. Gil, it's April tomorrow. Time we planned our future and got realistic about the circumstances. You've been working seven days a week. How about we take Sunday off? We could pack a picnic and drive north to the Quirimbas Park. It would be a pity to leave without visiting at least once. Then when we're far away from here, we need to talk turkey. It's time I filled in some gaps."

He traced her hairline with his fingertip. "Picnics are my favourite. Turkeys aren't bad either. Now let's sleep. I'll lock up and switch off the lights." By the time he came back to bed, Iris was capable of nothing more than a pat worthy of a spaniel.

19

———

April 1st had no significance in this corner of East
Africa. Pranks and jokes seemed crass to Iris's mind,
so she abandoned any hope of raising a laugh.
Instead, she asked Mafalda's permission for Sunday off,
cleaned the shower and toilets, swept the yard, dug out the
yard stones, filled in the gaps and set the white-painted boul-
ders as markers along the edge of the road. She leaned on her
spade and smiled. The place looked almost respectable.

Faith came skipping down the drive.

"Morning, Faith. You look full of beans."

"Katie's pregnant!" she announced, her smile splitting her
face. It took a second before Iris identified the name with the
goat.

"Fantastic news! She might have two kids if we're lucky.
This is what we need."

"It's exactly what we need! I'm coming with you on the
post run today; Joana wants to stay with Katie and Jenni says
the building crew can't do any more until they deliver the
cement."

"OK, I'll get the truck."

Faith dragged the bridge over the gully and waved Iris on. Once the Toyota was on the main road, Faith threw the makeshift drawbridge behind the wall and leapt into the car.

"Might be the last time we need to do that." Iris observed. "Gil's going to fill it in and erect a proper gate. Good thing too. That bridge is falling apart."

"The sooner the better. We can't afford to damage our only vehicle. Yes, if Katie has two healthy kids and they're both female, we have the makings of a herd. Chickens and goats will keep us, if we can keep them. That fence is everything to A Casa da Prata. Your man is solid. He knows what he's doing and why."

Iris pulled down her sunglasses to cover her eyes. "Yeah, he's reliable. What about your complicated love life? Are you planning a trip south on Nhamirre's coach? Where does that leave Mario?"

The Toyota hit a rock and skewed to the left. Iris righted the steering wheel, all her senses alert to the possibility of a blown-out tyre. "Shit! Do you think that was a trap?" she asked.

"Nope, I think that was you paying more attention to gossip than to the road. Yes, I will take my place on the CWI coach as the second most articulate and definitely the most elegant representative of A Casa da Prata. Gentlemen with an agenda will have to form an orderly queue."

Iris laughed.

"Iris?" Her voice grew serious.

"What?" She scanned their surroundings for any hint of danger.

"I think you should stay."

Iris didn't answer, still nervous about who had placed a rock in the road.

"Things have got so much better since you came. Now Gil is here, we have money to spend, the refuge is becoming famous and soon we'll have a proper farm. Why can't you stay?"

"Because I have to make a life of my own."

Faith folded her arms. "Mafalda says A Casa da Prata is her life."

"That might be true for Mafalda and I respect her devotion. But I always had other plans. Like everyone else, my aim is to do something useful and move on. You and Joana will make an exceptional team as the public face of A Casa da Prata. By the way, can you supervise lunch and dinner on Sunday? I am taking a day off with Gil."

When she got no response, she reached over to prod her companion.

Faith dodged out of reach. "If Gil stayed, would you?"

"That's why I need a free Sunday. He and I have to talk."

"OK, I can supervise the Sunday meals. What do you think of my outfit?"

She was wearing her green ballet flats, jeans and a brightly patterned shirt with the necklace Jennifer had made her.

"Very pretty! Is this for Mario or Nathaniel?"

"Why should it be for either of them? It's for me. Can we stop at the cycle shop? I want to see if they've finished the repairs on Demi's bike."

"The cycle shop where Filipe works? Sure we can." Iris grinned.

Faith shrugged and examined her fingernails, failing to hide a smile.

For the first time since arriving in Pemba, Iris was sending rather than just receiving post. She bought a simple card with a beach, palm trees and a view of the ocean. She composed her thank you carefully, purchased the stamp and put it into the post box.

Dear Senhor and Senhora Albarinho

Just a note to thank you for a stimulating discussion and delicious lunch. I feel privileged to have been invited. It was a pleasure to meet you and your friends. Our conversation gave me much food for thought. I very much hope to join you on a future occasion.

With all best wishes

Iris Simons

She collected the contents of their PO box, slightly intimidated by the amount of mail, and stuffed it into her backpack. After one obligatory trawl around the market to see if there was anything on special offer, she got back into the Toyota and drove to the bicycle shop.

Demi's bone-shaker had indeed been repaired. It took three of them, Iris, Faith and Filipe, to wrestle the thing onto the roof rack and tie it down. They paid the repair fee out of the housekeeping budget, and on the way home Iris gave into Faith's wheedling. They stopped at the roadside café for *churros* and hot chocolate.

When they arrived at A Casa da Prata, they couldn't access the driveway due to the presence of a large cement mixer pouring its contents into the gully. Gil spotted her and jogged up to the driver's window.

"Park outside the shed. We need to give this time to set before even allowing a chicken to cross it. They'll add the second load on Monday and until then, the driveway is out of bounds. Faith, you can help me tape a cordon around the area."

"Tape a cordon around the area?" Faith laughed. "Wow, you sound just like a cop."

Fortunately Faith's face was turned away so she couldn't see the look Iris gave Gil. The Land Cruiser bounced along the ruts made by Samuel Albarinho's HGV, shaking every bone in Iris's body. She untied the bike and was about to take the post into the compound when a bloodcurdling scream rent the air.

She dropped the bicycle and ducked under the fence, running on high alert. Nuno's mother was on her knees, wailing and cradling her son near the cowshed. The boy was grey-skinned and limp, his shorts soiled and legs streaked with diarrhoea. Iris crouched near the boy and took in his sunken eyes. Between her thumb and forefinger, she took a pinch of his skin. It stayed pinched, only relaxing into its normal position after three seconds.

His mother had stopped screaming, watching Iris with desperate hope. Other people came running to the shed and Iris searched the worried faces for their medic.

"He's got severe diarrhoea and dehydration. Has anyone seen Susie?"

Jennifer ran off with no clear purpose and everyone else shook their heads.

"OK, I must get him to a hospital. Faith, tell Mafalda to call CWI. I'm bringing in a seriously ill child, probably suffering from malnutrition, who will need urgent rehydration, possibly intravenous rather than ORS. Tawona?" She mimed picking up the child and pointed to the Toyota. Gil could have done the job but a man taking the child from his mother was a scene best avoided.

Nuno was completely inert as Tawona scooped him up and strode across the compound, over the fence and into the car. Jennifer joined Iris in the front while his mother cradled her baby boy in the rear. Iris handed over her own water filter bottle and Jennifer demonstrated how to get moisture into the little boy's mouth.

With as much gentleness as she could manage, Iris reversed down the tracks onto the road and sped towards CWI's hospital. *Two steps forward, one back.* But if Nuno died, that would be a tragedy from which the compound could never recover. She pressed her foot to the accelerator, listening to Jennifer's soothing tones and asking the same old question. *What the hell do you think you are doing?*

Two hours in the waiting area ground Iris into a slough of despond. Sick children, wrecked mothers, skin diseases she'd never seen and had no wish to see again, infant cries and hopeless expressions made her feel like a speck of sand standing in an ocean of agony. Jennifer sat like a statue, her focus on the floor. Once Iris walked along to the kiosk and bought two bottles of mineral water since her own had vanished with Nuno and his mother.

The noises of pain and grief grew overwhelming, bringing Iris near to tears. Her reaction on seeing Nathaniel Nhamirre was so powerful, she had to clench her fists and feet to keep a hold on her emotions. He sat on the wooden bench beside her, his reassuring smile not quite obliterating his concern.

"The boy is going to be fine. He is in good shape overall, but still recovering from malnutrition and a serious case of diarrhoea. What concerns me is the food he's eating. This child should not eat any raw milk products, none of the children under ten should. I don't understand why he has eaten yoghurt or unpasteurised milk. Your people should know this. Giving them bacteria in their food is incredibly dangerous, Senhora Simons."

"We don't! Everything is cooked, I swear. Nuno eats what everyone else eats so I can't understand what made him sick."

Nhamirre gave a signal to a nurse. "Sorry, I am required on the ward. Nuno can go home with you, but please make sure he has no more untreated milk. You told me you have a nurse on the compound, no? Make sure she supervises the children's food. Good evening."

On the journey home, Nuno was dozy but awake. His mother stroked his hair and kissed his forehead, murmuring to

Jennifer who responded in comforting tones. Iris mulled over Nhamirre's words. *You told me you have a nurse on the compound, no? Make sure she supervises the children's food.*

"Jenni? Ask his mother what he ate today, will you? Did he eat anything different to the rest of the compound?"

The two women conversed quietly until they arrived at A Casa da Prata. Nuno's mother carried her boy up the drive, avoiding the freshly laid concrete. Jennifer watched her go and turned to rest her arms on the Toyota.

"I'll go with her, help with the cleaning and all. Nuno ate as usual, she s-said, but S-S-Susie gave him some kind of pudding for his belly. He got s-s-sick after lunch and you know the rest." Jennifer ran up the drive without a glance backwards. After a few moments, Iris drove the Land Cruiser up to the shed, preoccupied by Nhamirre's words.

Saturday night was no different to any other night of the week. Dinner was cassava pancakes with vegetable and bean stew. The wind picked up although no storms were forecast and the evening was humid. Iris took a tiffin tin for Gil across to the shed. He still gave her his Labrador look every time she left him to eat alone, but he accepted the fact that her role at the refuge required her to be present at mealtimes. She suggested a stroll along the beach later and he agreed.

It seemed overdue to spend some social time with Susie because Iris had questions. She joined her table at dinner, offered to show her the route to the bar and invited her for a drink.

"That's very kind of you, Iris. I have to say, you all make me feel quite at home. I would love to walk down the beach with you and your young man for a drink. One of the best ways of getting to know a person, I would say. What sort of time where you thinking?"

"We generally wander down around seven o'clock. That gives us a couple of hours at the bar and time to get home before the generator goes off at ten. Early to bed, early to rise as always. Does that suit you?"

"That suits me down to the ground. I won't lie to you, Iris, I prefer to rest an hour after eating before heading out. At my age, my stomach takes more than a few days to get used to strange food. If everything is working as normal, I'd be delighted to accept your invitation. Is it just the three of us or is Mafalda coming along? I don't want to be a gooseberry."

Iris mopped up the remains of her dinner with a laugh. "You won't. Gil, Mafalda and I often stroll down for a drink together. The others aren't so keen on the bar. You're not the only one to suffer with digestive problems. I've learned to be very careful, boil water and wash everything twice. Talking of stomach upsets, Nuno had a serious reaction to something he ate this afternoon. We had to get him to the hospital."

"Poor mite! The water plays havoc with my digestion so what it does for a wee fella like him I can't imagine. That's why I always carry a hip flask. Gin for the journey, port for the first couple of days and whisky for emergencies. Mafalda tells me you're leaving at the end of the month. Shame, you seem to be very popular."

Iris noted her lack of interest in Nuno's welfare, "As you will be. Let's face it, your valuable experience outweighs my naïve enthusiasm by ten to one. Morning surgery is proving more popular than the school. Back to the point, though, Nuno's mother said you gave him some kind of pudding at lunchtime today."

Susie shook her head. "That woman is not the brightest light on the Christmas tree, unfortunately. No doubt trying to shift the blame onto someone else for her neglect. The children's welfare is my top priority, as I think I have demonstrated. So tell me about your plans. Where will you go from here? I imagine Brazil would be a wonderful place for the two of you to set up home."

Iris avoided the question. "That's a conversation we're going to have this weekend. Where were you before coming to Pemba?"

"Oh, I see! Forgive me, I'm a terror for sticking my nose in." She put down her fork. "Uh-oh, you may have to excuse me. If I don't return within the hour, may I take a rain check? These things are so unpredictable."

"Don't worry. Plenty of time to get to know each other. Hope you feel better soon."

Susie bustled off towards the cowshed with a little wave at some of the children. Absorbed by their food, none waved back. Looking at their reaction from Susie's perspective, it might seem like a snub. She made a mental note to ease her acceptance into the community. For these women and children, an endless stream of people passed through their lives, few able to speak their language or comprehend their history. Iris herself was only just chipping at the top of the iceberg.

A wail of pain came from the table of Makuhwa women. Iris rushed over to see Nuno had toppled off the bench. His mother lifted him to her chest, stroking his head. He clutched a chubby hand to his forehead, howling his pain and frustration the only way he knew how. Iris patted his shoulder and offered him a slice of dried coconut from the snack pack in her pocket.

"Nuno, Nuno, *olha aquí.*" Such was the volume of his distress, she went unheard. All the boy saw was a sweet thing he loved. With one arm around his mother's neck, he let go of his forehead to accept the treat. An egg swelled from his brow, a graze beading blood. Iris rinsed a clean handkerchief from her plastic water bottle and showed the boy how to press it to his injury. The other children watched with curiosity without a single break in their determined consumption of everything on their plates.

Iris checked the boy and found a smaller injury on the back of his cranium, explicable by the fall. The sandy ground and his own thick cushion of hair had prevented something worse. But what kind of missile hit a two-year-old, causing him to fall off his bench?

Amid the voluble debate around whose fault it was, she rotated her gaze. Everything appeared normal. She sat with the boy and his mother even after his tears became artificial and a ruse to get more coconut. It must have been one of the children, throwing something and missing the intended target. Tomorrow, she would speak to everyone about safety.

Mafalda strolled across the compound, wearing the silver jacket as if it was a royal cloak. Under her breath, Iris was humming Leonard Cohen's 'Famous Blue Raincoat', and half-wishing she'd never bought the damned thing. By seven o'clock, Susie had not reappeared and Iris chose not to hunt her down in the bathroom. She knew how mortifying an upset stomach could be. She collected her leather jacket from the empty shed and met Mafalda on the beach, lit as brightly as she had ever seen it on such a cloudless night.

They walked for a while, released from the pressure to talk.

"Where's Gil?" asked Mafalda.

"Already at the bar, I expect."

"What about Susie?"

"I did offer an invitation but she's got the squitters."

"She has all the skills we need. I was thinking of asking her to stay on."

Iris hesitated, thinking of Nuno. "Time will tell. Did we ever get any of her references? I'd like to find out more about her."

"None of her references have come through yet but we got lots more offers of sponsorship, including one providing recycled bikes. In theory, that means some of our young women can go to a public school."

Iris whistled. "Fantastic! Did Faith tell you our bike is road-worthy again?"

"She did, and we also have a pregnant goat. Good news at every turn. Tell me, if I offered you and Gil the management roles at A Casa da Prata, would you be tempted?"

Iris stopped walking. "What the hell are you talking about?"

"I'm talking about handing over the management role to two people better suited to run this place than me. Not just that ..."

"Mafalda?"

She walked on, taking her time.

"Mafalda?" Iris's patience was wearing thin.

"Yeah, well, it was just an idea."

"Don't do that! Either spit it out or shut up! I am bored of hints and suggestions. We're talking about people's future here which is far more important than one of your vague ideas. Would Gil and I want to take over A Casa da Prata? How can I answer on behalf of two people? From my standpoint, that's a flat no. As for Gil, I can't even begin to imagine because I don't know what you're proposing. For once in your life, Mafalda, give me a break and just say what you mean."

She stopped and wrapped her arms around her silver jacket.

Iris regretted her harshness. "I'm sorry. I shouldn't shout, I know that. I apologise for raising my voice and snapping your head off. Can we talk about this with Gil? Tomorrow is the day we plan our future and I'd like to have a realistic set of options."

"OK."

A song Iris recognised drifted from Divine's bar. A James Bond theme by Duran Duran.

"Mafalda, it's Saturday night. We should be having fun."

"Yeah, you're right. We should be having fun. I should be

having fun. You and Gil are so blessed, you could be happy anywhere. Me? I don't want to leave it too late."

"It's never too late." Iris linked arms with Mafalda and guided her along the sand towards the bar. "It's a question of choice. You have achieved something incredibly important and changed people's lives. You can choose to do the same for yourself. You really can."

Mafalda clutched her arm. "I can. We can change. Tonight, I am going to pet Rusty Nail."

"Really?" Iris questioned the need to start her friend's emancipation with befriending a dog, but shut her mouth. "OK, I'll be right beside you. This is April the first, a brand-new beginning for Mafalda Moutinho! I hope Divine has something appropriate on the cocktail menu."

Divine did not disappoint.

20

"**M**oonlight Martini! If you have to ask why, you better look up at the sky tonight. I'm not telling you the ingredients, you have to guess." She poured two yellowy drinks into martini glasses and popped in a maraschino cherry in each.

Gil was sitting at a table, wearing a black shirt and talking to Edson. Iris noted they were drinking beers from the bottle, not a martini glass in sight. They looked up with welcoming grins and Gil pulled two more chairs to their table.

"A martini is a martini, Divine," said Iris. "Gin, vermouth and usually an olive. Does adding a cherry turn this into a Moonlight Martini?"

"Oh no. This is something much more exotic. Taste it and tell me what you think."

Iris mugged a fearful look at Mafalda and took a sip. Strong alcohol, a hint of sweetness from the cherry syrup and something like fennel or aniseed. It couldn't be Pernod or the drink would be cloudy, but the presence of absinthe in a Pemba beach bar was unlikely.

"Is it my imagination or do I detect a green fairy?"

Divine pointed an index finger at her like a revolver, her mouth open with delight. "You're the first one! Nobody but you got my secret ingredient. Your prize, Tequila Sun-Iris, a cocktail on the house."

"She can have mine too," said Mafalda, pushing her glass along the bar. "This is way too strong for me. Sorry, Divine, can I have a beer?"

Divine rolled her eyes but cracked the lid off a bottle of 2M and handed it over. "Praise the Lord for Europeans, that's all I can say. Only the Swedes and those French guys have been brave enough to drink one. Even they said no to seconds."

"It's pure alcohol, Divine. Give me a bottle of sparkling water otherwise you'll find me curled up behind the bar with Rusty Nail." She didn't look at Mafalda while invoking the dog's name, guessing it would take at least two beers and maybe a smoke of the house special before her boss was ready to face her fear. They joined Gil and Edson, Iris carrying two cocktail glasses and a bottle of water.

"You thirsty tonight, Iris?" asked Edson, his grin broad.

"Polite and well mannered, that's all. And after two of these, someone will have to take me home in a wheelbarrow. What's new with you?"

"Just checking Gil got all the stuff he needs. You guys don't hang around, do you? The fence is looking great."

"Our team is doing a great job," said Mafalda, zipping up her coat.

Gil drained his bottle. "Easy with damn good workers. Edson, can I get you another beer?"

"Maybe later. I have to tune up my guitar. Hey, listen, Divine wants me to play moon songs this evening. Please think of a few more than Billie Holiday and Frank Sinatra, would you? Mafalda, you coming for a smoke?"

"Sure. Give me a minute, we gotta to talk shop."

She waited till he'd gone down the steps and spoke fast in a low voice. "I want to hand over A Casa da Prata to responsible people who can maintain and improve on what we've achieved. Sorry, that sounds like I'm writing a job advertisement. It's time for me to move on, for selfish personal reasons, but I can't just abandon the refuge. The place needs a manager, or better still, two. Iris, you've done a wonderful job and Gil is solid as a bull. My question is, would the position interest you? Maybe not immediately, but perhaps in six months or so? I know you have a free day tomorrow to make plans so I had to ask you tonight. Think about it, that's all I ask, and we can talk next week. I am a control freak, I'm aware of that, but for the first time, I'm ready to let go. For the refuge and for myself. Over and out. I'm going to smoke weed with Edson."

Gil spoke as Mafalda got to her feet and wrapped her coat tighter. "Thanks for your trust. Can I ask one thing? Why now?"

She swallowed down tears. "Because the clock is ticking. Because what happened in the past will not dictate my future. Because you two give me hope." She gave them a watery smile and rushed off to the beach.

"Changed my mind. I think I will drink one of those cocktails." Gil took a draught of a Moonlight Martini and coughed as the alcohol hit his throat. "Do you know what the hell is going on? I just don't understand that woman."

Iris took the other glass. "Neither do I. My vague theories can wait for tomorrow. What I do have is more moon songs for Edson this evening. Creedence Clearwater Revival, 'Au Clair de la Lune' or Van Morrison."

It was a marvellous night, filled with song and laughter and an unusual amount of dancing. Iris blamed the absinthe. Rusty Nail emerged to observe the stomping and reeling, his amber eyes judgemental. In a courageous move, with Iris at her side,

Mafalda stroked his head. The dog gave her a patronising look worthy of a president and retreated behind the bar.

At a quarter to ten, Gil herded them into a messy, far from sober group. Edson kissed Mafalda goodbye more than once, Iris hugged Divine, and everyone in the bar tried to persuade them to stay. Eventually Gil dragged the residents of A Casa da Prata away, stumbling and swaying up the beach, occasionally breaking into song. It was a beautiful evening, the sand silvery and a promising breeze floating across the whispering rush of the sea. Part of Iris longed to stay here, to put down roots and learn from this odd little promontory in East Africa.

Sounds of an engine rumbled along the sea road, louder than the average truck, and headlights swept the beach.

Gil tensed and came to an abrupt halt. "Mafalda! Come here. Let's stick together."

"What? Why?"

"Come here, please!" The fear in his voice chilled Iris.

A massive flash exploded from the road and a repeated pulse of bullets pounded the beach. Gil and Iris hit the sand. Another strafe of shots hit the shoreline. The vehicle switched off its lights and drove away.

Iris lifted her head the few millimetres she needed to breathe and reached for Gil. He was panting, whether out of fear or pain, she could not tell.

"You hurt?"

"Hit in my leg. Not serious. You?"

"Nothing."

"Good. Mafalda?"

There was no answer.

"Find her, Iris. Keep down."

Iris scrambled along the shore line until she located the silver-coated woman face down in the water. "Mafalda! No!"

She dragged her up the beach and felt for a pulse. Time and again, she pressed on her arteries and found no sign of life.

In the monochrome tones of the moonlight, Iris couldn't discern any injury, but the smell of blood and burnt flesh told a different story. She rolled her onto her back. Her T-shirt was no longer white, torn apart by two gaping holes, one in her chest, and another in her stomach. A bubbling sound came from her lungs.

She scrabbled up the sand to Gil. "I'm going to get the Toyota and take you both to hospital. Where are you hurt? Speak to me!"

"I'm fine." He spoke through gritted teeth. "Is she OK?"

"No. She was hit twice and I think it's too late. I'll be as quick as I can." She took off at a run and jerked to a sudden halt. "Gil, are you carrying a gun?"

"Yes. Are you?"

"No, but I have my knife."

She couldn't hear Gil's reply but assumed it was exasperated. Her knife and her wits had got her this far, why change now?

She sprinted along the shoreline where the sand was firmest, until she could see the compound. The new fence glinted in the moonlight, making the place identifiable, even though the generator was already silent. Iris veered left and heaved herself up the dune towards Gil's shed, her breath shaky. The Toyota was where she had parked it earlier. With an inward curse, she remembered the house rule. *Always leave the keys in the farmhouse.*

She ducked under the string marker and tiptoed past the cowshed, slower and more wary of unexpected obstacles. Everything was silent and in darkness. Almost everything. A dancing blue light up ahead caught her eye. It had been a while but Iris recognised the glow of a mobile phone when she saw one.

She dropped to a crouch and watched as a figure moved out of the shadow of the cowshed and in the direction of the beach. Whoever it was wore black with a hood covering his or her hair. No one at the compound, as far as Iris knew, possessed a mobile phone. So this had to be a stranger. She loped silently across the yard and watched as the figure opened the gate and descended onto the beach. The gait was determined and professional. Iris waited until the blue light and its operator moved right. Then she turned tail, pelted across the courtyard and ran back the way she came.

So there was only one conclusion. That person was heading down the beach intending to finish the job. Whether this person was one of the shooters from the truck or a backup in case one of their victims escaped, it made no difference. Gil Maduro lay injured and in desperate need of help.

Iris ran at a cautious jog, balancing safety and silence with speed. When she judged she had got some distance ahead of the assassin, she crouched by the dune and peered over the top. Her assessment was correct. A little more than fifty metres away, the blue light was visible if dimmer than before, bobbing in time with the person's walk. Iris scrambled down the dune to crouch behind a palm tree. As the figure approached, she realised the reason the screen was dimmer was because the user had changed from messaging to speech.

"… like the previous time. You do the job, I clear up the mess. I will ask you again, did you complete the job?"

Iris recognised the voice, dismissed it as the confusion of her own stressed imagination, and accepted she was right the first time. The person stalking down the beach with every intention of killing anyone left alive was a nurse, midwife, grandmotherly volunteer with an impressive CV and no references.

Susie.

In a second of revelation, it all made sense. The shooters weren't opportunist drunks out for a laugh, but organised, systematic professional killers, most likely sent by someone with a grudge. After all, Iris had made enemies across four continents. Their undercover agent, bug, walk-in or inside eyes, however she chose to phrase it, had given them all the essential information. To neutralise their target, they needed to know which beach, what time, how many people and what they would be wearing. Iris winced, visualising Mafalda proudly dressed in a silver raincoat.

One thing was certain, this was the cleaning lady, sent to mop up the mess and plant enough drugs, weapons or other incriminating evidence to deflect police attention. 'Susie' was striding down the beach with every intention of executing Iris. Without a second thought, she would shoot another bullet into Gil and probably kick Mafalda's corpse, just to make sure. She was a pro. But so was Iris.

The hooded figure had almost drawn level with the palm tree where Iris was hiding. Susie's phone was still pressed to her ear as she searched the beach with a torch. If Iris jumped her, the element of surprise might work to her advantage, but what weapons lay under that black hoodie was anyone's guess.

The woman's voice, dripping with poison, whispered into her phone. "You think I don't know that? I worked for Vovó before while you were still breast-feeding. Now fuck off and stake out the airport. I have a job to do. Comms to silent."

One word was all it took.

Vovó.

A deadly chill spread through Iris's entire body. *Kill or be killed*. It took fifteen seconds to make a decision. She shucked off her leather jacket, tightened the strap on her backpack and withdrew her knife. With a light step, she rushed up behind the hooded figure and caught her around the neck. The woman reacted fast, spinning on one leg and using her elbows to dislodge her assailant. They fell to the ground, Iris underneath. The sand cushioned the blow but the weight of the woman on top of her crushed Iris's chest. That momentary loss of power gave her target the slightest advantage. Susie threw her head back, cracking Iris's nose and reached for a weapon. Iris didn't hesitate. She tightened her forearm around the woman's neck, yanked her chin skywards and slit her throat. Blood pumped from her jugular vein, pouring onto Iris's face. She held her position, her left arm gripping tightly to the slackening torso and her slick knife poised in her right hand. Once convinced the woman was dead, she threw her off and snatched up her torch, shining it into her face.

The kindly grey-haired nurse was no more, leaving behind a rictus of rage. Iris turned away and shone her beam further down the beach, trying to discern the difference between clusters of rocks and an injured Brazilian policeman. She broke into a jog, wiping the blood from her face.

"Iris?"

She spun on her heel, searching for the source of his familiar voice. "Gil? Where are you?"

"Beside Mafalda. I tried to move her but I can't manage it. I'm losing a lot of blood. Where's the car?"

Iris angled the torch towards the sound of his voice and saw him hunched over Mafalda's body, shirtless, with a tourniquet around his knee.

"No lights! What if they come back to finish the job?"

"They won't," Iris replied, switching the flashlight to illuminate her face. "I finished the job."

"What do you mean?"

"Ssh! Someone's coming!"

From the opposite direction to the compound, two lights moved towards them. Iris flattened herself into the sand.

"Gil, give me your gun."

He grunted in pain and withdrew a revolver from his jeans. Just before he handed it over, he stopped to listen. "That's Divine. I hear her dog."

Sure enough, a throaty panting and Divine's constant monologue penetrated the night air.

"Divine, is that you?"

"Iris? What happened? We thought we heard gunshots!"

"Keep your voice down. Who's with you?"

"Me, Edson and Rusty Nail. We heard the shots and came down here to check. You OK?" Her torch flickered across the beach and found Iris's face. She let out a scream and dropped her light. Rusty Nail began a rumbling growl.

"We're hurt, Divine. Somebody shot Mafalda and Gil. We must get to a hospital ..."

"Edson, go get my truck! I don't care if you're high as a kite, my man, drive that vehicle down here right now." Edson stumbled backwards and started to run. "Wait! You're going to need the keys!" She held out an arm. "Fast as you can, you hear me? Rusty, hush now. You keep watch like a good dog."

She stayed the dog with a splayed hand and stared at Iris. "Where you hurt?"

"I'm not. But Gil took a bullet in his leg and they killed Mafalda."

"Mafalda is dead?"

"Divine, listen to me. You have to take Gil to hospital."

"No!" Gil's cry was pure agony.

Iris knelt by his side. "You need urgent medical attention. Go with Divine." She kissed his forehead. "I'll catch up with you later. Promise."

"Where are you going?" he asked, his voice weak. He was about to pass out, Iris was sure.

"To take care of some unfinished business."

Headlights swept the beach and the sound of an engine reached them.

"Here's Edson," said Divine. "What about Mafalda?"

"Take her with you and call the police to report a murder."

"Why would anyone want to kill her?" Divine's voice cracked.

Edson pulled up beside them, saving Iris from the obvious answer. She embraced Gil, who was barely conscious.

"Take good care of him for me. I have to run." She took off in the direction of the compound, her mind rushing in circles. *One thing at a time*, she told herself. *First, deal with Susie.*

"Divine?" she called. "Do you have a boat?"

21

———

Samuel Albarinho had never been one to sleep late, not even on a Sunday. He eased out of bed, slid his feet into slippers and closed the bedroom door, leaving his wife to continue her slumber undisturbed. His La Cimbali coffee machine ground, blasted and spat out his morning *meia do leite*, a noisy but welcome start to the day. He drank it in the living-room, absorbing the view over the bay. The weather was going to be warm, sunny and clear, he knew that in his bones. But until the sun heated the ground, he kept the windows closed. The morning air was piercing through a pair of silk pyjamas.

Fruit salad for breakfast, he decided, and the perfect time to try out his new waffle maker. Like many of his other labour-saving devices, it took a few tries before creating the perfect result. He was beating eggs, milk and vanilla essence for the batter when he saw a movement reflected in the brushed steel of the fridge door. Someone was standing outside the French windows, looking in.

Samuel was no stranger to burglars, intruders and other ne'er-do-wells who thought they could help themselves to his abundance. For that reason, he kept a Taser in the kitchen drawer. His security company had advised a gun, but in Samuel's experience, guns were a permanent solution to a temporary problem. With no hurried movements, he placed the bowl on the counter and reached for the weapon. At that moment, his visitor tapped on the door, using a fingernail, rather like the pecking of a bird.

He couldn't see the person's face as the rising sun kept their face in shadow, but he observed a knot of blonde hair, sunglasses, a sizeable rucksack and an apologetic wave. He placed the Taser in the drawer and moved to unlock the window. When he got close enough to recognise the individual, he was astonished.

"Iris! What a pleasant surprise! Would you like a cup of coffee?"

Sitting in Samuel's kitchen, eating waffles and fruit salad while drinking a coffee so good she might have been in Portugal, seemed perfectly natural to Iris. The last eight hours had provided enough surrealism to last her a decade. Samuel, whether through intuition or bewilderment, made coffee, provided food and sat at the opposite end of the table, requiring no conversation from his surprise guest. She had a request to make and it wouldn't wait but somehow she ate and drank and processed the nightmare.

The muscles in her backs, arms and legs burned from the near triathlon she had completed during the night. First she had run to Divine's bar and untied the boat from the little jetty. She rowed along the coast until she could identify the location of the corpse. Dragging the boat up the beach was the easy part. Getting the body into the small craft was a feat of pure will. Grazes on Iris's knuckles bore witness to her scrabbling around on the beach for a sufficient number of rocks to weigh down Susie's body. Added to weaponry and communications devices, none of which Iris wanted to touch, the would-be killer was heavy as a sandbag. Iris rowed her grim cargo out to the shelf where the ocean changed colour and the undersea cliff dropped into the abyss. There she tipped the weighted cadaver into the water and watched it sink. By the time she'd rowed back to shore and hauled the boat out of the water below the compound, she was desperately thirsty and fit to collapse.

Yet there was no time to rest. The police could be already on their way. *Act fast.* She was in a different kind of cleaner mode. *Leave no trace.* She stripped off all her clothes, located her own leather jacket and dumped it beside the dark stain where Susie had bled to death. *Muddy the tracks.* Then she waded into the sea, cleaning her skin and hair of blood, wincing as the salt pierced her wounds. Naked and shivering, she snatched up her backpack and scrambled up the dune to Gil's shed. Time to think was a luxury she could not afford. *Get out.*

Speedy packing, a skill she had honed over the years, had never been more useful. Everything she owned, except her copy of *Wide Sargasso Sea,* fitted into her rucksack. She borrowed one of Gil's baseball caps, stuffed her hair into a knot and crept through the compound to find Demi's bike. Even as she heaved it above her head and hauled it over the fence, she still had no idea where she was going. The airport was tantamount to suicide. Buses, coaches and taxis were too risky, always presuming she had a destination in mind. Her driving force was to get away, flee the scene and escape her pursuers. She cycled off into the darkness, leaving everything behind.

When the sun rose shortly after four in the morning, she climbed over the Albarinhos' garden wall. She sat in their pool house by the glinting water and waited for him to wake up.

.   .   .

"Sorry to turn up unannounced, Samuel. Thank you for breakfast, I feel better now. I don't suppose you've seen the news today?"

Samuel discarded a corner of waffle and wiped his fingers on a napkin. "News? No, never on Sundays. Other than the weather forecast, there's nothing that can't wait till next week."

"Hmm."

"Iris? I'm always pleased to see you but I would like to see you, if you know what I mean. Conversing with someone wearing sunglasses detracts from clear communication. Why do you ask if I have seen the news today?"

"I'm wearing sunglasses for your sake, because not even I know how bad the damage is. Last night, as my friends and I were walking back to A Casa da Prata from a beach bar, someone opened fire with a semi-automatic machine gun. My boss is dead, my partner is in hospital with a serious injury and I suffered some facial damage from one of our attackers. Samuel, I need to get out of Pemba, ideally to an international hub. Pemba airport is out of the question. I know for a fact people are waiting for me and I'm not talking about a VIP escort. I know we only met twice and I have no right to turn up here asking favours. The thing is, I can count my friends with personal helicopters on one finger. It may not look like it, but I can afford to pay you the going rate. I need to get out of Mozambique today. Will you help me?"

Samuel raised his white eyebrows. "Help yourself to coffee. I'm going to change and tell my wife I'm popping out for a while. The downstairs bathroom has a full first-aid kit. Around the corner and on the right."

Iris ate another waffle, filled her water bottle from the filter jug and took the Taser from the drawer before attempting basic repairs to her swollen face. By the time Samuel escorted her outside, she was ready to say goodbye to Mozambique.

· · ·

"My range won't get us to a major airport," said Samuel as he parked outside the warehouse. "I've been thinking about it and the best I can do is to take you to the island of Comoros. From there, you can take a scheduled flight to Tanzania and Dar-es-Salaam International Airport. I'm not going to ask you where you want to go because I have no desire to interfere. I will fly you to Moroni Prince Said Ibrahim airport in Comoros and wish you luck. Strap your baggage in the rear and I'll contact ATC."

Never in her life had Iris been afraid of flying. So the uncontrollable shakes as soon as they took off took her by surprise. Samuel noticed and said something reassuring she couldn't hear due to the buzzing in her ears. The company warehouses dropped away beneath them, their vastness shrinking as they rose into the sky. The helicopter hovered for a moment then headed east, across the peninsula of Pemba. Iris recognised the airport road she had driven only two days ago. Samuel pointed out the hotel on Praia do Wimbe where they had discussed Jean Rhys over a civilised glass of wine. Then they flew out over the Mozambique Channel in the Indian Ocean with nothing but blue beyond.

It didn't take long before the emotional shock and physical exertions took their toll and Iris's eyes closed. Twice her head jerked upwards until she gave in and used her small backpack as a pillow. The presence of Samuel at her side and the reassuring throb of the rotors eased her into an exhausted sleep.

Communications from air traffic control woke her and she listened to Samuel's confident voice responding to instructions as the approached the island of Comoros. Her body ached and her head pounded. The bridge of her nose was agony. It crossed her mind she might actually have a hangover to add to her troubles. How far away last night's celebrations seemed now. She twisted the cap off her water bottle and drank most of its contents as Samuel navigated the machine onto the helipad. The airport was small but efficient and within fifteen minutes, she was inside the terminal. While she waited for them to fetch someone from immigration to check her passport, Samuel went to the bathroom.

On his return, he held out a hand. "This is where I leave you, I'm afraid. I wish you every success in your future and I hope we meet again. Safe onward travels."

Iris shook his hand warmly. "I can't thank you enough for your generosity. I can and I will pay you for this trip. No, don't argue, I insist. Use the money to establish Pemba's first English-language library, perhaps? I know the language schools would love it. Thank you, Samuel, you really are a knight in shining armour."

"A white knight, indeed!" he laughed. "Before we say *adieu*, could you please return my Taser, if you don't mind? You'll never get it through security in any case."

Iris had almost forgotten she taken his household defence weapon and couldn't quite remember why she had done so. She pulled it from her backpack and handed it over.

"Sorry. Old habits die hard. Can I ask one last favour? When you get back to Mozambique, would you deliver a letter for me?"

"Of course. You said deliver, rather than post?"

"Yes, I did. The reason being there is no address. I want you to deliver this letter to your shed, which is currently sitting on a plot of land beside A Casa da Prata. The man who lives there is likely to be in hospital for some time but when he returns, I want him to have this." She slid an envelope from her jacket.

"I'll do it tomorrow morning on my way to work. Is there a way of contacting you? I'm not talking about something as traceable as an email or telephone number. If I have news, for example, I could publish this information, leaving you to read between the lines."

Iris looked at this beneficent soul with such admiration he grew embarrassed. "That's an excellent idea. How about a book club to go along with the English-language library? You could publish reviews or a summary of discussions every month. A creative mind like yours would find a way of concealing news within an innocent-looking text. Ah ha, here's the guy from immigration. Goodbye, Samuel, and thank you for everything. Give my love to your wife." She hugged him gently because few areas of her body were not in pain.

He patted her shoulder, took the letter and walked out of the building towards his helicopter, the sun shining on his panama hat.

"My apologies for keeping you waiting, madame. Could I have your name and your identification document, please?"

Iris faced the man with a smile, searching in her backpack. "No need to apologise, I'm grateful for your time. This is my first time in Comoros. Tell me, is it always this beautiful?"

"Always, madame. You should stay longer next time."

"Thank you, I will. Ah ha, here's my passport and my name is Ursula Brown."

22

———

2 *April, 05.00*
Dear Gil
I'm writing this with no idea if you'll receive the message or not, but I have to try. I don't know how badly you were hurt and I have no way of finding out. Turning up at the hospital would be a death sentence for both of us. All I can say is, I hope and pray you're going to be OK.

When you turned up in Pemba, I swore to myself I would never leave you again. You gave up everything for me and I know how much that must have cost you. But what happened tonight proves I have not outrun my past. No matter where I go, they will find me.

Whether they followed you to Pemba or my regular appearance on Mozambique news sites triggered an alert is immaterial. They found me. They always will.

I'm done. I don't want to live the rest of my life on my nerves, endangering everyone close to me and fearing for my life every time I see a stranger. In Brazil, I believed I could live like a recluse, forming no ties with other human beings. You changed my mind. Now I want to enjoy life with you, working together for something we both believe in, like the refuge. Nothing would make me happier.

But I can't. Tonight, I mean yesterday, you suffered injuries in the line of fire and a good-hearted woman lost her life. Because of me.

This is not my ego claiming celebrity status. I am absolutely sure who sent the shooters and who the target was.

Gil, the last time I suspected these people had caught up with me, I considered ending my life. To my mind, there were only two options: kill myself or wait for them to kill me. Sitting here, watching the sun come up, I realise there is an alternative.

Their organisation is broken, fractured and scattered around the world. Some of their operations continue, some have been shut down permanently. This is a self-perpetuating organism, able to regenerate and grow new limbs to replace those chopped off. It takes care of itself and doesn't waste its energy on vengeance. Of course not. It takes a human being to seek revenge.

I promised I would never leave you and I meant it. But if we have any hope of being together and living our future, I have to run one last time.

The only way of ending this constant pursuit is by cutting the head off the Gorgon. I can almost see your face as you read this. You're thinking it's the most insanely dangerous mission I have ever undertaken. You're not wrong. This could be my last attempt to derail these people. The bottom line is, I will throw them off forever or die trying.

Why? Because I want to live. And by live I don't mean a shadowy existence racing from one far-flung location to another. I want to live with you, relaxed and happy, not looking over my shoulder for the next wave of upstart assassins. It has to stop. One way or another I'm going to put an end to the whole sorry mess.

On the first night I went to Divine's place with Mafalda, she told me this: 'We're all trying to escape something. Like a shadow, you'll never outrun it. One day, you have to turn around and look it in the face and say 'Basta!' Enough is enough.'

That day is now. I say **Basta**. *Enough is enough.*

At the centre of this network is a festering, bitter soul. When I drive a stake through its heart, all this will be over and I can come home.

Let me do this alone. Any attempt to follow or assist will endanger my life and yours.

I love you, Gil Maduro. Wait for me.

X.

AUTHOR'S NOTE

Thank you for reading PEARL MOON. I hope you enjoyed our the fourth adventure in the Run and Hide series.

Coming next, the show-down to end them all. The Osman-Vargas criminal organisation has tentacles everywhere. There's only way to stop the beast – cut off its head.

BLOOD AND SAND (due 2023) is the penultimate book in the RUN AND HIDE series. To read the first chapter, simply turn the page.

BLOOD AND SAND – CHAPTER 1

One song reverberated through her brain for the first two days: 'Who Let The Dogs Out?' She couldn't remember the name of the band who sang it or any of the verses, but that chorus wormed its way into Ursula's ear morning, noon and night. The only difference was her brain substituted the word 'cows' for 'dogs'.

Goa was overrun with bovines. They slept in the street, ambled along the beach, grazed on any patch of greenery they could find and trampled through hotel gardens. No one lifted a finger to stop them. Ask anybody which animal is sacred in India, you'll get the right answer. From a cowshed to a cow paradise.

It had taken almost a fortnight to travel to this odd little pocket of western India, mainly because she had spent ten days in Mumbai, doing her homework and recovering from the injuries sustained on April Fools' Day.

Her focus was laser sharp and relentless. There was no time to look back and fret over recent events. She had a job to do, and faced the unpleasant truth – she was not up to the task. Her physical fitness was well below par due to months of sporadic activity and a lean diet. Her combat training was about was fresh in her mind as her schoolgirl French. As for the talents required by an undercover agent, she had neither back-up nor intelligence, nothing but memory.

The process of self-transformation must start with an image. *Who do I want to be?* In a similar kind of process to her A Casa da Prata application, Ursula began at the other end. What do they want? Who do they need? And how could she fulfil those requirements? The answer came as she soaked in the bath of her suite. They need a fixer: someone with connections, useful contacts and knowhow. A person who knew people. The only fly in the ointment was that Ursula knew no one. But that had never stopped her before.

If she wanted to convince people she was the real deal, she had to look the part and walk the talk. She gave her face and fingers time to recover from the events on the beach in Mozambique. In her heart, she knew the damage went further than skin deep, but repairing her psyche would have to wait. She had enough work to do, immersing herself in the identity of Ursula Brown.

Most tourists with a few days to spend in a city like Mumbai would take a tour, visit the highlights, sample the food and marvel at such an extraordinary city. Ursula stayed in her suite, scouring the web for information on the organisation she hoped to penetrate. It wasn't available through judicious use of any search engine, neither was it accessible from official records. The only way of establishing what aspects of racketeering these people currently controlled was by reading between the lines.

Thesis, antithesis, hypothesis. Ursula believed their headquarters was situated in Goa. However, that theory was built on nothing more than the word of a drunken old salt in a South London pub. She had no proof the people she was looking for were even on this continent. Any evidence would be well concealed, practically impossible to find, unless you knew what you were fishing for. Ursula selected her bait with care.

Step 1 was easy. Create an online persona, a rich young man with disposable income and a nose for a party. Step 2: fill invented persona's social media presence with generic images of jet skis, beach barbecues, skiing trips, scuba dives and indistinct suggestions as to his glamorous companions.

It took her most of the morning to lay her traps, because she wanted it to look especially authentic. The decision that took longest was the name. He had to sound like old money. She browsed the society pages of British newspapers for a first name, surname and a number, for maximum impact.

Harrington Locke III leapt into life at the touch of a button. Ursula felt like she knew him already and hated his guts.

Step 3: set up an email address for the fictional playboy's personal assistant. Step 4: have his assistant put out some discreet feelers as to where a young blood and his entourage could locate the right kind of venue, ensure every taste was catered for, arrange entertainment and source appropriate guests. All perfectly innocent and at the same time, for those in the know, it was 'Cristal' clear.

From there on, it was a question of cross-checking replies and joining the dots. Ursula thanked all her respondents and assured them her client would make a decision soon. Meanwhile she swam in the hotel pool, ate fresh food, slept in a king-size bed and focused on her mission. The psychological mettle was as important as the physical. Once her wounds healed, she hired professionals to help her shed a skin and invent a whole new personality. No big deal; she'd changed her appearance before. This time was different. This time, there was no going back.

Ursula Brown stepped off the plane, collected her shiny new suitcase and emerged into Goa's arrivals area. She wore jeans, trainers, a sports-branded T-shirt and sunglasses. Her glossy brunette ponytail swung as she walked, her skin glowed with health and her blue eyes sparkled. As arranged, a man was waiting with a sign bearing her name.

"Good morning! Directly to Da Gama Apartments, please. Could you take my bag?"

"Good morning, madam. This way, please." He wheeled her suitcase to a distinctly superior vehicle compared to the others idling in the pick-up bay of domestic arrivals. He opened the door and ushered her inside. It was dark, cool and sumptuous, with an array of soft drinks and snacks presented in a little box.

In comparison to Mumbai, Goa felt like a different country. The pace of life matched that of the ubiquitous, unhurried cows. People wandered rather than rushed, lingered over coffee or lunch, changed plans or direction at will and always had time to stop and sniff the roses. Instantly, Ursula wanted to get out of the luxury sedan and stroll the roads with the other inhabitants. She'd been confined to an air-conditioned set of rooms for ten days and yearned to eat something with her fingers instead of silver cutlery, smell something other than fabric conditioner and enjoy a constantly changing view. She didn't leave her seat, maintaining her image of the busy sophisticate here to judge the standards of service. But she watched, her nose pressed to the glass like a child in a sweet shop.

The Da Gama Apartments complex lived up to the photos on its website. A cool courtyard off the street sporting protective electronic gates protected 5-star accommodation complete with pool, restaurant and a concierge. It reminded Ursula of a place she had once stayed in Manaus, but this had fewer cats and gangsters. She checked in, rattled off half a dozen questions to the receptionist and accepted a local map. The journey from the airport to her lodgings had only taken half an hour, but convinced her the best way to travel in this area was by moped. She made up her mind either to rent or buy one before the weekend. Her first meetings were not until Monday, so she had three days to scope out her surroundings.

The apartment was a step down from her Mumbai hotel in terms of space and luxuries, but a whole lot more spacious than the stall she had called home for the previous five months. It boasted a double bed, a balcony overlooking the courtyard, a clean ensuite bathroom with a shower, a desk, mini-bar and wonderful street view from the window. Ursula Brown could be happy here.

There was one more thing she had to do before she let go of her previous existence. She set up her laptop, ensured access to an anonymous browser and masked her identity. This was the one and only time she would permit herself a check of news from Pemba or Cabo Delgado. It was already an old story, unless there was an active investigation. No news, as they say, is good news.

Her heart leapt into her mouth when she finally found a week-old article on page seven. *CANTOPRETO MOURNS TWO DEAD AT PEMBA REFUGE!* The angle was all about the politician's sense of personal loss, so it took a minute's frantic reading before Ursula could clarify the names of the victims in the unprovoked attack. Apparently Mafalda Moutinho and Iris Simons had lost their lives to a random gunman. One died in hospital, the other at sea. An adult male suffered injuries but had since been released from hospital. Arnaldo Cantopreto called for the community to come together at a memorial service on Sunday, in recognition of the women's work.

Nowhere in the newspaper report did they mention bodies, funerals, an ongoing investigation or the future of A Casa da

Prata. She was not surprised. Sad, but not surprised. She would grieve for Mafalda on her own terms.

To the world at large, her most recent identity was dead. That suited her fine. Because if Gil Maduro had received her letter, he knew different.

Wait for me, Gil. I'll be back.

ALSO BY JJ MARSH

Other titles in the Run and Hide series

WHITE HERON

BLACK RIVER

GOLD DRAGON

My Beatrice Stubbs series, European crime dramas

BEHIND CLOSED DOORS

RAW MATERIAL

TREAD SOFTLY

COLD PRESSED

HUMAN RITES

BAD APPLES

SNOW ANGEL

HONEY TRAP

BLACK WIDOW

WHITE NIGHT

THE WOMAN IN THE FRAME

ALL SOULS' DAY

My standalone novels

AN EMPTY VESSEL

ODD NUMBERS

WOLF TONES

And a short-story collection
APPEARANCES GREETING A POINT OF VIEW

For occasional updates, news, deals and a FREE exclusive novella, subscribe to my newsletter on www.jjmarshauthor.com

If you would recommend this book to a friend, please do so by writing a review. Your tip helps other readers discover their next favourite read. Your review can be short and only takes a minute.

Thank you.

ACKNOWLEDGMENTS

This book owes much to Florian Bielmann, VSO (Voluntary Service Overseas), Lília Momplé's book: *Neighbours, The Story of a Murder*, Rosa Maria Dias, Jane Dixon Smith and Julia Gibbs.

9 783906 256207